THE FOURTH MARCHIONESS

JAYNE DAVIS

Verbena Books

Manuscript development: Elizabeth Bailey

Copyediting & proofreading: Sue Davison

Cover design: P Johnson

ACKNOWLEDGEMENTS

Thanks to my critique partners on Scribophile for comments and suggestions, particularly Alex, Daphne, Jim, Rachel, Ysobel, Kim, David, Ann, and Violetta.

Thanks also to Beta readers Dawn, Helen, Kristen, Leigh, Mary G, Mary R, Melanie, Melissa, Patricia, Safina, Sarah, Sue, Tina, and Wendy.

CHAPTER 1

arch 1794, London

James Broxwood, the 8th Marquess of Harlford, shivered in the early evening chill as he descended from the hackney in Cavendish Square. It had been a tiring day, and he was looking forward to his dinner and a few quiet hours to go over his notes.

His butler awaited him at the front door. "Good afternoon, my lord. Lady Harlford wishes to see you. As soon as you came in, she said." His voice was barely audible.

James raised an eyebrow.

"Her ladyship is in the rear parlour," the butler added.

"Thank you, Haversham," James said, his voice as quiet as Haversham's. "Send Mitton up, could you? And bath water." He wasn't ready to hear Mama's demands, and he needed to get rid of the faint smell of sulphur that always clung to his clothing after a trip to the laboratories at the Warren.

"My lord." The butler bowed and headed through the baize door to the servants' quarters. James gave a wry grin and followed him, then used the servants' stairs, which guaranteed he would not encounter his mother until he had warmed up, bathed, and changed. He'd been doing this since boyhood, so the servants were never surprised. Belat-

1

edly, he thought he should have ordered something to eat, but when his valet appeared, a footman also arrived bearing a tray with tea and sandwiches. He really must check that Haversham was being paid enough.

Nearly an hour later, James entered the parlour clad in his normal, comfortable daytime dress of buckskin breeches tucked into top boots. Cassandra Broxwood, relict of the 6th Marquess of Harlford, sat in a chair near the fire, back stiffly upright and a novel in her hands. She wore an evening gown of crimson silk, embroidered all over with entwined flowers and lavishly trimmed with lace. At his entrance, her carefully shaped brows rose.

"Why are you dressed like that, James? We will be leaving shortly."

"Good evening to you, too, Mama," he said politely, knowing the irony would escape her. "You wished to see me?"

She looked him up and down, lips pursing in annoyance. "I asked to see you as soon as you came in."

"Mama, last time I came to see you straight from Woolwich you complained because I had not changed first. Do make up your mind."

"Well, you're here now. You will be ready in time if you hurry. The Cardingtons are expecting us for dinner before the ball."

"I don't recall accepting an invitation."

"I accepted on your behalf, naturally. Left to yourself, James, you'd never mix with other people."

"I go to White's often, and to Jackson's," he protested.

"Gentlemen's clubs and boxing salons are not what I mean, and you know it. Go and change; I don't wish to be late."

"No. I'm tired, and in no mood to attempt polite conversation with people I hardly know." He needed to write up today's meetings while the discussions were still fresh in his mind.

His mother's foot began to tap on the floor. "You put me in a difficult position—at such late notice your absence will upset Lady Cardington's numbers for dinner."

"In that case, perhaps in future you would do me the favour of not accepting invitations on my behalf?" He didn't try to keep irritation out of his voice.

"I am only acting for the good of the family. It's time you married and produced an heir, and if you don't attend social functions you will never meet a suitable girl."

He sighed—this again. It wasn't that he had any objection to marrying—as long as he found an acceptable woman. He had taken a full part in the last season, but his priorities had changed since then. The country had now been at war with France for more than a year and his research was more important than ever.

"You wasted your time last year—it was a shame I was unwell and unable to assist you."

"I did propose to a young lady, Mama, but she did not accept my offer." Amusement took over from annoyance as he regarded his mother's stunned expression.

"Rejected you? You are a marquess! You must have been the highest-ranking bachelor of last season. Who was she?"

Phoebe Deane was the only woman who had managed to talk about anything other than the weather, gowns, beaux, or the current gossip. Although she was the niece of the Comte de Calvac, her father had been a mere surgeon. Mama would not have approved.

"Who was she?" his mother repeated, more sharply.

"It's past, Mama." Miss Deane was married now. He hadn't loved her, but he had liked her. Her refusal had hurt him more than he'd expected, and dented his pride sufficiently to make him give up on the marriage mart last year.

Lady Harlford rose and sat at her escritoire in the corner of the room, taking out what looked horribly like a stack of invitations. "Are you engaged tomorrow evening?"

Could he claim to have engagements every evening for the next fortnight? No, that would not stop her; the only escape was to return to Herefordshire. He would do that soon enough, but he had to remain here until his next meeting at Woolwich, not to mention the business with his contacts in France, so he was stuck in Town for the moment.

"No, Mama."

"Good." She laid the pasteboard rectangles out on the writing flap.

"These are the invitations you have received. There is a rout tomorrow, and a ball. Then the next day a musicale, and then—"

"No."

"What do you mean, 'no'? James, you need a wife!"

"There is no hurry. I won't be thirty for several years yet."

"You never know what fate has in store. Look at what happened to poor Robert!" She dabbed her dry eyes with a corner of her handkerchief.

Of course. He spared a thought for his older brother, dead after attempting a hedge too high for his horse. While trying to catch up with the hunt, it was said, but more likely he'd been returning from visiting his mistress in the next village.

"There's always Uncle David." Who was living somewhere in Italy. James envied him at times.

"Nonsense—he wasn't brought up to be the next Mar—"

"Neither was I."

"Nor does he have any sons."

She had a point. Unfortunately. "One engagement per evening, Mama. That is all." He almost told her he would be returning to Harlford Castle within a couple of weeks, but thought better of it. "You may choose—except I will not sit in a stuffy room listening to some soprano screeching, or young ladies trying to play the piano." Or the harp; that was worse. "No musicales."

To his relief, she nodded and picked up the invitations, arranging them in rows. She looked like a fortune-teller laying out the cards that foretold his doom.

Once in his study, he poured a brandy and stood by the fire. Damn Robert for dying without securing the succession. It wasn't only that his death had made James the focus of his mother's matchmaking efforts, but he still missed his brother. He missed the friendly rivalry at riding and cards, the mutual teasing, and even telling Robert about his work. Robert hadn't been interested, really, but he listened because that's what brothers do.

Now it was his duty to find a wife. He'd rather be left to make his choice in his own time. But as Mama was likely to nag him into attending the events she selected, he might as well go and make an effort to get to know a few of this season's young ladies. As well as one could in the noise and crowds of a ballroom.

He swallowed his drink and spread his papers out on the desk. The scribbled notes he'd made during the day's discussions would make no sense in a few weeks' time, so he needed to write them up properly now.

He surfaced for a while when Haversham placed a tray of food on his desk, then again when the butler came back to remind him to eat it. At that point he decided enough was enough and his brain would work better after a good night's sleep.

Alice Bryant paid off the hackney and turned to gaze at the façade of Montagu House. The rows of tall windows and the wings that flanked the courtyard spoke of wealth, but gave no clue to the vast amount of knowledge stored within its walls.

Her young charge set off at a brisk pace across the courtyard towards the main entrance. "Can we look at the cannibal pictures again? And the mummies from Egypt?"

Alice strode after him. "We've come to learn about natural history, Georges. If you pay attention, we will ask our guide to take us to the exhibits from Captain Cook's voyages afterwards."

Georges scowled for a moment, then his naturally sunny disposition took over once more. Alice regarded him with affection—she was lucky in her position. Georges' father, the Comte de Calvac, was a generous and considerate employer, and Georges was an intelligent lad, even though his enthusiasm for learning currently leaned mostly towards the gruesome and warlike.

"Come, let us show the porter our tickets."

The porter looked down his long nose at Alice's plain pelisse and bonnet, but the comte's name on their tickets persuaded him that they were worthy to enter the hallowed halls of the museum. "Wait here, miss, until the other visitors arrive. Someone will come to show you around."

"I believe Monsieur le Comte made a particular request that we be allowed some time to examine the specimens in the natural history rooms." Alice had brought Georges to the museum before, and the guide had rushed everyone past the displays at a pace that allowed no time for learning. "Could you consult your list for the day?"

The porter sniffed, but before he had time to reply two more visitors walked up the steps. From the deep bow the porter gave to the elderly man in a full wig, he must be someone of importance. The other man was much younger, with a lean face and aquiline nose. His black hair was unpowdered and tied back with a plain ribbon that matched his unornamented coat. He looked familiar...

"Hello, Lord Harlford," Georges said. "Have you come to look at the exhibits, too?"

Of course—the marquess on whom Georges' sister, Hélène, had set her sights last year, but who had offered for their cousin instead. Phoebe had refused Lord Harlford in favour of the man she loved. Although the letters describing her new, adventurous life were entertaining, Alice missed her company.

"You took me to see a balloon ascension last year." Georges spoke before the marquess had a chance to reply.

"Georges," Alice hissed, embarrassed at his forwardness. But, to her relief, the marquess' serious expression lightened. He had some tiny scars around one eye that she didn't recall, but she hadn't been this close to him before.

"How could I forget? No, young man, I am not here to tour the galleries. This gentleman is one of the trustees. He has agreed to let me inspect some of the objects they have stored here." He glanced towards Alice, a slight crease to his brow. "Is there a problem, Miss...?"

Alice curtseyed. "Bryant, my lord. I'm Georges' governess." He had spoken only a few words to her last spring—she would have been surprised if he'd remembered meeting her. "Monsieur le Comte arranged for me to show Georges the natural history specimens."

"The book has no record of a request for an officer to explain the exhibits, sir," the porter said.

"But—"

The trustee cut off Alice's words. "There is no need for you to waste your time over this matter, my lord. If you will come this way." He raised a hand in the direction of the staircase.

Lord Harlford ignored the man's gesture. "I'm sure Miss Bryant will not interfere with the exhibits if she is allowed to examine them. Why do we not escort the visitors there on our way to your Chinese store?"

The trustee frowned, but Lord Harlford merely raised a brow and waited.

"Oh, very well. This way, if you please." Ignoring Alice completely, the trustee headed for the stairs.

Alice was grateful for the unexpected help. "Thank you, my lord." She nudged Georges.

"Yes, thank you, Lord Harlford." He marched up the stairs next to their benefactor. "Have you seen any more balloons, sir? Have you been up in one? I asked Papa, but—"

"I'm afraid I haven't, no." The interruption was firm, but not unfriendly.

"Don't bother his lordship, Georges. Look, here we are at the display of birds."

"They are labelled," the trustee said sourly. "I will see if I can find someone to explain them to you."

Alice put her chin up. "I am perfectly capable of explaining Linnaeus' binomial system of classification."

"It is a rather complex subject for a woman."

"Not at all." Alice looked through the door—the nearest cases held swallows and swifts. "The genus *Hirundo*, for example, includes the species *urbica*, *apus*, and *rustica*, commonly known as the house martin, the common swift, and the swallow. They are part of the order Passeres, based upon the characteristics of their—"

"Hmph." The trustee scowled.

"Have I made an error, sir?" Alice took a deep breath—she had let her annoyance show, but a curl to Lord Harlford's lips indicated he might be amused rather than irritated.

"I think Miss Bryant has ably demonstrated her ability to educate the Comte de Calvac's heir." Lord Harlford laid a slight emphasis on her employer's rank.

The trustee's scowl deepened. "Very well. This way, my lord." He stalked off along the corridor. Lord Harlford inclined his head at Alice, that trace of amusement still on his face, and walked off before she had time to thank him. She felt a flash of envy at the privilege given by a title, but she suspected the attitudes of the porter and the trustee had as much to do with her being female as with her position as a governess.

"Do I have to learn all that you said?" Georges asked, his tone doubtful.

"We are here mainly for you to understand the principles behind the system." They entered the room, stopping at the first case. The specimens, although competently stuffed, always looked sad to Alice. She'd prefer to study animals in their natural habitats, but here it was easier to show Georges the features common to the different species and orders so he could understand how the classification system worked. And seeing them in the flesh—in a manner of speaking—was more interesting than merely examining drawings in a book.

"Let us look at these birds first, then we may see if there are croco-diles or tigers."

CHAPTER 2

$\mathcal{J}$ames leaned against a pillar at the side of the ballroom, surveying the crowd. Although they had arrived fairly early, the air was already stifling; the sickly scents of perfumes mingled with odours of candle wax and perspiration. It looked the same as all the balls he'd attended last year—a confusing swirl of people with a dazzling mix of colours on the older women and many of the men, and the unmarried misses in their paler dresses.

And the noise—the scraping of the musicians could scarcely be heard above the hubbub of conversation. Give him a horse and some open countryside, with nothing more than the sound of birds and wind in the trees.

There must be a better way of choosing a bride.

Mama had been waylaid by an acquaintance as soon as they arrived, but he didn't need her to introduce partners. There would be enough mothers with marriageable daughters present to recognise him and recall his rank and wealth.

He was proved correct only a few moments later. The Comtesse de Calvac approached, her daughter in tow. Hélène was as beautiful as he remembered, her golden curls dressed with tiny flowers that matched the embroidery on her gown, a pretty smile on her delicate features.

9

"My lord." The comtesse and her daughter curtseyed. "How good to see you back in Town. I hope you are well?"

"My lady. Lady Hélène." He bowed his head in brief acknowledgement. "Are you enjoying the season so far?"

"Oh, yes, my lord. I've been much in demand at balls." Hélène fluttered her eyelashes. "Such a pity that you haven't been present until now."

What was there to say to that? He'd found Hélène's slightly breathy way of speaking entrancing last year—now it was irritating. He'd been captivated by her beauty until he realised how self-centred she was.

"It is a very pleasant room, don't you think?" she said into the following silence.

"Very pleasant." In truth, it seemed little different from most rooms people used for entertaining.

"I do so love dancing." Was there a hint of desperation in her voice?

At that moment the music ended and people moved about, finding partners for their next dance. He resigned himself. "Would you allow me the pleasure of the next dance?" She took his hand with a little giggle. The comtesse gave a satisfied smile as he led her daughter out onto the floor for a country dance.

"I met your brother this morning," he said as the music started. It was all he could think of to say to her. "Visiting the British Museum."

"Oh. I expect Bryant took him there for his lessons. Papa took me once—so tedious, all those dusty old relics." The dance separated them after this dismissal of all the learning inherent in the 'old relics', but she carried on talking as soon as they met again. "I'd much rather go to Bond Street. It is so important for me to be in the latest fashion."

Why? He wasn't about to choose a wife based on her fashion sense, and he could see little difference from last year—heads still sported ostrich plumes, knots of ribbon, or flowers.

She chattered on, not seeming to notice as the figures of the dance took him out of earshot, and he turned his mind back to yesterday's meeting. Would a different mix of propellant help—?

"The weather is rather cold, but the fashion for..."

He'd tried several combinations, but—

"I do so enjoy dancing, it is…"

And then there was the problem with the—

"… so many people here, that…"

James gave up his attempt to think about his work. If he had to converse, he'd rather talk to her brother. Or Miss Bryant, even though he knew little about biological classification.

"…fun it is to drive in the park." This time there was a pause when she finished speaking.

"Quite so." He may not be blessed with all the social graces, but he recognised a hint for an invitation when he heard one and he wasn't going to take that bait. "I'm afraid I haven't brought my phaeton to Town." She gave a little pout when he said nothing more, but the set had finally ended and James returned her to the comtesse with relief.

His mother found him soon afterwards, and introduced a Miss Chilton, who kept a conversation going without requiring much in the way of responses from him. A Miss Esham was next—he wondered if she had something wrong with her eyes, as she seemed to blink rather often. The sets blurred into each other—Lady Something-or-other, Miss Somebody-else…

How was he ever to remember their names? Mama would ensure they danced with him at other events, hoping he might take an interest in one of them. This one was a Miss Gearing—a pretty blonde who giggled at the end of every sentence. Miss Giggles—that might work. He smiled as he returned her to her chaperone.

"My lord?" Lady Hélène stood beside him, smiling prettily. "You promised me the last cotillion."

Had he? As he wondered how to avoid another dance with her, he felt a touch on his arm. Not another young miss, but a woman a decade older than himself, a little on the plump side, with light brown hair. He'd met her last year… Lady Jesson?

"Lady Harlford has need of you, my lord," she said. "Allow me to take you to her."

Reprieve, but possibly only from the frying pan to the fire. Nevertheless he gave Hélène a brief bow and offered his arm to Lady Jesson.

11

"Is my mother unwell?" he asked as they walked off.

"I have no idea." She looked up at him, with a smile that was almost a laugh. "I was rescuing you, on the assumption that you did not wish to dance with Hélène for a third time. Was I right to do so?"

Third time? He should pay more attention—that could have been taken as declaring an interest.

"Er, yes. Thank you. But how—?"

"Merely observation, my lord." She took her hand from his arm. "Lady Hélène may make some man a good wife, but not you, I think." She left him with a friendly nod.

Astounded, he wondered why she'd intervened. Lady Jesson was often talked of as an interfering gossip, but in this case she'd done him a favour.

He'd had enough for one evening. His mother was sitting with several other women of similar age, and he managed to take his leave without allowing her the chance to protest.

Mama would take the carriage home, and he decided to walk rather than have a hackney summoned. He reviewed the evening while he waited for a footman to fetch his coat.

The talk while dancing had been tedious—when his partners had talked at all. One young lady had been tongue-tied; the others seemed interested only in fashion or hinting at drives in the park.

His parents hadn't talked to each other often, and he had sometimes been aware of an air of hostility in their dealings. That wasn't what he wanted in a marriage. Love wasn't essential, but he should be able to respect his wife and hold a sensible conversation with her.

His lips twisted as he considered that his boredom may have been as much his fault as theirs. He had no aptitude for the kind of small talk that was expected in these situations.

"Your coat, my lord."

James donned his coat and set off towards Cavendish Square. The air outside was indeed cold, as Lady Hélène had so astutely mentioned, and the streets were full of jostling crowds, but the exercise helped to clear his head.

He wanted more than conversation from a wife. One of his chief pleasures at home was riding or driving around the countryside with no-one to bother him. Could he find a wife who would enjoy that, too? Provide companionship without constant chatter?

If he were to take this business seriously, he should make a list of questions to ask at tomorrow's ball. Did they prefer Town or country? Did they ride? Which plays had they enjoyed?

As he was changing for dinner, his valet held out a grubby bit of paper between finger and thumb, as if reluctant to touch it. "I found another note in your coat pocket, my lord."

James took it—at least one of the jostles on the way home must have been deliberate. How else the thing could have been placed there, he didn't know. He recognised the scrawled handwriting—Laurent wanted another meeting.

Mermaid. 4 Germ.

At the Mermaid tavern near the Billingsgate wharves—the usual place. The fourth of Germinal? He put the note aside—he'd have to consult his notes to translate the date from the revolutionary calendar that Laurent insisted on using, and those notes were in the library. He would do it in the morning.

It would be good news, he hoped—the last few letters he'd received had said only that little progress had been made.

Alice strode along the path around the edge of Hyde Park, wrapped up well against the chill breeze. Normally, she'd be admiring the new leaves unfurling on the trees and enjoying the feel of the sun on her face, but today her thoughts turned inwards. She'd just been given her notice.

It hadn't really been unexpected—she'd always known that Georges would need a tutor to prepare him for school this year—but she'd hoped to have a little more time before starting the round of applying for positions again. She would not be destitute if she could not find employment, but the prospect of going back to live with her brother was not an attractive one. She loved the old farmhouse on the edge of the Marlborough Downs, and she'd had a happy childhood there. However, things had changed after Papa died—Dan had married, and his new wife did not take kindly to having Alice living there as well.

The comte had been generous, offering to pay her salary for three months, even if he found a suitable tutor before then. And he'd allowed her some extra time off to visit employment agencies. She supposed she should have done that this afternoon, but she'd come to the park instead, hoping the fresh air and exercise would cheer her up. It had helped, a little, but the park was beginning to fill with riders and carriages as the fashionable hour approached. It was time to make her way back.

A row of carriages was parked on the opposite side of Berkeley Square to the Comte's house, outside The Pot and Pine Apple. Hungry after her exercise, Alice debated going in—tea and cake would be lovely.

No, that would be extravagant—but she looked in the window all the same. The display was mouthwatering. Little fancy cakes with pink and white icing, slices of seed cake and wedges of glazed apple tart—and Chelsea buns, their glistening coils dotted with currants.

Alice could almost taste the cinnamon and lemon peel.

She shouldn't...

But she did.

The tables near the windows were full, but there were several free at the back of the room. Alice sat down at the smallest and removed her bonnet. A waiter came and she asked for tea and a Chelsea bun. She'd brought Georges here several times last summer for the famous ices, and it felt a little strange to be sitting alone. Amidst the bright colours and elaborate styles of the other women's clothing, her plain garb felt out of place. By the time the waiter reappeared, she was wishing she hadn't come in. And he wasn't carrying a tray.

"Miss, the lady at that table requests that you join her." He pointed at one of the window tables, where two women were standing adjusting their bonnets. A third woman remained seated; Alice recognised her as Lady Jesson. They had met briefly last summer, when the comte's family were staying in Kent. She had been a good friend to Phoebe.

Lady Jesson smiled and beckoned. Mystified, Alice waited until the other two ladies left, then went to stand by one of the empty chairs. The waiter cleared away the used crockery, and set out her tea and bun.

"Lady Jesson?"

"Do sit down, Miss Bryant. Do I have your name correct?"

"Yes, my lady." Alice sat. "I'm surprised you remember me." They hadn't spoken last year.

"I remember most people, my dear. If you prefer to be alone, please just say so."

"I… no. I am happy to have company."

"Excellent." Lady Jesson raised a hand, and ordered more tea and cake for herself. "Have you come into some money, or are you consoling yourself?"

Alice shook her head, but couldn't help smiling. "Consoling, in a way. I need to look for a new position."

"Hmm. Calvac's son is to go to school in the autumn and needs to improve his Latin. So you are about to be replaced by a tutor."

Alice's mouth dropped open for a second, and Lady Jesson laughed.

"I am not a mind reader, my dear. I overheard the comtesse talking about it the other day. Are you looking for another position in London?" She took a bite of her cake.

"No. I've enjoyed being able to see the sights while I've been here, but I prefer to be in the country."

"Do come to me before you reply to any advertisements. I may be able to advise you if the situation will be suitable. It would not do to end up in a household where there is a husband or son with a wandering eye."

Startled, Alice tried to read Lady Jesson's expression, but could see nothing beyond friendly concern. She didn't know why Lady Jesson was offering to help, but she would accept it gladly.

"Thank you, my lady." She was lucky, she knew, to have had no such problems thus far. "Why are you...?" She stopped herself—it seemed rude to question Lady Jesson's motives.

"I am interested in people, my dear, and I help when I can. Are you in urgent need of employment? I could ask my acquaintance if—"

"I have three months."

"Not a great deal of time, in truth." Lady Jesson looked at Alice's plate. "Don't forget to eat. Then you may tell me a little more about yourself."

Alice obediently took a bite; the bun was as delicious as it looked.

"What subjects can you teach?" Lady Jesson asked when Alice finished eating. Alice wondered where to start.

"Beyond the basics, I can teach French, a little Latin, mathematics, the use of the globes, natural philosophy." Her first position had been teaching three young girls, with very different interests from Georges'. "Also drawing and watercolours, piano, embroidery..."

"You must have had a good governess yourself, my dear. Or were you sent to school?"

Alice took a sip of her tea. "Neither, my lady. Mama taught me the ladylike skills, and my father taught my brother and me mathematics and some Latin until Dan went off to school. I learned more when I helped him to run the farm."

She'd read a great many of Papa's books and the agricultural journals he subscribed to. Farming and horticulture fascinated her, but it wouldn't do to say anything about the occasional articles she contributed to the Society for the Improvement of Agriculture. Lady Jesson might disapprove of her encroaching on such a male preserve.

"Tell me more about the farm, Miss Bryant."

"It's on the edge of the Marlborough Downs..." Alice described the rambling stone farmhouse and the hill behind it, shopping trips to Marlborough, local assemblies...

Several cups of tea later, she realised she had related far more about her life and family than she had told anyone else. Lady Jesson was a comfortable person to talk to—kindly, and genuinely interested. No wonder she was reputed to have all the latest gossip. But their plates had been empty for some time, and the waiter was hovering. Alice had taken up enough of Lady Jesson's time.

"It was a pleasure talking to you, Miss Bryant," Lady Jesson said as Alice stood up. "It does make a nice change to meet someone who can talk about more than balls, fashion, and suitors. Do call on me in Henrietta Place when you have any prospective employers to discuss."

"Thank you, my lady." From another person, the offer could have been merely a polite platitude, but Alice thought Lady Jesson meant it.

CHAPTER 3

*A*lice knocked on the door of Lady Jesson's house. It had taken a fortnight to obtain the names of several families in need of a governess, and the three-month period the comte had given her was beginning to seem not very long at all. The afternoon was fine, and mild for early April, so she'd walked to Henrietta Place instead of sending a note to see if her ladyship was free.

Lady Jesson's butler looked askance at Alice's lack of calling card or accompanying maid. He pursed his lips as he indicated a hard chair in the hall and went to ascertain whether his mistress would receive her. The hallway was nicely furnished, although some of the pieces showed signs of wear. A console table was draped with an embroidered runner that didn't match the fabric on Alice's chair. Curious, she lifted one end to look beneath. It concealed a round stain where spilled water must have been left for too long. The comte would have banished the table to the attic.

Her observations were interrupted when the butler returned, and Alice hurriedly smoothed the runner back into place. The butler's manner was considerably more pleasant as he led the way along the hall. Alice caught several glimpses of furniture under holland covers as they passed half-open doors, before she was shown into a small parlour. Lady Jesson sat at an escritoire, sorting through what looked like a sheaf of bills. She put them to one side as Alice entered, and asked the butler to bring a tea tray.

"You said I might call, my lady, if I needed your advice," Alice started, a little uncertainly.

"I did indeed." Lady Jesson rose. "Come, sit by the fire, Alice. May I call you Alice?"

Taken aback, Alice could only nod. Then, once settled in a comfortable, if somewhat shabby chair, she took a list of names from her pocket. "An agency gave me these possibilities, my lady. I also have several advertisements from the Morning Post."

Lady Jesson perused the list, her brows rising once or twice, then handed it back.

"I would advise against the first three positions," she said. "I'm afraid I know little about the other two, or the names in the Post."

"What is wrong—?" Alice broke off as the butler knocked and entered, setting a tray with tea pot and cups on a side table. It seemed a menial job for such a starchy man.

"The first—a lecherous husband," Lady Jesson said once the butler had gone. "There is nothing wrong with the menfolk in the second household, but I have a mutual friend. From what she says, the children's mother is a pleasant enough woman, but of the type who thinks her offspring can do no wrong. Your life would be a misery."

Alice could imagine. "The third?"

"A son. The kind who blames the housemaids for leading him on when they fall pregnant, and parents who take his side."

Oh. Alice hadn't realised how fortunate she'd been in her employment so far.

"I can make enquiries about the others on your list, if you wish."

"If it's no trouble, my lady, I would be very grateful."

"Do call me Maria, my dear. I think we are going to be friends."

It didn't seem right to use her Christian name after so short an acquaintance. "I... thank you, but..."

"I am not quite old enough to be your mother, you know." Lady

Jesson smiled. "Or at least, I would have to have been a *very* young mother."

Alice looked away, rather embarrassed at being provided with this detail. Her gaze settled on a portrait above the fireplace. It showed a younger version of Lady Jesson standing in a woodland glade, one hand resting on the arm of a cheerful-looking man. Two boys played at her feet.

"My late husband."

"I'm sorry."

"It's more than eight years since he died. The boys are at school at the moment, although Simon should be going up to Cambridge in the autumn." She sighed. "When you marry, my dear, be sure to choose someone who isn't too fond of gambling."

There was a rather awkward silence, then she added, "But I'm sure you're sensible enough to know that."

"I have no plans to marry."

"Well, you are still young—who knows what may happen?"

Alice shook her head. The only time she'd come close to marriage —to a young man she'd met at assemblies in Marlborough—she'd been dissuaded by his announcement that she wouldn't need to bother herself with farming matters if they wed. He'd managed to make Dan sound weak for consulting her, and implied that he knew everything worth knowing about the subject.

Lady Jesson cleared her throat. "I sense a story there, but perhaps not for now. Do you like dogs?"

Alice was nonplussed at the sudden change of subject. "I...I like the farm dogs well enough." Yapping lapdogs were a different matter— was Lady Jesson planning on getting one?

"Good. Are you set on being a governess, my dear, or might you consider a position as a companion?"

A companion? "I... I hadn't considered it. I enjoy teaching..." The idea of waiting hand and foot on some old lady was not appealing. "It would depend on the situation."

"Sensible." Lady Jesson nodded. "The new... the *potential* new position is as my companion."

"You are not old enough to need a companion," Alice objected, wondering if this was a joke, or even some kind of test. "And..."

"And?"

"May I be frank?"

"Please do."

"Can you afford to pay another salary?"

To Alice's relief, Lady Jesson did not appear to be offended. "What leads you to ask that?"

"I meant no disrespect."

"I realise that. I really want to know."

"Well... You have holland covers on furniture, your butler serves the tea rather than a footman, and... and you mentioned your late husband's gambling."

Lady Jesson smiled. "Very good. In answer to your question, the situation is not quite as simple as I made it sound. I cannot tell you all the details at the moment, but I would like to know if you are at least open to the idea."

"Yes. Yes, of course." How could she not be? To work for a congenial employer, who talked to her as a friend—that would be far better than any teaching position she might find. She would probably have more time for her own interests, as well.

"Excellent. I gather Calvac has given you some extra time off to look for employment."

"Yes. With a little notice, I can rearrange Georges' activities to allow myself one or two free hours in the afternoon."

"I will send a note when I have more news, or if I find out anything about those other positions."

That sounded like dismissal, so Alice thanked her hostess and took her leave.

What a strange conversation it had been—but interesting. Time spent with Lady Jesson would never be boring.

The wind along the Thames blew the smell of rotting fish and other filth into the streets. James could almost feel it clinging to his clothing as he got out of the hackney. The alleys closer to the river were too narrow for the vehicle to get much further.

As it was, he felt uncomfortably conspicuous, even in his oldest clothes. The darkness helped make him less obviously an outsider, but dangers lurked in the shadows.

This damned business with the Frenchman had gone on long enough. Two weeks ago, Laurent had told him progress was being made. Then, yesterday, he'd received another note saying that Laurent —if that were even his name—needed more money.

A scuffle in a side alley had him thrusting one hand into the pocket that held his pistol, but a murmur of voices reassured him. A whore agreeing her price was unlikely to be a threat, and the man would have other things on his mind.

He'd been a fool to come to such a place this late in the evening. It wouldn't happen again, but he was here now—and if Laurent succeeded, his efforts would be worth this potential danger. Well worth it.

As James turned the last corner, a dark shape moved against the light spilling from the open door of the Mermaid Inn. He pulled his pistol out of his pocket, quietly cocking it.

"C'est moi, Broxwood." Laurent's voice was hardly audible against the sound of drunken arguments and off-key singing. "Put that thing away."

James lowered the pistol, but kept it in his hand. "I've brought what you asked for. I want results, Laurent, for all this money."

The man shrugged, his features invisible in the gloom. "Bribes cost gold. I am doing my best."

James took the leather purse from his inner coat pocket. Laurent weighed it in one hand, then nodded and hid it somewhere inside his clothes.

"Good. I return to Paris tomorrow. I will send word if there is any progress."

"Send it to me at Harlford."

Laurent grunted his agreement and melded back into the shadows.

Perhaps Laurent *was* doing his best. Or James was being taken for a flat.

He might never know.

The air was still cold the following morning as James rode along Oxford Street towards the corner of Hyde Park. These morning rides were one of the pleasures of his day in Town, before the park became busy in the fashionable hour. Rotten Row was almost empty, and he urged his mount into a gallop.

His horse became less fidgety after they had ridden along the Row and back, and James slowed. Although early for members of the *ton* to be abroad, it was mid-morning and Mama would be breakfasting by now. And waiting to berate him, no doubt, as he'd left the butler to pass on his apologies for missing last night's event. Craven, possibly, but it had saved him from having to prevaricate about his destination. No-one must know about his meeting at the Mermaid.

Instead of going back through the streets, he turned his mount parallel to Park Lane. He'd make a circuit of the park at a more leisurely pace before heading back for breakfast. He set off towards the band of trees that edged the park, admiring the crocuses and daffodils that brightened the grass between them. As often happened, his mind wandered to his research, and he was within a few feet of a woman kneeling on the ground before he noticed her. Her face was close to the grass and a boy crouched beside her. Not beggars or destitute—both wore respectable clothing.

He drew rein. "Do you require assistance?"

The woman gave a start and scrambled to her feet, her face hidden by the rim of her bonnet as she brushed bits of grass and twigs from her skirt. The boy turned and gave him a beaming smile. Young Calvac and his governess.

"Oh, hello sir! That's a splendid horse. Does he go fast? Have you been—?"

"Georges." Miss Bryant put a hand on the boy's shoulder. "What

23

have I taught you about polite greetings? "She looked up at James. "I do apologise, my lord."

"It is no matter, Miss Bryant." Now he could see her face in brighter surroundings than the museum, he took in clear skin and faint lines beside her mouth that suggested she smiled often. Her gown was a particularly unbecoming shade of brown, but a sensible choice if she was going to kneel on damp grass. "What were you doing?"

Her cheeks reddened, and she glanced at an open book lying on a folded blanket. "I was… we were—"

"We were looking for beetles, Lord Harlford," Georges piped up. "I've been learning the proper names. I can do trees, too." He pointed at the one they were standing beneath. "That is *Quercus robur*, that one is *Acer*—"

"Georges, do not bother his lordship. Thank you for stopping, Lord Harlford, but we are not in any difficulty."

"Such enthusiasm is to be commended," James replied, rather surprised to find that he meant it. He'd had little to do with children, but the lad's curiosity and thirst for knowledge was endearing— although he was glad he didn't have to deal with such enthusiasm on a daily basis.

"Are you interested in insects, too, sir?" Georges held up one hand, opening it to reveal a small, black beetle. The governess coloured again, the look of chagrin on her face almost comical.

"I was when I was your age," he admitted, "but I became more interested in chemistry." He touched the end of his riding crop to his hat. "I must be on my way. Good hunting."

The governess curtseyed and Georges said goodbye as James rode off. How different the lad was from Hélène. He hoped his sons would turn out like that.

If he found a suitable wife.

～

Mama's opening salvo at the breakfast table came straight to the point. "The Eshams were most disappointed by your absence last night."

"It was a small ball, then?" James took a mouthful of coffee.

"No, of course not. Why would you think that?"

"They can't miss one person at a large ball." Accepting his plate of sausages and mushrooms from a footman, he started eating.

"Of course they did. They were expecting you."

"Let me guess, Mama. They have a daughter to marry off and thought I might do?" Esham... Miss Eyes? The auburn-haired girl who continually fluttered her eyelashes at him.

"James, you are not taking this seriously." Her words became clipped as her annoyance grew. "You owe it to the family to marry a suitable girl and produce an heir. And I am offering to help you."

Offering to help? It felt more like demanding he do as he was bid. Would her definition of suitable bear any resemblance to his own?

"I will attend whatever you wish this evening, but I am returning home in a few days' time."

He was looking forward to being at Harlford again, even though he'd only been away for a few weeks. He'd be back to his horses and his laboratory, and away from the ceaseless round of what passed for entertainment in the *ton*. And back to Lucy; it didn't seem right to leave his sister in the country with no-one but her governess and Grandmama for company.

His mother's lips formed a thin line. "You cannot go back to Harlford, James. It is the season! Where else will you meet suitable marriage prospects? You must—"

"Understand me, Mama," he interrupted. "I came to Town because I have business here, *not* because I wished to spend my time at these endless balls. I am returning to Harlford because I need to attend to my research. There must be someone in the neighbourhood at home who would do as well as the young ladies you have been introducing me to." He might attend some assemblies in Hereford, or even return to London when he'd made more progress with his research, but he wasn't going to commit himself to that. "I shall be ready at eight this evening for whatever event you've chosen, but I *will* be returning home later this week."

He stood, dropping his napkin on the table beside the uneaten food on his plate.

"Very well, James. There is no need to storm off like that and leave your breakfast. If you must return home, I will say no more about it." She raised a finger to summon a footman with the coffee pot.

"I'm afraid I've lost my appetite, Mama."

It was only as he settled himself at his desk in the library that a feeling of unease started to grow. Mama had capitulated far too easily —she must be planning something.

Whatever it was, he suspected he wouldn't like it.

CHAPTER 4

our days after their last meeting, Alice and Lady Jesson alighted from the hackney in Grosvenor Square. "Who are we visiting?" Alice asked, looking at the imposing mansion before them.

"Marstone."

Alice's hand hovered over the knocker. The Earl of Marstone had been involved in Phoebe's adventures last year—if adventure was the word for getting involved with spies and being kidnapped. And now Phoebe was sailing the Mediterranean with her husband, working for Lord Marstone in some way.

She took a breath and knocked. Lady Jesson had implied that this visit was something to do with her possible employment as a companion. Was 'companion' really the job that would be on offer? "Lady Jesson..."

"Don't worry, my dear. You will not be committing yourself to anything by hearing what Marstone has to say. I know nothing we discuss will go any further."

"I... well, yes, of course..."

There was no time for more, as a footman opened the door and took their coats, and a butler ushered them into the library. Alice scarcely had time to envy the number of books at the earl's disposal before another footman came in and set down a tray of refreshments. The earl entered shortly afterwards. He wore his brown hair unpowdered and tied back, and his clothing was unadorned but clearly cut by an expert tailor.

"My lord." Lady Jesson dipped her head in greeting. "May I introduce Miss Alice Bryant?" Alice made her curtsey. Lord Marstone examined her for a moment, his blue eyes piercing, then he smiled and waved towards the chairs set near the fire.

"Will you pour, Lady Jesson?" He waited until cups and plates had been passed around before speaking again. "Miss Bryant, I understand Lady Jesson has discussed with you the possibility of becoming her companion?"

"She has." Alice glanced at Lady Jesson, who continued to sip her tea. "I assume there is more to the position than the usual duties of a companion?"

Lord Marstone nodded. "Indeed." He steepled his fingers beneath his chin, then nodded. "I have made enquiries about you, and received excellent reports of your intelligence and honesty. I trust that you will not repeat anything said in this room?"

Alice nodded, not sure whether to be annoyed that he'd asked people about her, or pleased at the good reports. It was little different, though, from a prospective employer asking for a character.

"You also speak French, I believe."

"Yes, my lord, although not nearly as well as Phoe—Mrs Westbrook. I could not pass for a Frenchwoman." She felt a prickle of unease; Lord Marstone didn't want to send her to France, did he?

"Do you know what the Westbrooks are doing now?"

"Not exactly, other than the fact that they work for you in some way." The earl said nothing. "Gathering information, I understand."

"Some might say that what the Westbrooks are doing is dishonourable, Miss Bryant. They misrepresent themselves and deceive people."

"Such is the nature of spying." There, she'd used the word—and

Lord Marstone did not contradict her. "I assume the information they gather will be useful for our army and navy."

The earl nodded. "And you, Miss Bryant. Would you be willing to serve your country by doing similar things?"

Her unease grew. "I...I mean, what would be involved? I don't know whether I can..." Whether she had the courage, but she didn't like to admit to that.

Lady Jesson put her cup down. "We would be working together, Alice, and Lord Marstone assures me there should not be any physical danger."

Should not wasn't the same as *will not.*

"The task involves information gathering only," Lord Marstone explained.

Lady Jesson would be good at that, but Alice wasn't sure that she would be. "I've never done anything like that before."

"Neither have I," Lady Jesson said calmly, helping herself to more cake. "This will be my first, er, adventure, too."

"You seem doubtful, Miss Bryant? You would be doing a service for your country."

"I understand that, my lord. But... I mean, I would like to know a little more about the task before I make a decision."

"Very well, but there is one matter to confirm before we go further," the earl said. "That extra member of the team we talked of, Lady Jesson." He got up to ring the bell, and waited until the butler arrived. "Langton, please ask Chatham to bring Tess in." As the butler left, the earl reached for a small, covered bowl on the tea tray and handed it to Alice. She lifted the cover.

Chopped ham?

"Good heavens, Marstone!"

Alice looked up at Lady Jesson's exclamation. Her eyes were wide in surprise, staring towards the door.

"That is rather larger than I had in mind."

Alice turned to see one of the footmen leading a huge dog. It was an Irish wolfhound, almost half her own height at its shoulders. It looked around the room, ears up, then fixed its gaze on Alice and Lady Jesson.

The earl smiled. "Chatham, please introduce Tess to my guests."

Tess? How could a hound that size have a dainty name like Tess?

The footman brought the dog close to Alice's chair and unhooked the leash.

Realising what the ham was for, Alice held out a piece. Tess' tail waved and the animal came up to her, sniffed, and carefully took the ham, leaving Alice with wet fingers. This must be why Lady Jesson had asked her if she was used to having dogs around—but what task did Lord Marstone have in mind that required a dog like this? Or any dog at all?

Was this interview the reason that Lady Jesson had befriended her? Her spirits lowered at the thought, but she pushed the idea to the back of her mind. Even if their connection had started that way, she felt there was genuine friendship between them—as much as there could be between two people of their different stations.

Alice obeyed the pleading in Tess' eyes, and fed her another piece of ham. "Sit, Tess." The dog looked briefly at the footman then sat, her face almost on a level with Alice's, tongue lolling.

"Good girl." Alice offered another piece of ham, then put the bowl on a side table and used her dry hand to find a handkerchief. Tess looked longingly at the bowl, but made no attempt to eat what was left. The animal had been well trained.

The earl had watched with a smile of approval. "You are used to dogs, I understand, Miss Bryant?"

"Farm dogs, my lord, yes. But nothing as large as Tess."

"Good, good. Chatham, sit down, if you please." Although this was a highly unusual request, the footman did not seem at all surprised and seated himself beyond the dog. He was in his middle years, and his features were unremarkable, apart from a slightly bent nose. Alice wondered if he'd been a pugilist at one time.

"Lie down," Chatham said softly to Tess. The wolfhound looked around before appearing to decide that nothing interesting was about to happen and complying.

"How on earth can I explain... that?" Lady Jesson stared at Tess. "I thought you meant a pug, or something similar. Horrid, yappy things, admittedly, but manageable. At least one can pick them up!"

"A recently deceased relative, perhaps?" Marstone suggested, a gleam of humour in his eyes. "An *eccentric* relative, who left you a modest annuity as long as you looked after his... or her... beloved Tess. I'm sure you can provide sufficient detail to make such an implausible tale sufficiently convincing."

Lady Jesson sighed. "Oh, very well."

The earl leaned back in his chair. "My problem, Miss Bryant, is that a member of the peerage has been sending clandestine messages to France. In addition, it has come to my notice that the French are in possession of certain confidential information to which this peer is also privy. Details which could be of material help to their army. We have intercepted one or two of the letters, and taken copies. Their contents, however, are vague in the extreme, and give no indication whether the correspondence is concerned with the information that has gone astray. The two may be linked, or not."

"What kind of information?" Alice asked. Movements of troops or battle plans?

"I will let you have more information if you accept the task."

Alice nodded.

"I am reluctant to believe the man is guilty," the earl went on, "but I must be sure."

"And if he is not, then you must look elsewhere for your traitor." Alice bit her lip, wondering if she should not have spoken up, but the earl seemed pleased rather than put out.

"Exactly. I am following several lines of enquiry, but I need people inside his house."

Alice looked at Chatham, still sitting impassively near the dog. "Can you not arrange to have a footman or maid taken on?" People who would have reason to be in almost any room in a house from time to time.

"Lady Jesson made the same suggestion when I first broached the subject. There is no time to do that, but in any case, servants have very little free time in which they might search for evidence. Guests, on the other hand, will have access to most of the house, and be able to move about the grounds without being questioned."

"And you can see I'm not the best person to explore the grounds," Lady Jesson put in, patting her waistline. "You will be able to walk much further than I."

"If you accept, you will accompany Lady Jesson to a house party early next month at this man's estate. Between you, you will endeavour to find out what you can to clear him, or to confirm his guilt. Chatham will accompany you, and exercising Tess will provide an excellent excuse for either you or him to be wandering around the park and grounds, if necessary."

"What would we be looking for?" Alice asked.

"Documents, letters, people where they should not be. That kind of thing."

"Why the grounds, my lord? Wouldn't documents and so forth be kept in the house?"

"I, or Lady Jesson, will explain that, should you accept. This is a lot to take in at once, Miss Bryant." The earl's tone sounded encouraging. "Lady Jesson has agreed to help, but will manage better—much better —with a companion such as yourself."

She expected him to say it was her patriotic duty to agree, but he didn't.

"Who are we to investigate? Oh, I will find out if I accept?"

The earl nodded.

"Come back with me, Alice, and we can discuss it." Lady Jesson rose as she spoke. "Lord Marstone, we will let you have an answer within a day or so."

"It all sounds rather underhand, and nebulous," Alice said, once they were alone in Lady Jesson's parlour. That reminded her of something. "When did Lord Marstone ask you to do this?"

"A week or so ago. Oh, you are thinking this is why I befriended you?" Lady Jesson shook her head. "No, Marstone contacted me after we had tea and cakes together. I felt I would like you then—I'm usually very good at sizing people up. All Marstone's approach did was to make me speed up the process of getting to know you." She reached over and patted Alice's arm. "My dear, it would be too difficult to pretend friendship for an extended period with a companion I did not like!"

Lady Jesson sounded sincere, and Alice's last lingering doubt disappeared. "Why did Lord Marstone choose you?"

"Because I'm a gossip."

"You're not..." Alice stopped as Lady Jesson shook her head.

"I am, my dear. It's a well-known fact. But I do my best not to pass on anything I know isn't true, or would harm someone."

"Phoebe spoke well of you," Alice acknowledged. "But how does that help?"

"What else did Phoebe say?"

"You... you use information to influence people. For the better."

Lady Jesson nodded. "I try, when there is the opportunity. I think this might be one such instance—I have obtained an invitation to the house party in question."

"Why me? I mean, how do you know you can trust me?"

"As I said, I am usually a good judge of character."

"I'd still like to know more about it before I commit myself."

"Marstone told me that stolen information is connected with a new type of weapon, so it is possibly more serious than the loss of a single battle plan. It could remove any advantage our army has over many battles."

This *was* an important task. But if the information was so significant...? "If this man is guilty, or if there is someone else spying, it may be dangerous. Aren't you worried by that?"

"Not really. Marstone himself does not really believe that... that our subject is guilty, and nor do I. We would be in no danger from him."

Alice decided to trust Lady Jesson's judgement on that.

"If there is someone else spying, Alice, we would only report what we know to Marstone. We would not confront him. And we will only be at the house party for the fortnight it lasts—Marstone hopes we will find some evidence one way or another in that time. However we may leave at any time if we become worried about our safety."

"Lord Marstone said that?"

Lady Jesson shook her head. "No. *I* said that. Marstone has no hold over us to make us stay in a situation in which we are not comfortable."

Alice mentally ticked off the points in her head: she could be of real service to her country, she would be helping to clear an innocent man of suspicion or identifying a traitor, and there should be very little risk. And she would enjoy Lady Jesson's company.

If she did not accept, she would have to continue searching for a new position. The discovery that three of her five first possibilities were not suitable had not been encouraging. It might take her longer than she'd anticipated to find a good opportunity, and she could end up having to live with Dan and his unpleasant wife until she did.

Alice took a deep breath, hoping that she was not making a dangerous mistake. "Very well, Lady Jesson. You have employed a companion!"

Lady Jesson smiled. "Thank you, my dear. Now, if we are to be together much of the time, I insist that you call me Maria. Do you have time to discuss some of the details before you return?"

Alice nodded.

"Good. I will ring for tea, then we may be comfortable."

Alice considered the situation while the tea was being prepared. "The house party—will a paid companion not be treated more as a servant than a guest?" Her gowns were plain and dark, as befitted a governess, and with lower waistlines than the current fashion. She would stand out amongst the guests.

"I will introduce you as a distant relation. Do not worry about your appearance. Marstone isn't going to pay me a salary, but I intend to get new wardrobes out of him for both of us." Maria's gaze focussed on Alice's hair. "And Simpson, my maid, will dress your hair in a more becoming style."

Alice laughed. "I wish her luck. It will not hold a curl, no matter how hard I try."

"Hmm. We'll see. As I was saying, Marstone will meet my expenses, which will include a year's salary for you. You will have plenty of time to look for a new position once the..."

"Spying?"

"Investigation. Once the investigation is finished."

The clink of china interrupted them, and Alice waited until the butler had left before asking her next question. "Who are we to investigate?"

"Lord Harlford. You will have seen him last year when he was courting your employer's daughter, and then Phoebe."

Lord Harlford?

"He doesn't seem..." Phoebe had spoken well of him, and he'd been helpful with that obnoxious trustee at the museum, but that didn't mean he wasn't a traitor. "I suppose a good spy must be able to seem something he is not."

The idea of spying on someone she'd talked to, and who had been friendly towards her, seemed even more underhand—dishonourable, even—than she'd originally thought.

"As I said earlier, I do not believe Harlford capable of treason." Maria sipped her tea. "Nevertheless, he *has* been corresponding with someone in France, and there is the question of information being where it should not. Both matters need investigation."

That was true, and she'd agreed to the plan. The identity of the person they were to investigate should make no difference.

"Why do we need a dog?"

"I understand that Harlford carries out his experiments somewhere in the grounds. Exercising her will provide an excuse for you or Chatham to explore beyond the formal gardens."

That made as much sense as any of the rest of the plan.

"The house party is being hosted by Harlford's mother, with the aim of providing a selection of young ladies from which he will be expected to choose a bride. I doubt he knows about it yet. She is unlikely to tell him until invitations have been accepted."

"So he cannot cry off?" Alice had some sympathy. He was handsome, if rather stiff and formal, but most of the mamas pushing their daughters at him would have their eyes on his title and wealth rather than his personality. It could not be pleasant to be pursued purely for those reasons.

Lady Jesson laughed. "Yes, poor man—I've seen him at balls. He looks... hunted at times. It is an interesting household we will be visiting. There are three Lady Harlfords."

Three?

"The current marquess' grandmother lives in the Dower House, or so I gather from gossip. Harlford's mother rules the roost in the main house, and his widowed sister-in-law lives there too."

"Three marchionesses..." Alice said, thinking out loud.

"Soon to be four, if his mother has her way."

CHAPTER 5

arlford Castle, Herefordshire

James recognised his mother's handwriting on one of the letters waiting for him at the breakfast table, and pushed the whole pile of correspondence to one side. He'd eat breakfast first, and look at the newspaper. Outside, the early morning rain had stopped, and gaps in the clouds allowed a few shafts of watery sunshine through.

When the footman had cleared the plates away and poured him another cup of coffee, he turned to the letters, leaving his mother's missive until last. An answer to an enquiry he'd made about a mare was welcome, and he put that aside to deal with later. Several invitations to summer house parties from families with whom he had the barest acquaintance must be prompted by the possession of marriageable daughters; he supposed he should accept one or two of them, if he were serious about finding a bride. He put those to one side as well —more interruptions to his work.

He broke the seal on the final letter and ran his eyes over his mother's neat script, cursing under his breath. *This* was what Mama had been planning last week.

As he'd refused to stay in Town to select a wife, she wrote, suitable candidates would be brought to Harlford. The invitations had already been sent. Any faint hope that people would decline to travel to Here-fordshire in the middle of the season was instantly dispelled by the second sheet, which listed several people who had already accepted.

Damn. He couldn't cancel the house party now without causing offence to many families and embarrassing Mama. Not that he would mind the latter—she had brought it on herself—but it wasn't worth the endless complaints that would result.

The guests would arrive at the beginning of May, which gave him only a couple of weeks of peace.

"Bad news, Jamie?" Lucy spoke from the doorway. He looked up with a smile—he'd arrived late yesterday evening, with only time for a few words with her before she retired. Her black curls were loosely tied back with a ribbon, and she wore a plain round gown suitable for a morning of lessons. It wouldn't be long now before she made her debut in society, but ensuring Lucy married someone she would be happy with was a problem for another year.

"We're to have a house party," James said as she sat at the table and reached for a piece of toast.

"Oh, good. It will be nice to have lots of people around." She gazed at him, her smile fading, and he realised he'd been scowling. He made an effort to lighten his expression—it wasn't fair to take out his bad mood on her.

"Mama is bringing some young ladies. She wants me to select a wife."

"That's good, isn't it? You need a wife."

"So she keeps telling me, but I'd rather have one of my own choos-ing." Not that she'd pressed any particular candidate on him so far, but she was clearly expecting him to choose from the guests she'd invited.

Lucy frowned. "I see what you mean. Robert and Arabella weren't very happy together."

"At least Arabella doesn't interrupt people while they are having breakfast."

"Oh, don't be stuffy, Jamie. Anyway, you've finished eating. You were sulking."

James opened his mouth to reply, but caught the laugh she was trying to hide. He couldn't help a rueful smile. "Well, you would sulk, too, at the prospect of having to dance attendance on guests for two weeks."

Lucy laughed. "Just tell her no. You're the marquess, aren't you?"

"Of course, that always worked well for Robert, didn't it?" He suspected his older brother hadn't tried very hard to avoid Mama's matchmaking. He'd married the quiet mouse his mother had presented as a suitable bride, and continued hunting, fishing, and gambling as he'd always done. And continued to visit his mistress in the village. That was not something James approved of, but it wasn't up to him to interfere.

"I wonder if the house party is the reason why Arabella went to visit her family?" Lucy said.

Bellingham had mentioned her absence when James arrived yesterday. If that was indeed the case, she'd shown more initiative than he'd credited her with—he wished he could avoid the party as easily.

"Is there really no-one you liked at all, Jamie? Not last year either?"

It seemed Lucy was not going to let the subject of his future wife drop. He toyed with the idea of telling her about Miss Deane, but rapidly banished the thought. "I don't know any of them well enough. It's impossible to converse properly in a ballroom."

"It looks as if Mama has invited lots of fathers and brothers." Lucy had risen and was reading the letter over his shoulder, leaning on the back of his chair. "She must be trying to keep the numbers even."

"Lucy! You'll have to behave better than this when we have guests."

"Mama will say I'm not due to be out until the year after next, and keep me locked up with Miss Sullivan in the schoolroom," Lucy said, some of the fun leaving her face. "What are these ladies like?"

James looked at the list of names again. Mama had invited the Comtesse du Calvac and her daughter, although they were on the shorter list of people who had not yet responded. "This one is bird-witted and vain." The others... "Miss Eyes," he muttered. And Miss Chatterbox—the brunette who talked a lot. The one so determined to please him that she agreed with everything he said, even totally ridiculous statements.

"Miss *Eyes*?" Lucy sat in the chair next to him and peered at the list. "Do you mean Miss Esham? Why did you call her Miss Eyes?"

James felt his face flushing. "She always seems to have something in her eye."

"You mean, like this?" She gazed up at him, eyebrows raised very slightly, head tilted a little to one side, and blinked rapidly.

"Yes, exactly like that." James had to laugh, his mood lightening at her silliness. "Who taught you do to that?"

"I'm merely observant," Lucy stated. "I've seen the housemaids do that to the young footmen. But Jamie, that can't be the only thing you know about her?"

"She excels in all the ladylike accomplishments." He took a sip of coffee. "She told me so herself."

Lucy laughed. "What about the others? Miss Gearing?"

"She giggles a lot. After every sentence."

"Miss Sullivan tells me off when I giggle—she says it is annoying."

"She is correct."

"And she says it makes people think I am silly or nervous." She took a second piece of toast and spread a huge dollop of jam on it.

"Or both."

Lucy pouted, before her ready smile took over.

Was that why Miss Gearing had agreed, with a giggle, to every observation he'd made?

"I expect you make them nervous, Jamie. I'm surprised they say anything at all. If you weren't my brother, I'd be terrified of you."

"I'm not terrifying," he protested.

"Trust me, Jamie—when you look like that, anyone would be terrified." She laughed at his grimace. "What is Miss Stockhart like?"

"Miss Shy." A short girl, if he recalled correctly, with pleasant features. She'd been almost silent at first, but when he'd asked what she liked about her home, she'd talked about the gardens and how she enjoyed painting flowers. The way her face became animated as she talked had made him think she truly enjoyed it, rather than it merely being one of the accomplishments expected of a young lady.

"Lucy, I am not going to go through the whole list with you. You'll meet them when they arrive."

The door opened. "It's time for your lessons, Lady Lucy."

"Sorry, Miss Sullivan." Lucy crammed the last piece of toast into her mouth and waved a slightly sticky hand at her brother. "Will you take me riding later?"

"If it's dry. Four o'clock?" He'd have done enough work by then, and he would see little enough of her once the house was full of Mama's guests. Lucy rewarded him with a beaming smile and followed her governess out of the room. He finished the last of the coffee and checked the clock—there was enough time to write about the mare before his steward was due to meet him.

Terring knocked on the library door at eleven o'clock precisely. James sighed. The steward's fortnightly sessions were necessary, but another drain on his time.

"Good morning, my lord." Terring put the ledgers on James' desk and opened them to the pages needing to be signed off. James ran his finger down the columns of numbers, adding up in his head as he went, and checked the totals at the bottom. He cast a cursory glance at the items of expenditure—nothing seemed to be out of the ordinary.

"The leases for Ryader and Wyeford Farms are due for renewal within a few weeks, my lord," Terring stated as James closed the ledger and pushed it back across the table. "I recommend increasing the rent in both cases."

James rubbed one temple. He knew little about farming, but he did have a healthy distrust of his late brother's management method of agreeing without question to everything suggested by the steward. "Why?"

"The overall revenues are not keeping up with expenditure, my lord."

Sitting up a little straighter, James looked Terring in the face. He had expected to be told agricultural profits had risen since the last rent review, or that improvements had been made to the land.

"Revenues have dropped? How so? No land has been sold recently, has it?"

"Er, no, my lord." The steward's face turned a dull shade of red.

"Rent arrears elsewhere? Poor harvests?"

Terring shook his head. "It is the expenditure that has increased, my lord. The contractors for her ladyship's plan to extend the formal gardens require an initial payment for materials."

Not again—last year he had vetoed his mother's plans to redecorate and refurnish all the ground floor rooms in the latest style. "When did I agree to this work?"

Terring swallowed. "Her ladyship had a Red Book done by Mr Repton some years ago, my lord. It suggested several ways in which the grounds could be remodelled to provide more attractive prospects. That was while your late brother was alive."

James waited.

"Er, the late marquess did not object, my lord."

"The estimates." James held his hand out.

"Um, I can fetch them, my lord, if you wish." Terring shuffled his feet.

"Tell me the total." The steward hesitated and James' brows drew together. "The total, if you please, Mr Terring!"

"J...just under three thousand pounds."

James stood abruptly, his chair almost toppling behind him. "Three thousand pounds?" He leaned forward, hands resting on the desk. "And you were going to start spending this money without checking with me?"

"Her ladyship—"

"Her ladyship is not in charge here." James regained his composure with an effort. "She runs the household only, until such time as... as my brother's widow decides to take the reins." An unlikely eventuality, unfortunately. "Is that clear?"

"Er... yes, my lord."

"You will offer the leases for those farms at their current rents.

Cancel the contractors, and authorise no additional spending whatsoever without referring to me first. Is that also clear?"

"Yes, my lord."

What else had Mama been spending money on?

"Tomorrow morning, I wish to see a list of all expenditure you have authorised since my brother's death, beyond the standard amount Lady Harlford is allocated for household expenses."

"Yes, my lord." Terring bobbed his head again, smiling weakly.

"And Terring—in future, pray do remember who actually employs you." James jerked his head to dismiss him, and Terring picked up the ledger and scurried out of the library.

His mother seemed to view the Harlford wealth as a bottomless pot. James recalled arguments several years ago, when Mama had badgered his father to buy Bourton Manor, in Sussex, then renovate it. All because Brighton was becoming a fashionable place for the *ton* to spend the summer. It had only been completed a few months before his father's death, and as a result of the mourning period for that, and then for Robert, Mama had never used it. Money wasted. If he indulged Mama in this, she would want something else redesigned or rebuilt next year.

As if this damned house party weren't enough, he would have to confront Mama about her spending soon. Luckily for her, she wasn't planning to return here until a day or two before the guests were due to arrive.

He stalked out of the library and along to his rooms, telling the butler as he passed to send his valet up and have Ventus saddled. A good gallop would put him in a better mood to see his grandmother. He'd have to wait until tomorrow to see what his laboratory assistants had done while he'd been away.

"Hello, Grandmama, how are you?" James bent over the thin hand the Dowager Lady Harlford held out to him.

"Well enough, thank you." Her hair was white, and she walked with a stick, but she was nowhere near as frail as her appearance implied. As was her habit, she sat near the glass doors that opened onto the terrace. This side of the Dower House looked across the knot garden and the lake to the Castle beyond. "When did you arrive?"

"Yesterday evening." He sat down.

"Hmm. In that case, Cassandra must have started organising the house party before you left Town."

"You've heard about that already?"

"The servants told me, of course. Cassandra had the sense to give them plenty of warning."

"Will you be joining in?"

Grandmama shook her head. "Tempting though it might be to put a spoke in her wheel, I don't think you would appreciate having Cassandra in a temper because of my presence." She tilted her head to one side. "What do *you* want out of this house party, James?"

"I didn't want it at all—I only received Mama's letter this morning. She's determined I should choose a bride."

"That is the way of things."

"I know." He sighed. "I *am* trying to get to know some young women—and some of them do seem *very* young—but I don't like feeling pushed into it. If I'm going to wed, I want to find someone who has some similar tastes to mine."

"And doesn't mind you shutting yourself away in your laboratory?"

He nodded.

"So, not a wife who will want to spend most of her time in Town."

"Exactly."

"This house party is not such a bad idea, then," she pointed out. "Going to Town to find a wife who does not like being there is somewhat contradictory, is it not?"

"True." All the young women he'd asked had assured him they enjoyed spending time in the country, but he suspected many of them had only said what they thought he wanted to hear. He began to feel a little better about the forthcoming party. It would, as she had pointed out, help him to get to know the young women and what they really thought about spending most of the year in the country. And Grandmama, at least, had his happiness in mind, not merely the production of an heir.

"Poor James. Never mind, you must bring them all to see me. Not all at once, mind!" She picked up a letter from the table beside her. "I have some news for you. Good news."

"Oh?" The only good news he could think of would be the cancellation of this damned party.

"Your uncle David is coming home. Permanently, I suspect. He has sold his place in Italy."

That *was* interesting. "I don't remember much about him. In person, that is. It was a pity he was in India when I visited Italy on my Grand Tour." There had been plenty of letters over the years, and his father or grandmother had read them to him, but they were mainly descriptions of the places where Uncle David had travelled.

"How should you? You were only ten when he left on his travels. I do recall you got on well with him then."

His memories were flashes of different things: Uncle David and his father taking him riding, swimming in the lake with him on a hot day, getting him out of a tree that was harder to climb down than it had been to get up. James also remembered Mama arguing with Uncle David. Not quite arguments, he corrected himself. He could recall his mother's angry tones, but only quiet replies from his uncle. He had never been able to work out what they had argued about.

"What brings him home now?"

"Oh, this and that. I asked him to come home when Robert died, and I think he started to wind up his affairs then. Now, James, tell me all about your time in London. Which young ladies did you get to know?"

James resisted the impulse to loosen his neckcloth. "There was Lady Hélène, Calvac's daughter."

"You're not still considering her, are you?"

"No, but she was considering me."

Grandmama tutted, but waited for him to continue. James settled back in his chair—he'd do his best to recall details, but he suspected it would feel more like an interrogation than a conversation.

CHAPTER 6

$\mathcal{A}$lice observed the passing countryside with interest as the familiar chalk downland gave way to the fertile clay soils of the Cotswolds and then the rolling fields and apple orchards of Herefordshire. Apart from a brief trip to Sussex and her journey to Scotland with the Calvacs last summer, she had only ever travelled between Wiltshire and London, and those trips had been in crowded and often smelly public coaches. She enjoyed the comfort of Lord Marstone's well-sprung coach, and there was plenty of room even with Tess taking up as much space as a person. Chatham must have exercised the dog well, for she spent most of the journey asleep at their feet.

They spent their second night on the road at the Kings Head in Hereford. Alice hesitated in surprise the following morning as she stepped out into the inn yard. Lord Marstone's coach was nowhere in sight, and Chatham was supervising the loading of the luggage into a much less appealing vehicle.

"Lady Harlford knows I'm not well-to-do," Maria explained as they climbed in. "It would be difficult to account for a luxurious coach, let alone one with Marstone's crest on the door."

"I suppose so." There were many details she hadn't thought of.

"How well do you know the dowager marchioness?"

"Not at all—she's decades older than I."

"Lord Harlford's mother?"

"Oh! No, his grandmother. Technically, there are three dowagers, but Harlford's grandmother is the senior one. It will save some confusion if we only use the term dowager when we are referring to her. His mother's in her mid-forties, I think. I haven't encountered her often in Town, but have heard some talk. Arabella, Harlford's sister-in-law, was married in her first season—a pale little thing, but with good lineage and a hefty dowry. Cassandra—that's Harlford's mother—will be after another meek girl she can keep under her thumb."

"How did you get the invitation if you are not friends?"

"I don't know." Maria's lips twitched. "What I mean is, I don't know the reason Cassandra allowed herself to be persuaded. All I did was mention that it would be a pity if her son found out what happened before Lord David Broxwood—Harlford's uncle—left for the continent. She soon sent me an invitation."

The maid sniffed.

"Simpson doesn't approve," Maria said.

Alice wasn't sure that she did, either. "What *did* happen?"

"I have no idea." Maria smiled, then laughed. "That's the beauty of dealing with people who have guilty secrets. I always thought there was something a little havey-cavey about Lord David's sudden departure. That was in my first season. I remember there being some gossip at the time, but it was pure speculation, as far as I know, and mostly not intended for debutantes' ears."

"So you only *suspected* she'd done something she's ashamed of?"

"Not ashamed of, necessarily, although she may be. There's something she doesn't want Harlford to know about. It may be of little importance—who knows?"

"What would Lord Marstone have done if she had not sent the invitation?"

"I'm sure he would have thought of something. You might have found yourself governess to Harlford's younger sister."

"On my own?" Alice shook her head. "I wouldn't have liked to undertake this alone."

"Well, it doesn't matter now." Maria turned towards the window. "These villages are very pretty, are they not, with the black and white houses?"

The coach jolted on for a couple of hours, and at last slowed and turned between a set of high pillars topped with stone lions, then passed over a small stone bridge. The gravelled drive led through a band of woodland shielding the estate from the public road, then across a park, with deer grazing beneath clumps of trees in the distance. The building itself was hidden from view until the chaise rounded a low hill.

Harlford Castle really was a castle, facing a smaller building across a lake. A square crenellated tower with an arch beneath occupied the centre of the frontage. As the coach came to a halt, Alice saw that this opened onto an inner courtyard. High walls extended either side to smaller towers at the ends of the façade. But its days as a proper castle were long gone, as the old walls were pierced with windows. A more modern extension stretched backwards, its south-facing wing looking over formal gardens.

"Very impressive," Maria said, eyebrows raised. "I can see why there is some competition for the position of fourth marchioness."

"It's probably cold, draughty, and inconvenient." Alice smiled; in spite of her prediction, she was looking forward to exploring it, and the gardens. She jumped down without waiting for the approaching footman to let down the step. Beyond him, a stately individual who must be the butler came towards them.

Alice turned to look across the lake. The house there was an elegant Palladian mansion, separated from the water by gardens. She must be looking at the back of the Dower House.

"Welcome to the Castle, my lady, Miss Bryant," the butler said with a bow. "My name is Bellingham. If you would step this way, please? I will have a maid show you to your rooms."

"Well organised," Maria whispered as they followed the butler through the arch into a courtyard, then up a flight of steps to the main doors.

Alice had another moment of hesitation as she entered the building, but straightened her spine and followed the butler across the echoing hall and up a wide staircase. She was committed now.

James checked the letter Terring had prepared for the landscaping contractors while Lucy sat reading at the far end of the library. Over the last couple of weeks he'd examined the account books and found nothing more than Mama overdrawing her allocated allowance. He didn't know what she'd spent it on, and wasn't going to try to find out. The money was gone, and it wasn't so much that it would materially harm the estate's prosperity, but he did abhor waste. The steward would be more careful in future, but James resented the time stolen from his research to check the books.

"There's another carriage, Jamie." Lucy jumped up to peer out of a window. "That must be the last one."

"For goodness sake, Lucy, can you not sit still for more than five minutes? Don't make me regret giving Miss Sullivan a holiday."

James regarded his sister with amusement. She had asked him if she could be included in the activities Mama had planned. He didn't see why not, and said so—she was only a couple of years away from being introduced to society, and it would be unreasonable to expect her to concentrate on lessons while their guests were playing croquet or charades. Some of the young women might even be company for her—it must be lonely for her at times; there were only a couple of families in the neighbourhood with girls of a similar age.

Lucy had suggested that it would be kind to allow the governess to visit her family in Cheshire for the fortnight, and James had agreed to that, too. When Mama, on her return to Harlford two days ago, had discovered that the governess was missing, it was far too late to get the woman back. James said so, and refused to listen to Mama's complaints.

His lips twitched. He should be cross with his sister for manipulating the situation, but she had certainly got the better of their mother, for once.

"Oh, there's another one arriving." Lucy opened the window and leaned out precariously. "A hired carriage, by the looks of it. I thought everyone was here. Jamie, have you Mama's letter to hand?"

James opened a drawer and flicked through the pile of labelled folders, extracting the letter with the list of guests.

Lucy read through it. "More carriages have come than this list suggests. Shall we go and see who the new ones are?"

"No." James held his hand out for the letter. "You go, if you wish. I'm busy."

"How can you concentrate on stuffy business with all this excitement?" Lucy picked up his brass paperweight and examined it, before setting it down again impatiently. "Mama wasn't pleased about Arabella not being here either—I expect she wanted her to chaperone me."

James reached out and replaced the paperweight in its original position. "I expect she did."

Lucy's hand drifted towards the cut-glass inkwell. James put his hand on it. "Lucy! Leave me alone, or I'll suggest to Mama that you stay in the Dower House for the duration."

"Oh, very well."

Lucy flounced out of the room, and James restored the folder to its place, lining it up with the others in the drawer.

The account books lay on his desk, next to his research notebook. He would have to tell Mama to restrain her spending, but with the house filling with guests, this was not the time.

He locked his notebook in its drawer with regret. He wasn't going to get much work done in the next few weeks. If he chose one of the young women his mother had invited, it would be a decision that affected the rest of his life. It behoved him to spend most of his time getting to know them.

He would greet the guests formally this evening, but now he'd head for the stables. Athena was due to foal within a week or so—he'd go and check how she was coming along.

~

The maid led Alice and Maria along the corridor, two footmen following with their trunks. Alice's supposition that the place would be cold and draughty had been mistaken—the two wings behind the old stone frontage were much more recent, with wood panelling on the walls and a thick carpet muffling the sound of their feet.

They were shown into a room halfway along the corridor. It was not large, but the bed appeared comfortable enough even though the embroidered hangings were a trifle faded and didn't match the fabric on the chairs by the fireplace. A door in one wall opened onto a small dressing room, and the tall sash window overlooked a stable yard, with parkland beyond. Trying to work out directions, Alice thought this room was on the opposite side of the house to the formal gardens.

Simpson sniffed, then directed the footmen where to leave the trunks.

"You're upstairs, miss," the maid said to Alice. "If you will follow me?" She led Alice and Maria back to the main landing, and through a door that Alice hadn't noticed earlier—there was no doorframe, the edges of the door cunningly arranged to coincide with joins in the panelling. Narrow stairs led upwards and opened onto a plainly painted corridor, illuminated at the moment only by light coming through open doors.

"Is this the nursery floor?" Maria asked.

"Yes, my lady." The maid pushed open a door giving onto a small room. "There are a lot of guests here, so Miss has the head nurse's room."

"I thought Lady Harlford—the youngest Lady Harlford—had a baby?" Alice asked. That was why Harlford had not taken the title until months after his brother's death, when the new arrival turned out to be a girl.

"Yes, miss, but she likes to have little Lady Mary with her. There are only a couple of nursemaids now, and they sleep in one of the dressing rooms in her ladyship's suite. But her ladyship has taken Lady Mary to see her family."

Alice's room had a narrow single bed set against one wall, and a threadbare armchair near the fireplace. She thought with regret of the comfortable room she'd occupied in the Comte du Calvac's townhouse, and the much larger one Maria had given her in London. Looking on the bright side, there was a bucket of coal standing ready by the fire.

"This is not—"

"This will be acceptable." Alice interrupted Maria's complaint.

The maid looked relieved, and bobbed a curtsey before leaving.

Maria waited until the door closed behind the maid, her lips pressed together. "This is an insult—to you and to me. Cassandra—"

"It gives me an excuse to be on this floor, if I need to be, and the window overlooks the opposite side of the building to yours."

Some of the tension left Maria's shoulders.

"It must be part of Lady Harlford's revenge after your... persuasion. Really, Maria, it's perfectly all right. As a governess, I've not been used to better accommodation than this." She tilted her head to one side and grinned. "Shall we explore this floor while we're here? We need a bit of exercise after sitting in the carriage all morning."

"Very well. After you."

The room along the corridor was almost empty. Cupboards against the wall and small frames without mattresses indicated it must once have been a bedroom for children. The adjacent room was much larger, with several windows giving it an airy feel. A round table occupied the middle of the floor, holding a globe and an untidy pile of books, together with a notebook, pencils, and an inkwell.

Alice went over to the bookcases, as if drawn by a magnet, but was disappointed to find that most of the volumes were dry histories or stories for young children.

"Hello." The voice came from behind them. "Were you looking for anything in particular?"

Alice started, turning abruptly. She'd have to pay more attention—her career as a spy was not going to last long if she didn't notice people entering the room.

The young lady—for it was a lady, not a servant—had glossy black curls confined in a bandeau, laughing brown eyes, and features that showed she was related to Lord Harlford. Her words could have been a reprimand, but her face contained only curiosity.

"My room is a few doors along the corridor," Alice said, "so I thought I'd look around before going back downstairs. I'm Alice Bryant, and this is Lady Jesson."

"Oh!" The girl's eyes grew round. "You have only just arrived?"

"That's right, Lady..." Maria said.

The girl blushed, dropping a small curtsey. "I'm Lucilla Broxwood, but I prefer to be called Lucy. I'm pleased to meet you, my lady." She waved at the books on the desk. "I'm still in the schoolroom, but my governess is away so I will be allowed to join the guests." Her brows creased. "Why have they put you in the nursery wing, Miss Bryant?"

"The maid said you have a lot of guests," Alice explained. "I don't mind. There's a splendid view over the gardens from here; I'm looking forward to exploring in them."

"Oh, there's a much better view from the library, on the next floor down, but Jamie—my brother—uses it and doesn't like to be disturbed. I was trying to read but it was too exciting, looking out for all the new people arriving, so he sent me away for talking too much." She put her hand to her mouth in dismay. "Oh dear, I'm doing it again, aren't I?"

Maria laughed. "Don't worry about that. But could you show me back to my room, Lady Lucy, if you know which one it is? This is such a large house."

"Of course." Lucy led the way back down the narrow stairs onto the first floor landing. "Would you like me to show you around the house? And please, don't bother with the 'lady'; it makes me think I'm being reprimanded for something."

"You must call me Alice, and I would love to be shown around." Alice glanced at Maria. "Would you prefer to rest?"

"I think I'll get settled in my room," Maria said. "Simpson can get me some tea. I'm along this corridor, I think. Come to me there later, Alice."

CHAPTER 7

"May we start our tour by going to the stables?" Alice asked.

Lucy smiled. "Yes, if you wish. I didn't see a horse arrive with you."

"Lady Jesson came into some money from an aunt recently," Alice said, recalling the story they'd agreed upon. "She had to take the old lady's dog as a condition of the inheritance. I help to look after her."

"Oh, a dear little dog!" Lucy's eyes lit up. "I always wanted one, but Mama doesn't like having animals in the house."

That might complicate things. All the more reason to exercise Tess in the grounds, though.

"Doesn't Lady Jesson want her dog in the room with her?" Lucy continued.

Alice laughed. "I'll introduce Tess to you if you like." She paused, feeling a pang of guilt about using Lucy to further their nefarious ends. "I wonder, is there a servants' stair I could use if I need to bring Tess indoors?"

Ten minutes later, Alice's head was spinning with the details, but she had been shown the servants' passages that gave access to one end of the library, to the two main corridors, and to the stairs that led down to the kitchen levels and on out to the stable yard.

Lucy hesitated, then set off to the far side of the yard and knocked on a half-open door. "Pritchard, is there a new dog?"

A short man with a jockey's build came to the door. "I should say so, my lady." He looked curiously at Alice.

"This is Miss Bryant," Lucy said. "It's her dog."

"Ma'am." Pritchard touched his forehead, then pointed. "End door. Found a room where your man can sleep with her."

By the time they reached the end door, Chatham had emerged with Tess on a leash.

Alice smiled at Lucy's round eyes and open mouth. "You can see why it's best that Tess sleeps in the stables."

"Oh, yes," Lucy laughed. "Mama would have a fit!" She took a hasty step backwards as Tess moved towards her, but the dog only sniffed at her and sat down, the end of her tail moving gently. Lucy reached out a tentative hand and stroked her head.

"She likes being scratched behind her ears, my lady," Chatham said. Tess' tail wagged further as Lucy tried that.

Alice stretched her back. "Lucy, Tess and I have been sitting still in the chaise all morning. Would you mind showing me around the grounds? We could take Tess with us."

"That will be fun." Lucy set off towards the rear exit from the stable yard. "You saw the front when you arrived, so we'll start in the formal gardens."

Alice took Tess' leash from Chatham and followed Lucy around the back of the building, through the edge of a shrubbery and past a high brick wall. The terrace she'd seen from the coach stretched the length of this side of the building, one tower of the crenellated frontage marking the far end. A gnarled wisteria trained along the wall and between the windows was almost in flower.

"This is lovely," Alice said, coming to a stop at a flight of shallow steps leading down to a lawn that paralleled the terrace. Tess pulled on the leash, her nose twitching, but sat when Alice told her to.

"It's better in summer." Lucy pointed to the parterre garden beyond the lawn, its box-bordered beds separated by gravelled paths converging on a circular pool in the centre. "I love to come out here to paint when the fountain is on and the roses are in bloom." She looked at Tess. "There's an orchard beyond the garden. Would you like to go there so your dog can run around?"

Tess, although still obediently sitting, was shuffling her front paws, so Alice readily agreed. As they crossed the formal garden, a pair of women approached arm in arm from one of the other walks. The older woman, in a pelisse of rich burgundy, wore her hair powdered and dressed high. The younger had auburn curls visible beneath her bonnet, and an elaborate amber walking dress. As they came nearer, Alice could make out regular features, with long eyelashes and a rosebud mouth.

"Friends, Tess," she said quietly, as they came to a halt. She wasn't sure how Tess would react to strangers, but the dog merely sat down and waited.

"Lady Esham, Miss Esham." Lucy curtseyed as she spoke, and Alice followed suit. "May I introduce Miss Bryant? She is here as Lady Jesson's companion."

"Pleased to meet you, Miss Bryant." Lady Esham's voice was flat. Miss Esham raised one eyebrow and raked her gaze over Alice's pelisse, the prettiness of her face marred by disdain. She nodded, a mere twitch of her head, then took her mother's arm and walked on.

Lucy frowned. "Did I do it wrong? She looked down her nose at me when we were introduced earlier. I can't have said anything wrong then, as Mama did the introductions."

"I wouldn't worry about such an impolite person." Alice set off along the path again. "Come, let us take Tess to the orchard." She would like to enjoy the blossom for half an hour without worrying about how she and Maria could begin to investigate their host.

"But I *do* worry—she might become my sister-in-law!"

"Hmm. Your brother might have more sense than to marry someone so rude."

"I doubt it," Lucy muttered.

~

James checked his neckcloth in the mirror, adjusting his ruby pin so it was exactly in the middle. He allowed Mitton to give his coat a final brush, then straightened his shoulders and headed for the drawing room. He was not looking forward to this evening—or the rest of the fortnight, come to that. Although there were other unmarried young men in attendance, he would be the main target, as if he were a piece of meat on display.

Exactly what had he said to his mother when she arrived at Harlford? Had he actually *promised* to choose one of the young ladies she had invited? Surely he had not been so stupid.

No—he had agreed only to take part in the activities she planned. He would give the young women a chance to show more of their true selves here than they could in the confines of a ballroom or a carriage ride in Hyde Park. He should not dismiss any of them without getting to know them better.

A footman opened the parlour door and announced him. The hum of conversation ceased and clothing rustled as everyone turned to face him. There were around twenty people in the room, slightly more women than men. As he looked around, the younger women curtseyed, while the older ones and the men nodded or bowed.

His mother hurried to his side. "Come, James, let me introduce you. This is Mr Ashley Gearing, Miss Gearing's brother. You know Miss Gearing, of course, and her mother, Lady Gearing."

"I am pleased to meet you again, my lord," Miss Gearing said, with a high-pitched titter and downcast eyes. Had Lucy been correct about nervous giggles?

"And you remember Miss Chilton..."

Miss Chatterbox. When he asked, she'd professed to enjoy the theatre, but hadn't been able to recall much detail about the last production she'd seen.

There were Miss Chilton's parents to greet, and two brothers, then Miss Esham of the eyelashes, and Miss Stockhart, who was almost too shy to speak at all but had admitted to enjoying painting. He had more difficulty keeping track of the names and faces of brothers and parents.

"James, do be polite and talk to people," Lady Harlford admonished, when she had toured most of the room with him. "And I mean the young ladies. No talking about hunting or boxing with their brothers."

"No, Mama." Really, must she speak as if he were still in the schoolroom?

She left him, and James looked around. Two women sat on a sofa in the far corner—Lady Jesson, and a younger woman. Why hadn't Mama introduced them? He hadn't thought Lady Jesson was old enough to have a daughter of marriageable age.

He made his way towards them, but it was only as he drew close that he recognised the younger woman—her primrose coloured gown suited her complexion far better than the drab things she'd worn at the British Museum and in Hyde Park, although her hair was still pulled straight back with none of the elaborate curls the other women sported.

But what was Miss Bryant doing here? He thought the Calvacs had declined their invitation. Had they changed their minds?

"Good evening, Lord Harlford." Lady Jesson held out a hand, and James bowed over it. "I believe you have met Miss Bryant before, although she was not my companion then."

James let out a breath—he would not have to fend off Lady Hélène's machinations.

"Miss Bryant." Unlike the other young women he had just been introduced, or re-introduced to, she wasn't looking up at him expectantly, fluttering her eyelashes or giggling. In fact, she looked uncomfortable. "I hope you both enjoy your time here at Harlford. Did I see you in the gardens earlier, with my sister?"

"Lady Lucy was good enough to show me the gardens, my—"

"Oh, Lord Harlford, I wanted to say how lovely your gardens are."

"Excuse me, Miss Bryant." He turned towards the woman who had so rudely interrupted them. The fluttering eyelashes...Miss Esham.

"I took a walk in the gardens with Mama this afternoon," Miss Esham went on, undeterred by his lack of response. Or possibly not even noticing. "It would be lovely if you could show me around tomorrow."

"You are interested in botany, Miss Esham?"

"Oh, yes, I find it a fascinating subject."

He smiled, not believing it for one moment. "I will arrange for the head gardener to give you a tour. Do let Bellingham know what time would suit you best."

Miss Esham's lips drooped, before she pasted on a wide smile. "It would be so much more enjoyable if you—"

"Fowler knows much more than I about the subject, Miss Esham. I'm sure you will benefit greatly from his expertise."

Her smile this time appeared forced. "Thank you, my lord." She turned and walked away.

"I would enjoy being shown around by your head gardener," Miss Bryant said.

James studied her face, but detected no insincerity or mockery there. "I'm sure Fowler will be happy to take both of you."

As she thanked him, Bellingham announced that dinner was served. At the far side of the room, his mother moved in his direction, Miss Gearing beside her. A dinner full of giggles wasn't appealing, even if the girl couldn't help it. He cleared his throat.

"Lady Jesson, may I escort you into dinner? And Miss Bryant?"

"I think I will talk to Lady Harlford," Lady Jesson said. "But thank you for your invitation. Alice will be happy to accept." She smiled at him, and moved off to intercept his mother.

He looked around—Miss Esham was hovering hopefully, but beside her, gazing at a landscape on the wall...

"Miss Stockhart, may I escort you, too?"

A blush rose to her cheeks and she fixed her gaze on the top button of his waistcoat. "I... That is, thank you, my lord."

In the dining room, he ignored his mother's frown at the disruption of her seating plan, and ushered Miss Bryant and Miss Stockhart to the facing chairs on either side of his place at the head of the table. From beside his mother, Lady Jesson commented, in a voice that was surely a little louder than necessary, that it was such a nice change to have an informal seating arrangement, and it took a woman confident in her social position to allow it. His lips twitched as he watched Mama register what Lady Jesson had said and decide not to protest.

"I recall that you enjoy painting flowers," he said to Miss Stockhart, once both ladies had a selection of food on their plates. Her face reddened again.

"I... yes, I do." She cut up a piece of chicken and pushed it with her fork.

"Miss Stockhart might like to join tomorrow's garden tour." Miss Bryant spoke into the following silence.

Miss Stockhart raised her head.

"Lord Harlford's head gardener will show Miss Esham and me around the gardens."

"Would you like that, Miss Stockhart?" James hoped she was not going to be silent for the whole meal.

"I would, thank you." Her voice was almost inaudible, but at least she'd replied.

"If you wish to paint, ask my butler for a footman to assist you with your easel and other equipment." Or whatever else she needed.

A small frown creased her brow. What had he said wrong now?

"I understand that Lady Lucy—his lordship's sister—enjoys sketching and watercolours," Miss Bryant said. "If you have not brought your own materials, she might let you borrow hers."

Miss Stockhart smiled.

"She'd be happy to," James confirmed, grateful that Miss Bryant seemed to have identified the problem. "Do you paint, Miss Bryant?" he asked, when the silence began to feel uncomfortable.

"I can produce a passable image, but it is not my preferred pastime..."

That was surprisingly honest. He tried—and failed—to imagine someone like Miss Esham admitting that her drawings were merely passable.

"...I enjoy the beauty of a garden as a whole, as well as the individual plants."

"Do you make a study of botany then, in addition to your interest in classification?" He remembered with amusement the stunned expression on the trustee's face in the British Museum when she had started to explain the Linnaean system.

"I am interested in many things. As you would require from a governess, I think?"

He'd forgotten for a moment why she'd been at the museum. "I would expect knowledge, Miss Bryant, not necessarily interest beyond that required to teach effectively."

"But I think someone who is truly interested can more easily inspire enthusiasm in her charges than someone who merely delivers facts."

"I think that is true, my lord." Miss Stockhart looked almost as surprised as he was that she had spoken up. He gave what he hoped was an encouraging smile.

"My first governess did not like painting. It was only when Papa took on a different woman who enjoyed it herself that I really started to learn."

He wasn't sure that was always true—it had been his tutor's disdain for matters scientific that had spurred him on to learn what he could from books.

"I think there are some illustrated botanical volumes in the library," he said. "Please feel free to look or borrow them while you are here. You, too, Miss Bryant."

"Thank you, my lord." They spoke almost in unison.

Had he just made a foolish offer, inviting two women to make free of his sanctuary? Perhaps not—Miss Bryant appeared to be a sensible woman who would use the library for its intended purpose, and Miss Stockhart was too timid to take advantage.

"Does your home have a large garden, Miss Stockhart?" Miss Bryant asked. James was happy to listen as his two companions talked of their gardens at home, and he described the local countryside when they asked about beauty spots in the vicinity of the Castle.

Altogether, it was the most pleasant dinner he'd experienced in some time. This fortnight might pass more easily than he'd feared.

～

Alice curled up in the chair beside the fire in Maria's room and opened the latest copy of the *Agricultural Journal*. She'd been startled by Lord Harlford's sudden invitation to escort her into dinner, but enjoyed it more than she'd expected. He'd been a little stiff and formal at first, but once Miss Stockhart had gathered enough confidence to take part, the conversation had flowed more easily. His descriptions of riding the nearby hills and valleys had shown a love of the countryside that was similar to her own.

Being seated beside Lord Harlford, and at his own request, had earned her poisonous looks from two of the other young women present and their mothers. When the ladies withdrew, she'd come up here instead of joining them in the parlour, unwilling to subject herself to the questions that would have initiated any conversation, such as who her family was and how she was connected to Lady Jesson.

She smiled at the idea that she could be a threat to them, and turned to an article on breeding pigs.

"You escaped very quickly."

Alice folded the journal as Maria came into the room and sat in the chair opposite. "Lady Harlford looks through me as if I am invisible."

"She'd do the same to me if she dared, I suspect," Maria said. "The next few days should be interesting—in many ways."

"Did you gather any gossip?"

"Only the usual who is courting whom, how much money they have, and so on. And Cassandra boasting about the size of the estate here, and the Castle." Maria shrugged. "Nothing useful for our purposes."

"That's not really surprising. I found out nothing useful either—although Lord Harlford did say I might borrow books from his library."

"Excellent. Simpson says, via servants' hall gossip, that Harlford spends a lot of time there. It is a likely place to find any incriminating documents."

Alice sighed. "Finding a time to do so without being caught might be difficult."

"Well, we have a fortnight. Chatham may find something useful from the outdoor staff."

"We're taking Tess for a walk early tomorrow morning—I can ask him then." Alice still found it difficult to believe Lord Harlford could be a traitor—he'd been helpful and friendly whenever she'd talked to him. But a good spy must be able to deceive people.

"What did you think of Miss Stockhart?" Maria asked, with the air of one settling down for a good coze.

CHAPTER 8

*T*he morning air in the stable yard was pleasantly brisk on Alice's skin. It lacked half an hour to the time she'd arranged with Chatham, but the blue skies visible from her bedroom window and the sound of birdsong had tempted her out into the dewy morning. Maria would be abed for another couple of hours.

Chatham took only a few minutes to ready himself when she knocked on his door. Tess' tail waved enthusiastically as the three of them left the stable yard via the same archway Alice had taken with Lucy the day before. This time they carried on walking through the shrubbery instead of skirting the house.

Alice waited until they were on a worn path beneath the apple trees in the orchard, and well away from the buildings. "I saw a rider coming this way from my window. Did you see who it was?"

"Yes, miss. Lord Harlford, that would be. From what I heard, he goes off most mornings, early. Sometimes he's away all day, but he's expected back mid-morning today."

"Do they know where he goes?"

"There's a quarry out that way, marked on the plans Lord Marstone obtained. In the middle of them woods, most likely." He pointed in the direction they were walking.

They followed the same track Lord Harlford had taken, stepping out briskly across the gently rolling grass of the park. Chatham let Tess off the leash once they left the orchard, and she ran around, sniffing at the bases of the trees that dotted the park, and following invisible trails on the ground.

"Is the quarry where he does his experiments?" Alice asked.

"I reckon so, Miss. I got talking to the stable lads last night—there's bangs now and then, and his lordship sometimes smells of fireworks when he comes back."

"The information going to the French is something to do with a new weapon."

"Aye, so I was told." Chatham scratched his head. "A couple of men work there—folks here have seen them come and go, but they live out. Walk in from the villages to the east, like as not, and come in the back of the park."

"You've found out a lot in one evening."

Chatham shrugged. "The lads are happy enough to talk, especially if I give them a hand with the mucking out."

The path became muddier as they entered the woods. Carpets of celandines and wood anemones glowed in the light slanting through the still-bare branches. Further on, banks of wild garlic held furled buds above their smooth leaves, soon to be in bloom. She could wander here for hours—but she had a job to do. "Can we look at the quarry today? I don't have to be back for at least another hour."

"We can look for it, Miss, yes. We'd best be quiet though."

Alice shrugged. "If we're spotted, we can claim that Tess ran off." Tess looked around, then continued her exploration of smells and sounds.

Eventually more sky became visible ahead, and they slowed as they approached a thinning of the trees where the path joined a track that came in from their right, its origin hidden by a rising shoulder of land. Could that be the quarry?

Chatham must have had the same thought, for he stopped, then gestured for her to follow him back the way they had come. He halted around a bend in the path, and surveyed the woodland sloping above them.

"I might be able to look down into the quarry from up there."

"*We* might," Alice corrected him, and followed him up the hillside, lifting her skirts to avoid them tangling in the undergrowth. She kept her eyes open for dead branches—the crack from stepping on one would carry for some distance. But other than an occasional muttered curse from Chatham when his clothing caught on old bramble stems, they managed a quiet ascent.

The ground disappeared a few yards ahead, and they edged forward slowly, doing their best to keep tree trunks between them and the quarry. It was about thirty feet deep and roughly circular, with piles of shattered rocks at the base of the walls. An opening to their left must be where the track came in. A long low building stood near the entrance, with several metal racks beyond it, surrounded by blackened earth.

There were no people visible, and if there were windows in the building they must be on the far side. Alice backed away from the edge. She turned her head to speak to Chatham, but he wasn't there. Retreating into the trees a little way, she carried on until she came across him bending to examine a patch of grass that ran up to the quarry edge. Tess, her nose deep inside a bush, whined, and Chatham went to investigate, carefully moving the branches aside to peer in.

"There's a folded tarpaulin in there, Miss," he reported when he emerged from the bush. He stepped away, waving a hand for her to follow him. "That grass was flattened when I got here. I reckon someone comes here to watch the quarry."

Alice peeped over the edge—from here the track was clearly visible, and she could see enough of the far side of the building to make out a door and several windows.

"Just as well they're not here now," Chatham added absently, his eyes on Tess. The animal was sniffing around the tiny clearing, then set off away from the quarry, heading further north along an indistinct path through the undergrowth.

"Following a scent?" Alice asked, putting from her mind the question of what would have happened if they *had* run into a spy.

Chatham nodded. "She'll let us know if she smells the same thing later. I'll follow her now, Miss, but you'd best get back before you're missed. Can you find your way?"

Alice nodded—she only had to go down this hillside until she crossed the path they'd arrived by. If Chatham did encounter the man they were looking for, he'd do better if he didn't have to protect her.

If she hurried, she might be able to report to Maria before she went down for breakfast.

"James, a moment, if you please! I missed you at breakfast."

James paused with one foot on the bottom stair, then turned to face his mother as she crossed the hall towards him, Miss Chilton following a few yards behind. "I told you I'd be at the quarry this morning." And he was here, as arranged, in plenty of time to join the guests for refreshments at one o'clock.

"Miss Chilton wanted to ask you something."

"I hoped you could show me the best places from which to sketch the lake, my lord."

That was only a slight variation on wanting a tour of the gardens, but at least this one didn't keep blinking at him. "I'm afraid I have no eye for the artistic, Miss Chilton. My sister will be pleased to help you, I'm sure." Perhaps she would not make such a transparent excuse to seek his company in future. "Mama has already arranged a walk this afternoon."

"At two o'clock," Mama confirmed.

"Oh, well, I will join you then. Thank you, my lord." Miss Chilton smiled prettily, and James wondered if he'd done her an injustice. He shrugged—he would invite Lucy along as well, and see if Miss Chilton did ask about sketching spots.

In the library, instead of dealing with his correspondence, he went to stand by the window. A group of four figures strolled between the box hedges in the gardens below—Fowler was giving the garden tour Miss Esham had requested. His lips twitched as he wondered how she was enjoying it.

The door opened, and footsteps approached. His shoulders tensed as he turned to see who had invaded his territory, but he relaxed when he saw it was only Lucy.

"What are you looking at, Jamie?"

"The garden."

"Oh, don't be grumpy!" She crossed the room to stand beside him, following his gaze. "Who are they?"

"Miss Esham, Miss Stockhart, and Miss Bryant."

"Do you like Miss Stockhart? Are you going to marry her?"

"Good grief, Lucy, I've only talked to her a few times!"

"You took her in to dinner last night. Bellingham told Mrs Finch, and Sally—my maid, you know—overheard and told me. I haven't met Miss Stockhart yet, but Miss Bryant is friendly."

He supposed a governess would be good at befriending girls of Lucy's age. He wondered what else his sister had found out from servants' gossip, but decided it was wiser not to ask. "Miss Stockhart merely happened to be standing nearby when Mama brought Miss Gearing over."

"Miss Giggles?"

"Don't call her that, Lucy. That was only to help me remember their names." If he wasn't careful, he would end up using his silly names to someone's face.

"I didn't think someone like Miss Esham would be interested in talking to the gardener." Lucy had turned her attention back to the gardens.

"She said she was interested in botany, and asked me to show her around. Fowler knows more about plants than I, so I arranged a tour for her."

"Jamie, you are hopeless!"

"Really?"

"She wanted *you* to escort her. How else can she get you alone to flutter her eyelashes at you?"

"Why do you think I suggested Fowler show them round?" He'd be hopeless indeed if he hadn't worked that out by now.

"Perhaps you're not as bad as I thought." Lucy dimpled at him.

"Thank you for that compliment, dear sister. Miss Chilton wanted me to show her the best places to paint the lake."

Lucy rolled her eyes.

"Indeed. Will you accompany us on our walk this afternoon so you can show her?"

She grinned. "Of course. I will let you know if she really is interested. I'll see you later."

She left the door open behind her as she went. James crossed the room to close it, then sat down at his desk. He should try to get *something* done before he had to go and be polite.

His concentration didn't last long. He replied to a couple of letters, then looked out at the gardens again. The little group now stood near the far door into the kitchen garden. As he watched, Miss Esham left them and stalked towards the house, irritation plain in the way she moved. He couldn't help smiling—she had enjoyed the botanical tour as little as he'd expected.

He watched the remaining two women a few minutes longer. They stood with Fowler by a bed of seedlings; the gestures, and the way the women were standing, indicated they were putting Fowler's knowledge to the test. The little group appeared more animated now Miss Esham had left.

Hmm. He had agreed to escort some of the young ladies on a walk this afternoon. Apart from Miss Chilton, his mother had not specified *which* young ladies. He would do well to make his own choice before she did so for him.

Not wanting to encounter Mama, he used the servants' door at the east end of the library to head for the garden.

The refreshments at one o'clock appeared more formal than the normal selection of foods laid out on a sideboard, but James managed to evade any seating plan Mama might have made and took a place next to one of the Chilton brothers.

That hadn't been a good move, he soon decided. James would have been happy to discuss horses, but Julius Chilton subjected him to a long and tedious anecdote about his hunting exploits. Across the table, Lord Chilton concentrated on his plate, ignoring Lord Gearing's attempt to talk to him—politics, from the few snatches he overheard.

"...took a toss, right into a ditch. But I didn't let..."

There was quite a contrast between the Chilton menfolk. The man beside him bore little resemblance to Lord Chilton's rotund figure and fleshy face.

"...fool couldn't manage a four foot hedge, and went..."

The other brother... Augustus? His pale blue coat and embroidered pink waistcoat contrasted with his brother's more sober attire, but he, at least, did not appear to be boring his companion. Miss Stockhart was taking a full part in that conversation.

Perhaps Lucy was right and he did make some of the young women nervous. He must try to be more friendly.

"I say, Harlford, is there any chance of a run out while we're here? I know the season's over and all that, but this is new countryside to me."

The sudden stop to the flow of words brought James' attention back to Julius Chilton. Riding? Not with Chilton, if he could help it. "I'm afraid I'm too busy. Ask Pritchard, my stablemaster, to assign you a groom to show you the best rides."

"Thanks, Harlford. Did I tell you about the time...?"

He was relieved when his mother rose as a sign the meal was over. That feeling was short-lived.

"James. Miss Esham would like to join your stroll around the lake with Miss Chilton."

"Very well, Mama. Lucy, Miss Stockhart, and Miss Bryant will be joining us, too." He ignored Mama's frown when he mentioned the last name. "I will see anyone who wishes to come in half an hour in the courtyard."

CHAPTER 9

*W*hen the walking party gathered in the courtyard, James found that Augustus Chilton and Lady Jesson had also joined them. James offered his arm to Miss Stockhart, who hesitated for a moment before laying her hand on it. Miss Chilton reluctantly accepted her brother's escort, leaving Miss Esham to choose between Lucy, Lady Jesson, and Miss Bryant.

James hid his amusement as he watched Miss Esham's expression change from dismissive as she looked at Lucy to wary as her gaze turned to Lady Jesson. She settled on Miss Bryant, taking her arm, and then manoeuvred the pair of them so they were walking directly behind him. They set off towards the path around the lake, and the cool shade of the courtyard gave way to warm sunshine.

"How did you enjoy the gardens this morning, Miss Stockhart?"

"Very much, thank—"

"Such a splendid garden, don't you think, Miss Bryant?" Miss Esham's voice drowned out his companion's much quieter tones. "Much bigger, I imagine, than anything you have seen."

"Yes, indeed." Miss Bryant's voice was quieter. "The display of *Parus major* was particularly impressive; planted out in such a beautiful design. The *Erithacus rebecula*, too."

Miss Stockhart turned a surprised glance back at their companions, her eyes wide.

"Oh, er, yes," Miss Esham said. "Very beautiful."

James felt movement where Miss Stockhart's hand rested on his arm. She was pursing her lips, and her shoulders shook.

"Do you recognise the plants she named?" He kept his voice low as Miss Esham loudly changed the subject.

"They're not plants, my lord. I think they may be birds."

James only just stopped himself laughing out loud.

Behind him, Miss Esham was describing the gardens at Blenheim Palace, talking as if she had been an invited guest. He caught a glimpse of a smile beneath Miss Stockhart's bonnet.

"Miss Stockhart?"

"Our home is in Oxfordshire—the Palace does have splendid gardens. My parents took me there on a public open day."

He chuckled. "I suspected as much."

They reached the turning, and he guided the group onto the path that skirted the water, helping the women around a puddle without having to step onto the soft grass.

Somehow, he found Miss Esham beside him when they all set off again. He glanced behind—Miss Stockhart held Augustus Chilton's arm and appeared quite happy in his company. Then Lucy came up on James' other side, and he had little choice but to walk on.

"Do you have extensive parkland, my lord?" Miss Esham fluttered her eyelashes.

Why did women do that?

"Oh, it's enormous, Miss Esham." Lucy spoke before he could answer. "I'm sure, if you wish for a guided tour…"

A smile spread across the hopeful face turned up towards his.

"…my brother can arrange for Terring—that's the steward, you know—to drive you around."

"Oh. Oh, but it would be much nicer if—"

"Terring is much more knowledgeable about the estate than I am, Miss Esham," James interrupted.

"I have no wish to tour the grounds, thank you." Miss Esham spoke through tight lips. "Excuse me, I think I have a stone in my shoe." She released James' arm and stopped, bending down. So abrupt was her movement that Miss Stockhart, walking behind, bumped into her. Miss Esham toppled over, letting out an unladylike screech as she fell into a muddy puddle at the side of the path.

"I'm so sorry, Miss Esham." Miss Stockhart offered her hand. "Do let me help you up. Oh, dear, your lovely gown—"

"Stay away from me, you stupid fool! You've done enough damage!" Miss Esham slapped away the offered hand.

"I say," Augustus Chilton protested. "Miss Stockhart didn't intend… you stopped…"

"Don't make any more of a cake of yourself than you have already, Miss Esham," Lady Jesson snapped. Miss Esham scowled, got to her feet and stalked off, rubbing at her dress but managing only to spread the mud further.

Miss Stockhart was almost in tears. "I really didn't mean… she was suddenly there…"

"Now, my dear, don't take on so." Lady Jesson patted her shoulder. Looking up, she met James' eye and made a waving motion with her hand. "Do carry on, my lord. I will see to Miss Stockhart."

James obeyed, relieved to let Lady Jesson and young Chilton comfort Miss Stockhart. He had no idea what to do with females in tears.

Lucy fell into step beside him as he set off for the Dower House again. Miss Chilton and Miss Bryant paired up behind.

"James, you're not going to marry Miss Esham, are you?" Lucy hissed, quietly enough for only him to hear. "Please?"

"It is not an attractive proposition," James admitted.

"Oh, good. Miss Stockhart seems to have caught Mr Chilton's eye. I expect he has found out about her dowry."

James frowned, mindful that Chilton's sister was within earshot. "Lucy, that's an unkind thing to say."

Lucy flushed and hung her head. "Sorry."

"Never mind now." He patted her hand, and they walked on in companionable silence until they reached the gate into the garden.

"Miss Chilton, Miss Bryant, have you had enough for one day, or would you care to look around the Dower House gardens? My grandmother keeps up a knot garden based on an Elizabethan design, she tells me."

"That would be interesting, thank you," Miss Bryant said.

"Yes, indeed." Miss Chilton's expression didn't quite match her words.

James ushered them into the garden. "I will see if Grandmama is receiving guests this afternoon."

James found his grandmother in her customary place in the parlour overlooking the gardens, with the glass doors standing open to admit the spring air.

"Well, James, have you brought someone for my inspection?"

He shrugged. "Mama arranged for me to escort them on a walk."

"Yet you have shaken off several of them already. There's nothing wrong with my eyes, you know."

James ignored the reading glasses lying beside her book on a side table. "I know, Grandmama. It was not my doing."

"Never mind. Talking to all five of your potential brides at once would be too much, especially with Lucy here too."

Five?

"There would have been only four." He followed her gaze to where the two women stood with Lucy by the lake, a few hopeful ducks swimming near their feet. "Miss Bryant is companion to Lady Jesson, and—"

"Maria Jesson? You must bring her to see me some time."

"You know her? She is much... I mean, not of your generation." Two generations younger, possibly.

"She was just a green girl when I was last in Town, but I know of her. She'll have all the gossip. Send her over, James, do."

"Very well." If Grandmama were busy with Lady Jesson, she could not be quizzing him about which woman he would choose.

"Who is the other young lady with you?" Lady Harlford prompted.

"Miss Chilton." He racked his brain. "Father's a baron."

"Invite her up for tea, James. You may entertain Lucy and Miss Bryant in the gardens while I talk to her. Meeting more than one fawning young miss at a time is too much for me."

James didn't believe it, but she had given him an excuse that might prevent Miss Bryant feeling slighted. "Do you wish to appoint times to interview the other candidates for the position?"

"Less of your cheek, boy!" She chuckled as she waved him off.

Miss Chilton simpered when he relayed his grandmother's invitation, casting a triumphant glance at Miss Bryant as she walked off. The companion didn't seem at all put out—but then someone in her position wouldn't expect to be singled out in such a way.

"Is Grandmama unwell, James?" Lucy frowned. "It's not like her to—"

"She's perfectly well."

Lucy's face cleared. "Oh, I expect she wants to interrog— I mean, find out all about Miss Chilton."

"Lucy!"

A muffled sound from Miss Bryant distracted him. She had a pursed-mouth look similar to Miss Stockhart's earlier. Amusement?

"Miss Bryant?"

"Sorry, my lord—but now you know how I felt when young Georges was so outspoken."

He had to laugh. "Tell me, Miss Bryant, does my grandmother's garden include *Parus...*?" What was it she'd said?

"*Parus major.* I'm sure it does, although they are most likely incubating eggs at the moment." She turned to Lucy. "Miss Esham agreed with me earlier that the great tits and robins were laid out in pretty designs in the gardens."

Lucy snorted with laughter, and covered her mouth with one hand.

"What do you think of the garden here, Miss Bryant?" He'd always admired the neat lines of the low box hedges and the symmetry of the patterns as they appeared to weave under and over each other in knots.

She considered before answering. "It is impressively intricate, and interesting if it is a historical design. Her ladyship's gardener must work hard to keep it trimmed so precisely."

"I sense a 'but' coming."

Miss Bryant gave an apologetic smile.

"Be honest, Miss Bryant."

"Very well. I prefer the parterre at the main house—the flowers within the beds there provide a variety of colour, and change with the seasons."

"This is a bit gloomy on grey days," Lucy put in. "Mama says it is out of date, and she'd have it removed if it were up to her. "

"It's not up to—" James stopped himself. "Pardon me, Miss Bryant." He wouldn't have thought of saying that in front of Miss Esham, or even Miss Stockhart. Somehow, it was too easy to let his guard down with Miss Bryant—perhaps it was the way she seemed to get on so well with Lucy.

"Miss Stockhart might like to see this garden," Miss Bryant suggested. "It could be a challenge to paint—the effect would depend on an accurate depiction of the lines and knots. In fact, a pen and ink drawing would be more dramatic."

"That's why I prefer the other garden, too," Lucy said. "It's easier to make a pretty picture…"

He'd invite Miss Stockhart to walk to the Dower House again, James thought as Lucy chattered on. Without Miss Esham, next time. However it would not do to be seen alone with any of the young women his mother had invited as prospective brides. That might indicate an interest he did not feel. Lucy or Miss Bryant might accompany him.

Alice gave Miss Stockhart an encouraging smile as a round of applause greeted the end of her rendering of 'Robin Adair', and returned the music to the stack on top of the piano.

"Encore!" Augustus Chilton called, still clapping.

Miss Stockhart blushed. "Oh, I couldn't, not—"

"Miss Esham will sing next." Lady Harlford's voice was loud enough to carry from her place several yards away. "Miss Esham, Lady Jesson's companion will play for you. You may show us your skills on the keyboard later."

Alice grimaced, then smoothed her expression before anyone noticed. She had willingly accompanied Miss Stockhart—the girl needed a friendly face beside her to help her confidence. It was a different matter being instructed to accompany the hostile Miss Esham, although there was little point in protesting.

"'Der Hölle Rache'," Miss Esham said, laying a sheet of music on the stand. "The Queen of the Night's aria from *The Magic Flute*. You can play it, I trust?"

Lord Harlford had winced as Miss Esham announced the aria. He didn't have the appearance of a man enjoying the evening. Alice flicked through the pages—it was too complex for her to play on sight, particularly in front of an audience.

"I'm afraid not. Have you a different piece?"

"Something very simple, you mean?" Miss Esham looked down her nose. "If—"

"Alice, my dear," Maria interrupted. "Would you fetch my fan from my room?"

"Excuse me, Miss Esham." Alice didn't wait for a response, but stood and left the parlour, waiting in the cooler air of the corridor.

Maria joined her after only a few minutes. "I thought we might escape to the library. And *from* Miss Esham's attempts to impress Lord Harlford." She raised a hand, and the footman on duty in the hall hurried over.

"Will she? Impress him, I mean?" Alice asked as they followed the footman.

"I doubt it. Miss Chilton announced that she would play it. That aria is lovely when sung properly, but I'd be surprised if Miss Esham has the ability. Or Miss Chilton, come to that." She smiled. "Poor Harlford."

Poor everyone, Alice thought.

In the library, the footman lit two branches of candles on tables near the fire and several in wall sconces, then left them alone. The room felt cavernous, its polished wooden floor appearing to stretch half the length of the building. One wall was broken by a series of full-length windows, hidden now by heavy curtains. A leather-upholstered sofa faced the fireplace near the door where they had entered, flanked by two armchairs, all set on a thick rug. The wall opposite the windows was lined with bookcases reaching almost to the ornately plastered ceiling. Bookshelves stuck out from the wall, forming a series of bays.

"Shall we see what the library has to offer?" Maria picked up one of the branches of candles.

Alice had been wanting to explore it from the moment Lucy told her how large it was. She picked up the other branch and walked the length of the room, looking briefly into each bay. The first held shelf upon shelf of parliamentary proceedings, collected in leather bindings. Later bays held bound copies of various magazines, and books enough to interest anyone: histories, travels, texts in Latin and Greek and in translation, and a section of recent novels. One bay had a stepladder on wheels, taller than Alice. She wasn't about to tackle that in skirts and holding a candle—the top shelves would have to wait for daylight.

There was another fireplace at the far end, but instead of a sofa and chairs, this end of the room had a desk with a blotter set neatly in its centre and a paperweight, inkwell, and pen holder arranged in a straight line next to it.

"A very tidy man," Maria said. "A pity—our task would be simpler if he'd left some secret letters lying around."

Alice's pleasure in being surrounded by so many books faded.

"There might be something of use in the desk." Maria pulled on one of the drawers. "Locked. Did you bring those little tools?"

"No, I wasn't anticipating needing them tonight."

"That's probably just as well. If the singing's as poor as I imagine, Harlford could escape and come here at any moment."

"Do we really need to search his desk?" Gathering information by exploring the grounds and talking to staff was one thing—opening locked drawers was taking matters into criminal territory.

"Yes, we do. The fact that someone is apparently watching the quarry does not mean that Harlford is innocent," Maria pointed out. "For now, let us see if the books in this last bay tell us anything. If he spends his time at his desk, then the books he uses most will be here."

The large volumes on the bottom shelves had cloth spines, and were marked only with numbers. Opening one, Alice saw rows of figures.

"Estate ledgers?" Maria suggested.

"Probably." A close examination might reveal if Lord Harlford was in need of money—a possible motive. But she had neither the time nor the expertise to go through them in enough detail to find out. She put the ledger back and moved on. The higher shelves held books on natural philosophy—some old, some recent—and bound copies of journals. A whole shelf was filled with the *Philosophical Transactions of the Royal Society*, the dates on the spines going back over a hundred years to when the Society was formed. Pulling out a few of the most recent volumes, she found slips of paper marking pages, often with comments in a neat, masculine hand. Other books, mainly connected with scientific matters, also had markers in them.

"Have you found anything useful?" Maria asked.

"Not really. We already know he's doing something with explosives—these only show he's interested in several areas of natural philosophy. I'll come back tomorrow for a better look."

"Very well—I'll risk the singing and return to the parlour. Are you coming?"

"If you don't mind, I'd rather retire."

"With a book?" Maria laughed. "Very well then. I'll see you at breakfast."

"Goodnight." Alice picked up the candles and headed for her room. She was going to have to use those picklocks after all.

CHAPTER 10

"Hello, Tess."

Tess jumped up at the sound of Alice's voice, her tail waving and tongue lolling. It wasn't a propitious day for a walk—dull grey clouds covered the sky and there was a damp feel to the air. Puddles in the stable yard indicated overnight rain.

"'Morning, Miss Bryant." Chatham emerged from his room with a steaming mug in one hand, and no coat. "Looks like more rain to come."

Alice looked around—all the stable hands were busy about their own business. "Did you discover anything else yesterday?"

"The signs Tess found led off north towards a well-used track—I think it goes between some of the local villages. There's nothing to see right by the track, though. It's as if someone leaves the track at a different place each time."

"Are you sure the path isn't made by animals?"

"It could be, but Tess was following a scent from that tarpaulin, and I found this on some brambles." He fished in his pocket and pulled out a tiny scrap of cloth, loose threads showing where it had torn. It was a drab green, a common colour for coats. "Can't tell much from it."

"Just that someone *is* using the little path."

"Miss Bryant!"

They both turned towards the main house. Lucy was walking towards them, clad in a dark blue pelisse and plain bonnet.

Chatham tucked the fabric back into his pocket. "I'll take another look at the place later today, miss." He nodded and retreated into his room.

Lucy came to a halt in front of Alice. "I saw you from my window. Are you taking your dog for a walk? May I come with you?"

Alice glanced at the clouds. "We're likely to get wet."

"I won't melt in a drop of rain! Jamie goes out riding in all weathers, and if it does rain, I'll be cooped up inside the house all day."

That accorded so well with her own thoughts that Alice had to smile. "I would be glad of your company." She unfastened Tess' leash from the ring in the wall and they left the stable yard. "Are we going anywhere in particular?"

"There's a pretty little stream in the woods—we can get there most easily by walking down the drive."

"That sounds lovely." And sensible; the grass would be wet and probably muddy. Alice let Tess off the leash when they were well away from the Castle, and the dog ran around them as they walked but never strayed far.

"James gave my governess two weeks off," Lucy confided as they strode along the hard-packed gravel, a wistful note to her voice. "I thought it would be fun to join in the party."

"You are not finding it so?"

Lucy shrugged. "Mama won't let me attend the evening entertainments, and the only guests who have been friendly are you and Miss Stockhart." Her eyes lit up. "Although I understand it was a musicale last night?"

"It was indeed."

"Ha—Jamie *hates* those. He says most young ladies cannot sing and play as proficiently as they think they can."

"I played last night," Alice said, interested to see how Lucy took that.

She coloured, one hand flying to her mouth. "Oh dear. I'm sorry."

Alice laughed. "Do you play?"

They walked on towards the wood that bordered the southern edge of the park as Lucy told Alice about the music teacher who came once a week, her failure to master the harp, and how she was looking forward to having a season the year after next.

In the woods, the trees turned the world grey, filtering the feeble light from the sky. Even the fresh green buds on the trees and patches of bluebells failed to brighten the gloom. Lucy came to a stop at the stone bridge near the gates and rested her hands on the low balustrade. The stream ran silently here, between low grassy banks. Tess darted off into the undergrowth, and splashing indicated that Chatham would have a very wet dog to deal with later.

"It really is pretty when the sun shines." Lucy turned to Alice with a wry smile.

"I'll make a point of coming back when the weather is nicer. Is there a way—?" Alice broke off as Tess barked. A rabbit, she assumed, until she heard the sound of a male voice—the words were unclear but the angry tone was not.

Could Tess be barking at the owner of the green coat? She shook her head—it could as easily be a member of Lord Harlford's staff Tess had met in the stables. With Lucy here, she could not go and investigate, but she would tell Chatham about it when she returned.

"Tess! Come here!" The barking stopped, and so did the voice. "Tess!"

Crashing in the undergrowth drew nearer, and Tess trotted onto the gravel. Alice pulled Lucy away quickly as the dog shook water off. "I'm sorry—it sounds like she was bothering one of your gamekeepers."

"Not necessarily. There's a path through these woods that goes towards Luncot, a mile or so that way. It cuts several miles off the road between there and Harlford Green."

That could be the track Chatham had mentioned earlier.

"We'd better go back," Alice said, as tiny spots of moisture landed on her. Lucy agreed, and they called Tess to follow them.

The Castle was in sight through a veil of drizzle when Tess barked again. The sound of hooves made them turn. Lord Harlford was cantering along the drive.

"Jamie!"

Lord Harlford dismounted next to them. Unsure of Tess' reaction, Alice put a hand to the dog's collar.

"I am happy to see that the two of you are so well protected." Lord Harlford smiled. Here, with only his sister present, his expression seemed friendly, more open than when in the company of his guests. His face, already handsome, now seemed more attractive.

He turned and the three of them started walking as the drizzle became rain. "Will you introduce me to your guardian?"

"This is Tess. Lady Jesson... inherited her."

"I'd offer you a ride, but I don't think Ventus would take three," Lord Harlford said.

"Take Lucy, my lord. I'm used to getting wet, and it's not far."

"I can't leave you alone," he protested.

"Of course you can. The longer we discuss it, the wetter we all get."

"Are you sure?"

"Go!" She made a flapping motion with her hands, and increased her pace. She heard a masculine chuckle, and a squeak from Lucy, then Ventus was beside her with Lucy sitting across her brother's legs.

Lord Harlford bent towards her, laughter in his eyes. "Now I know what Georges must have felt like." He touched his hat and urged the horse forwards.

Had she been too assertive? Possibly, but it seemed he didn't mind. And he had unbent enough to tease her about it.

As the horse and riders grew smaller and greyer through the rain, she felt a fleeting wish that *she* had been the one to be carried off like that.

Changed and breakfasted, Alice sought out the butler. "Bellingham, Lord Harlford said I might look at his library, but I don't wish to disturb him."

83

"I believe his lordship is engaged with guests in the parlour, Miss. I will accompany you."

Alice thanked him, and followed him upstairs. Maria had braved the rain—with the help of Chatham and a huge umbrella—to visit the Dowager Lady Harlford. Alice was happy to be left alone to explore the library further—mostly for her own interest, this time, as she couldn't risk using the picklocks in her pocket if Lord Harlford was in the house. She wasn't sorry to have a good reason for putting off intruding into his private papers.

Bellingham opened the library curtains, then left her alone. Although clouds still darkened the sky, it was easier to take in the scale of the room and read the titles on the book spines than it had been by candlelight. The browns and reds of the leather-bound volumes blended with the polished wood of the shelves and the floor. Combined with the dark red of the curtains and the smell of beeswax polish, the whole had a very masculine feel. A *comfortable* masculine feel.

She headed straight for the end bay and the bound journals that had caught her interest the previous evening. Seen in daylight, the end wall of the bay looked slightly odd. As she examined it more closely, she found that the middle section was actually a door, its counterfeit book spines creating the illusion of bookshelves. Pulling gently, Alice found that it opened onto a narrow corridor with rough matting on the floor—this was the servants' entrance Lucy had mentioned.

Pushing the door closed again, she turned her attention to the journals concerning horticulture and farming, amused to find they included the Society for the Improvement of Agriculture. Some older volumes had markers in them, but in a different hand from the notes in journals shelved near the desk. It looked as if Lord Harlford's father had been interested in agriculture, and the current marquess was the natural philosopher. The older brother had spent most of his time in London, Maria had said.

The latch on the far door clicked, and Lord Harlford entered with an older man wearing a grey wig and running slightly to fat. "The parliamentary proceedings are here, Gearing. Do feel free to consult them at any time."

"Good of you, Harlford. Nice and quiet in here—I'll take you up on that." He nodded in Alice's direction but didn't address her. Lord Harlford turned, brows rising as she walked towards him.

"I'm sorry to intrude, my lord. You did say I could use the library."

"You are welcome, Miss Bryant. I was merely surprised to find you here."

"I will leave you in peace, sir."

"No need, I..." He turned his head away at the sound of approaching voices.

"Ah, there you are, James!" Lady Harlford's voice was over-loud in these studious surroundings. Miss Esham and Miss Chilton followed her into the library. "Miss Esham would like to see the portrait gallery and, as you know, Miss Chilton is interested in painting."

"Anyone may visit—" He took a breath. "I mean, I'd be delighted to tell them all about my ancestors."

Alice bit her lip—he had almost managed to sound sincere.

"Miss Bryant, would you care to accompany us?" The words were neutral, but his expression held a trace of pleading.

"Yes. Thank you, my lord."

She'd be interested to find out more about the Castle, even if she didn't care for Miss Esham.

The portrait gallery was in the original part of the Castle, stretching the full width of the building, with chairs and sofas grouped at intervals. Alice could just make out the Dower House through the rain running down the windows. A fire blazing in a central fireplace gave the gallery a cheerful air on this still-gloomy day. At the far end, Lucy, Miss Gearing, and Miss Stockhart sat on a sofa with sketch pads on their laps, the two Chilton brothers nearby.

Julius Chilton's chair was drawn up very close to Lucy's end of the sofa, but he looked around and moved away a little as Lord Harlford followed Alice and the other two women into the room. Lucy's expression was hard to make out from this distance, but her tense posture relaxed a little. Augustus Chilton, resplendent this morning in a lime green and white striped waistcoat, sat almost as close to Miss Stockhart's end of the sofa, leaning on its arm. As Alice watched, Miss Stockhart tilted her sketchpad towards him.

Lord Harlford gave a brief history of the family as Alice and the other two young women followed him along the gallery, his words sounding like a recital of a tale too often told. Alice, paying more attention to the little tableau at the end of the gallery, only caught snatches of it.

"...first Earl of Bedstone, in Elizabeth's time..."

Julius moved closer to Lucy now that Lord Harlford's attention appeared to be elsewhere. Lucy showed him her sketch, but leaned away as she did so.

"...built the Castle that this gallery..."

Now they were drawing closer, Alice could make out expressions. Julius' lips thinned as Lucy laughed at something Augustus said.

"...must have done something at the restoration to become the first marquess, and..."

Lucy closed her sketchbook and stood, a frown visible even from this distance. Julius rose as well, and put a hand on her arm.

"...built the new wing—"

"Lady Lucy," Alice called, moving a few steps away to a portrait of a young girl with a spaniel in her arms. "Do you know the story to this portrait? Will you tell us?" She turned to Lord Harlford. "Can you tell me, my lord?"

Julius dropped his hand, looking furious, and Lucy walked over, her lips trembling. Lord Harlford joined her, his expression changing from puzzlement to concern as Lucy approached.

"What's wrong, Lucy?" he asked, his voice low.

"Mr Chilton..." Her voice sounded shaky.

At the end of the gallery, Miss Stockhart and Augustus seemed oblivious to the little drama just enacted. Julius stood with a polite smile on his face.

"Was he annoying you?"

Lucy nodded, and put a hand on his arm as he frowned. "Please, Jamie, don't make a fuss. Mama..." Her voice tailed off as she glanced towards Miss Esham and Miss Chilton.

"Do you wish to carry on sketching, Lucy?" Alice asked.

"Yes, but not, not if..." She glanced down the gallery. Julius Chilton smiled as if nothing was wrong.

"You could tell us about the rest of the portraits, then I will sit with you."

"Thank you, Miss Bryant," Lord Harlford said. "I will see if Mr Chilton would enjoy a tour of the stables." He walked back to the other two women and made his excuses, then headed for Julius Chilton.

Alice squeezed Lucy's shoulder, and they rejoined the others.

"Did my brother explain this painting?" Lucy asked.

"I'll wait until Lord Harlford can relate the rest of his history," Miss Esham snapped, and walked off.

Miss Chilton glanced at Augustus, still concentrating all his attention on Miss Stockhart. There was calculation in her expression. "I would be pleased if you would continue, Lady Lucy. My brother would be interested, too. I'll fetch—"

"Oh, no," Lucy said. "I've already told him all he wanted to know. The new wing you can see in this portrait was begun in..."

Miss Chilton scowled behind Lucy's back, hastily resuming a smile as Lucy turned towards her.

Poor Lucy, if she ended up with either of those two as a sister-in-law.

～

"A very nice pair." Chilton stroked the nose of one of the greys that James used with his phaeton.

"Never mind that, Chilton. Stay away from my sister."

Chilton turned towards him, hands held out sideways. "But what have I done? I was merely admiring Lady Lucilla's sketches."

"That's not what she thought."

"She's young, Harlford, and must have misunderstood. I wouldn't reward your hospitality by accosting a member of your family."

James couldn't detect any prevarication in Chilton's face, and wondered if he'd done the right thing by speaking to him. He hadn't noticed anything wrong himself—had Lucy read too much into whatever Julius had said or done? But Miss Bryant, too, had thought Julius' behaviour was not appropriate, and she was a sensible woman who said things plainly.

"Nevertheless, she *was* uncomfortable with the situation, so I do not wish you to be in her company for the remainder of your visit."

Chilton gazed at him, his expression unreadable, then shrugged. "Of course, if you wish it." He turned and headed back towards the house.

His polite agreement revived James' doubts. But the important thing was that Lucy had not enjoyed the man's company. Perhaps she *was* too young to be taking part in the house party, but it did seem unfair to keep her away from everyone. He might advise her to keep company with Miss Bryant when she could, and tell her to come to him immediately if Chilton gave her any more trouble.

As he was here, he'd take a look at Athena. Calling for Pritchard, he went to rub the mare's nose and patted her neck as she snuffled into his shoulder. He'd bred her with Ventus, his favourite stallion, last year, hoping for another foal that could be part of a matched pair when old enough.

"She's due soon," Pritchard said. "She's looking well, though."

"Excellent. Send for me when she starts. At any time."

"Yes, my lord." Pritchard touched his forehead, and started to stroke the mare's nose himself. James reluctantly left the stables—too long there and he would smell of horse and need to change his clothing.

Looking into the portrait gallery on his way to the billiards room, James saw Lucy happily sketching in one of the window seats, Miss Gearing beside her. Miss Bryant sat nearby, absorbed in whatever she was reading. Miss Stockhart and Augustus Chilton formed a separate grouping at the next window along. There was no sign of Miss Chilton.

Lucy looked around and waggled her fingers at him with a smile. Miss Bryant would look after her. He returned her smile and left them to it.

CHAPTER 11

*A*s the party in the portrait gallery broke up for refreshments, a footman presented Alice with a note from Maria, asking Alice to join her at the Dower House. Quite happy to avoid Lady Harlford's cold shoulder, Alice went to get her pelisse. She declined the services of a footman to hold the umbrella that Bellingham provided, and set off.

Maria was sitting with Lady Harlford in a parlour overlooking the knot garden and the lake. The dowager's skin was a papery sheet of fine wrinkles, her hair white without the use of powder, but she sat with her back straight. Alice could see where Lord Harlford got his patrician nose.

"Sit down, Miss Bryant." The dowager waved towards a nearby chair as Alice made her curtsey. "I understand you are a distant relation to Maria."

"Er... Very distant, my lady."

The dowager's brows rose. "Really? As far back as the conquest, perhaps?"

"It's certainly possible," Maria said. "Lady Harlford—your daughter-in-law, I mean—would have relegated Alice to the servants' quarters if I had not said that."

"A falsehood?" The dowager's words were stern, but Alice detected a movement at one corner of her mouth.

"An exaggeration," Maria contradicted. "Alice is a friend as well as my companion."

"The manipulator manipulated." The dowager nodded, and this time smiled properly. "Where are you from, Miss Bryant?"

For the next ten minutes the dowager questioned Alice about her parents and grandparents, education, governess positions, and how she preferred to spend her time.

"And do you pay attention to happenings in the world?"

"I read the newspapers when I can, my lady."

"The disturbances in France—what do you think of that?"

"What any sensible person does, I assume." Was the dowager looking for republican sympathies? "I don't understand all the reasons behind the events, although I do believe there were—are—many injustices."

The dowager's brows drew together. "You sympathise with the rebels, then? Traitors, many would call them."

Alice glanced at Maria, surprised at the turn the conversation was taking. Maria shrugged.

"I have sympathy with some of their complaints, but I do *not* agree with the way they are going about things. The executions..." Alice shook her head. "The cure is worse than the disease."

"Hmm." Finally, the dowager nodded. "You are certainly better informed than some of the other young ladies Cassandra has invited here."

"Did you subject Miss Chilton to a similar set of questions?" Maria asked.

The dowager smiled—a friendly smile. "Not the ones about France, not after she denied all knowledge of 'unladylike' topics. In *my* day, an intelligent woman took full part in political and literary salons. I'm not surprised Harlford didn't take to the Chilton chit. Who else did you spot Harlford with in Town?"

Alice gazed at the raindrops running down the window as the

dowager and Maria talked about people she had never heard of, and was unlikely to meet.

"Miss Bryant?" The dowager's voice was sharp, but her lips curled up at the corners. "Are we boring you?"

"No, of course—"

"We are," the dowager contradicted, before Alice had chance to apologise for not paying attention. "But you cannot wish to be out of doors in such weather."

"No, my lady. I…" She hesitated—it seemed rude to explain where she would prefer to be, when the dowager had invited her to call.

"I expect you'd rather be in the library, Alice?" Maria suggested.

Alice nodded—she could borrow some of the agricultural journals, and reply to some of the letters she had brought with her.

"Of you go, Miss Bryant, and leave us to our gossip. Enjoy your bookish afternoon." The words could have been a reprimand, but the dowager was smiling as she waved a hand towards the door.

"I will see you before dinner, Alice," Maria said, as Alice curtseyed and took her leave.

James applauded obediently as someone finally guessed what the current tableau was supposed to represent. He shifted uncomfortably on the hard chair, and glanced at the clock on the mantelpiece. Only ten o'clock? It felt as if he had been sitting here for hours.

"My lord?"

James looked around hopefully as Bellingham spoke quietly behind him. He'd welcome any excuse to get away from having to pay attention to cryptic scenes enacted by mostly unwilling performers and guess the names of uninteresting objects.

"Pritchard sent, sir, to say the mare is foaling."

James nodded, and Bellingham left as unobtrusively as he had arrived. If he had counted correctly, the next charade should be the last—he could stay that long.

Perhaps he was being unfair. Some of the guests were clearly enjoying the game, and Lucy had a smile on her face. She had begged to join in, and Mama had relented once Lucy had suggested that Miss Bryant might be willing to act as a chaperone. Lucy should not need to be chaperoned in her own home, but after that morning's encounter with Julius Chilton, James felt it was wise that she had someone with her.

He frowned as he recalled Mama's response—if she had to entertain someone like the Jesson woman and her companion, they might at least make themselves useful. Why, then, had she invited Lady Jesson?

Another round of applause roused him from his thoughts, and he excused himself before anyone could engage him in conversation. An evening spent watching charades had not helped him to learn anything more about the young women his mother had invited, but he shouldn't complain. He hadn't helped himself by spending most of the afternoon in the billiards room.

In the stables, Pritchard was leaning calmly against the side of Athena's stall, lanterns providing plenty of light. The mare shifted restlessly, her flanks damp with sweat.

"How is she?"

"No problems, my lord, and no reason to expect any difficulties, but you did ask to be told."

"Yes, yes, quite right." James found himself a bucket to sit on, and leaned back against the same wall. He was likely to be here for some time. Certainly until the guests had retired to bed. He and Pritchard readily fell into a conversation about the possibilities for the new foal, and whether to have Ventus sire Athena's next offspring, when the time came, or to choose another animal.

"It's the only way, Alice," Maria said. "Now Harlford has given Lord Gearing the run of his library, as well as Miss Stockhart, and possibly others we're not aware of, the risk of doing this at any time during the day is too great."

Alice sighed. "I know."

"I'd go, but I didn't learn to use those things nearly as well as you did." Maria poked the bits of metal laid out on the dressing table in her room. A few looked like keys; most were just metal strips with varying shapes filed in the ends.

Alice spread them out, then abruptly rolled them back into their strip of cloth and put them into the pocket of her robe. They had decided between them that, however improper it might be for Alice to be found wandering the house in the early hours of the morning in her night-rail and robe, being found fully dressed would be impossible to explain. The robe had been made for warmth, not style, and was a serviceable dark green. A very useful colour, under the circumstances.

"It's three o'clock," Maria added. "No-one else will be about."

Alice shook her head. "You know it's not that. I *like* Lord Harlford. It's wrong to spy on him in this way."

"We're trying to clear his name, remember? And you agreed."

"I've got to know him a little better since then." The care he had for his sister, friendliness to a mere companion… "Why don't we ask him? You don't believe he's a traitor, do you?"

"No, but I am not *always* right. Come, Alice, you don't think Marstone will accept our 'innocent' verdict if it's only based on asking Harlford if he's a spy?"

"I suppose not."

"And in the extremely unlikely event that he *is* a spy of some kind, Marstone will be able to deal with it better if he—Harlford, that is—doesn't know that we know."

"You're enjoying this, aren't you?"

"Not really, no. I've been keeping afloat via gossip for too many years." Maria shrugged. "Sometimes it is entertaining, making connections between what various people let fall in conversation, but that wearies after a while."

"Very well. I'll be glad to get this over with so I have an appetite again." The hollow feeling in her stomach was nothing to do with hunger, even though she'd been unable to eat much at dinner once they'd decided she needed to search Lord Harlford's desk tonight.

Taking a single candle, Alice crept across the corridor and through the servants' door, turning left along the passageway that Lucy had pointed out as leading to the library.

The door at the far end of the passage moved at her touch. She pushed it gently. No line of light marked the opening gap between the door and the wall, so there was no-one in the library. She slipped through the door and pushed it to behind her. There were no pale patches where the windows were, so the curtains must be closed, and it was safe for her to use the candle. The library was so long that she would hear anyone entering by the main door in plenty of time to escape the way she'd come.

Not that anyone would be wandering around outside, she told herself firmly. Or coming into the library at this hour.

She crouched beside the desk, standing the candle on the floor and spreading the picklocks out next to it. After a great deal of poking and wriggling with the small tools, the lock opened with a quiet click.

A pile of card folders was neatly centred in the drawer. She lifted them out and opened each in turn. The letters and notes in the first folder were in the same hand as the markers in the books on natural philosophy. These letters were about buying horses. Other folders in the stack concerned carriages, enquiries about ways of managing equine illnesses, and other topics connected with stable management.

Putting the folders back, she checked that the drawer looked as it had when she first opened it, then relocked it. She was pleased to find that the same tools worked on the next drawer down. The contents of the second drawer concerned investments. She scanned each document quickly, feeling more and more uncomfortable about prying into Lord Harlford's business. These letters included a lot of numbers —could they be coded messages? She felt a sick feeling in her stomach at the idea that Lord Harlford might be guilty of espionage after all. She wouldn't be able to work out what they meant, but perhaps she should copy one or two and send them to Lord Marstone.

What was that noise?

She held her breath, wishing her heartbeat did not sound so loud in her ears.

Footsteps?

The sounds came from the servants' corridor behind the bookcase, not the main door. Hastily putting the picklocks into her pocket, Alice replaced the folders in the drawer and pushed it closed, then licked her finger and thumb and pinched out the candle. With luck, there would be less of a smell in the air than if she blew it out.

~

The foal stood on spindly legs, wobbling slightly as he staggered towards his dam. Nuzzling her, he started to suckle. James rubbed his eyes, tiredness suddenly hitting him, but he loved these moments of new life. He stretched and said good night—good morning, rather—to Pritchard.

Bed—but first he would write the foal's birth date in his record book. Lucy would enjoy thinking up a name for him later. At the back entrance he scraped as much straw and stable muck off his boots as possible, and took the servants' corridors up to the library.

His candle flickered in a faint draught, and he guessed someone had left the hidden door slightly ajar. Once in the library he took his breeding book from the shelf and opened it at the current page. He noted the date and time, blowing on the ink gently to help it to dry, then put it back in its place.

~

Alice sat on the top of the stepladder in the next bay along from the desk, trying to breathe silently. The glow of candlelight moved, then she caught sight of Lord Harlford as he sat at his desk. The ladder was far too close to the open end of the bay.

Had she left the drawers locked?

If she hadn't, would he notice?

What was he doing?

Don't look this way. Don't look up.

Her racing heart calmed a little as he appeared to do nothing more than write in a book on the desk before him. He vanished behind the bookshelves, and she breathed a short sigh of relief.

The sounds of his movements stopped, and all she could hear was the blood rushing through her ears.

Had she made a noise?

She started breathing as the candle glow dimmed, then everything went dark. The click of the door closing was barely audible. Lord Harlford had left the same way he had arrived.

Alice swallowed hard, suppressing a sudden impulse to giggle. She was *not* cut out for this business.

After ten minutes or so—long enough for Lord Harlford to have come back if he was going to—she climbed down. Her hands shook a little, but she should investigate the remaining drawers, at least.

Opening the curtains wouldn't provide enough light to read by, as the dark clouds had shown no sign of clearing before she retired to Maria's room last evening. What light there was, though, might help her to see if there was a tinder box on the mantelpiece without knocking anything to the floor or falling over the fire irons.

The faintest of lines was visible if she didn't look directly at the window, and she moved cautiously forwards, feeling in front of her with each foot before taking the step. When her outstretched hand met fabric, she worked her way to one side until she brushed against the curtain cord. She pulled very slowly, hoping the rings did not make a noise. Gradually the darkness lightened enough to make out the looming shadow of the desk, and a glimmer reflected from the mirror above the fireplace.

There *was* a tinderbox on one end of the mantelpiece. Alice struck the flint, cringing at the noise, but the tinder caught and she lit her candle. She closed the curtains and went to the desk. She took a deep breath to calm herself, then locked the second drawer and opened the third. This one contained only a couple of large, thin books with plain covers. They were notebooks, their pages filled with writing in Lord Harlford's hand, interspersed with tables of figures, chemical notations, and a few diagrams. She replaced them, wondering if this was some of the information being sent to France—but whatever it was, it was not the correspondence she was looking for.

The bottom drawer held that: a folder of letters written in French.

The sick feeling in Alice's stomach intensified. Here was proof that his lordship *was* communicating with France. But this was not news, as Marstone had told them he was doing so. What Marstone wanted to know was the content of the letters.

Ten minutes later, Alice still didn't know exactly what Harlford was doing. He was trying to obtain something, or buy something—that much was clear, both from the copies of letters he must have sent, and from the replies. Various sums of money were mentioned, some of them large enough to buy a farm or two, and there were references to 'the goods' and 'a messenger', but nothing more explicit than that. And there was no name—the letters had no salutations, and were signed only with the letter L.

Alice replaced everything as she found it, locked the drawer, and slipped out through the servants' door again, pulling it closed behind her. None too soon, either, for the maids would soon be up and about cleaning the public rooms.

The hollow feeling inside her was no longer due to the fear of being caught. It was at the idea that Lord Harlford really might be a spy.

CHAPTER 12

"What did the letters say?" Maria asked. They were walking in the sunlit gardens after breakfast. Tess trotted beside them, having been well exercised by Chatham earlier.

"Mostly things like 'we are making some progress but need more', or 'someone will be in communication in two weeks'. No names, no signatures." She showed Maria the list she'd written when she returned to her room in the early hours, hoping that what she could recall would be enough.

To Alice's relief, Maria didn't suggest that she should go back and copy them out. It wasn't just the embarrassment and shame if she were caught—there was also a fear that she *would* find something incriminating. She still found it difficult to believe that Lord Harlford could be a traitor, in spite of the letters.

"Nothing conclusive, then," Maria said, handing the list back.

"No, other than the fact that he *is* corresponding with someone in France, and Lord Marstone already knew that. I don't see what else we can do."

"Tell Marstone what we have found, and ask for suggestions," Maria said. "I will write later, and give the letter to Chatham. However, it might take up to a week to get a reply. Then there is the matter of information being sent to France. You are sure Harlford's letters contained nothing of that nature?"

"Only that he appears to be trying to buy something. *Buy*, not sell."

Maria nodded. "However, a lack of evidence that he is selling or transferring information on weapons does not prove that he is *not* doing so. But it is also possible that someone else is responsible. According to Chatham, Harlford's assistants live in Woodley and Luncot. I am told they are pretty little villages, with one or two shops, so we could ask to borrow a carriage and visit them this afternoon. I'm sure Cassandra will be quite happy to have us out of the way. We will invite Lucy, and possibly Miss Stockhart or Miss Gearing. You young things will wander around together while I rest my ageing legs—"

"Hmpf."

"Ageing legs," Maria repeated. "That will give me an excellent excuse for talking to people. Relieving the boredom while my young friends have inconsiderately left me alone."

Alice chuckled. "Laying it on rather too thick!"

"That's better. No need to look so glum, my dear. There might well be an innocent explanation for those letters. Now, we have a plan for this afternoon, so I will arrange that, and then I am going to walk to the Dower House. Would you like to accompany me?"

Alice shook her head. "If you don't mind, I'd rather look around the kitchen garden again." And *not* subject herself to another interrogation by the dowager. "Are you going to introduce Tess to Lady Harlford?"

"Ha. No—if Tess causes a nuisance, get a footman to take her back to the stables."

They parted company, and Alice went through the door into the kitchen garden. She'd enjoyed the tour with the elderly head gardener a couple of days ago, listening as Fowler described his cultivation and propagation methods for flowers. However, Lord Harlford had joined them before they could look around the kitchen garden, and Fowler had excused himself.

The kitchen garden was laid out in neat rectangles separated by paths of hard-packed gravel only just wide enough for a wheelbarrow to pass. There were beds with pea sticks and supports for raspberry canes, others full of bushes that must be gooseberries and blackcurrants, and row upon row of young leaves poking above the soil. Espaliered fruit trees in blossom lined the east and west walls, and a glasshouse occupied most of the north wall. The whole garden was many times the size of the one at home, but had to feed a lot more people. She wondered if the way the planting was organised to ensure a variety of crops were available was the same as at home, or if there were factors she had never considered due to the different scale.

"Can I help you, miss?"

Alice jumped, not having heard the man approach. He was young, perhaps thirty, with the same dark hair and eyes as the head gardener. From his clothing he must be also be one of the gardening staff. He had the bland expression of a servant not expected to show his feelings, and touched a finger to his forehead.

"Griffiths, miss." He eyed Tess uncertainly, but after sniffing at his legs, the dog waved her tail and lay down on the path.

"Miss Bryant," she introduced herself with a nod and a smile. "I'm interested in how a garden this size is managed. Are you related to the head gardener?"

"My uncle, miss. I'm the undergardener. What was it you wanted to know?"

"I used to manage the garden at my home, but it was tiny compared to this." She had so many questions; where to start? "Tell me about the varieties of fruit trees you have. At home, our soils are on chalk—I think you have more loamy soils here?"

Griffiths smiled, and they spent the next twenty minutes walking around the edge of the garden while Tess dozed in the sunshine. Griffiths' enthusiasm for his work was clear; Alice wished she'd brought paper and pencil with her, but hoped she could remember enough of what she was told to make notes when she returned to her room. Her conscience finally allowed him to get on with his work, and she strolled around the beds again as he headed for the glasshouse.

She was examining the salad crops, recalling Griffiths' explanation of his planting succession, when she noticed Tess' attention on something behind her. She turned to see Julius Chilton entering through the door from the formal garden. He stopped just inside, looking around until he saw Alice, then headed towards her. His gait was stiff, his mouth pursed in a scowl.

"Tess, come here," Alice called. The dog's ears twitched, and she trotted to Alice's side. She must have sensed Alice's unease, for she began a low growl.

Chilton stopped, his scowl deepening, and Alice's heart began to race in spite of Tess' presence.

"You keep your nose out of my business in future, do you hear?" He was close enough to be heard without raising his voice, but the very quietness made the menace in his tone more frightening.

"I don't know what you mean, Mr Chilton. Excuse me, I am expected indoors."

He stood between her and the door, but there was another exit beside the glasshouse. "Come, Tess." Alice turned and walked away, Tess beside her, trying to still the faint trembling in her hands.

Was Griffiths in sight? He might help—but how many servants would risk challenging a guest of their employer? Tess, still growling low in her throat, would protect her, but what would happen to the dog if she attacked one of Lord Harlford's guests?

Chilton muttered a curse, and followed. "Do *not* presume to walk away from me when I am addressing you." His voice was becoming louder. "For a hired companion, you are getting well above your station."

Alice turned to face him. "I am no employee of yours, and you have no authority over me." She raised her chin. "Which business is it you want me to stay out of, Mr Chilton? Your unwelcome advances towards Lord Harlford's sister?"

A red flush spread up his face. "I intend to marry Lucilla."

"She's only just turned sixteen, Mr Chilton."

"Old enough. You will not interfere again, or you will learn what happens to women who cross me." He took a step back, running his eyes from her face down to her bosom and lingering there. "You will not always have that animal with you." He turned on his heel and stalked off.

Alice swallowed hard—his threat was plain. She put a shaking hand to her face, feeling as if her knees were about to give way.

~

James leaned closer to the window, as if that would help him see better. He had only come up to the library to check something in his breeding records, and happened to glance out of the window. Miss Bryant stood near the vegetable beds, that huge dog standing alert by her side and Julius Chilton before her.

About to turn back to his breeding book, he saw Miss Bryant turn and walk away, but Chilton followed. She did not wish to talk to Chilton—that was clear. They were alone in the garden, apart from the dog.

James swore—he was a fool to have believed Chilton yesterday. An animal that large should be protection enough, but he couldn't be sure. Cursing the size of the house, he rushed outside. Even taking the shortest route, it was several minutes before he'd sprinted through the stable yard, causing a handful of grooms to stop and stare at him, and around to the kitchen garden.

There was no-one in sight. He walked on a few yards, gazing about in case they were hidden by bushes somewhere.

"My lord?" It was the undergardener.

"Where is Miss Bryant?"

"Sitting down in there, my lord." Griffiths indicated the glasshouse, and he could see the pale shape of her bonnet through the glass. "She was distressed, my lord, so I took her in to sit down. The gentleman's gone."

No gentleman reduced young ladies to hiding in glasshouses. "Thank you, Griffiths."

He pushed open the door. Miss Bryant sat on an old wooden chair, the dog lying at her feet. She was bent forward with her elbows on her knees and her forehead resting on her hands. The dog raised its head at James' entrance, then sat up, but made no other move.

"I'm all right, Griffiths," she said, not looking up.

James cleared his throat. "Er, Miss Bryant?"

"Oh!" She sat up, her eyes wide in a white face.

He took a step back, and some of the tension in her body relaxed. "I'm sorry, I didn't intend to alarm you. I mean you no harm."

"I know you do not, my lord." She rubbed her face.

James felt unaccountably pleased at her statement, a warm feeling stirring within his chest. "I saw Chilton talking to you from the library window." He tried to keep the anger out of his voice—it was not directed at her. "What did he say?"

"He... he told me to mind my own business."

"Lucy?"

She nodded.

"He threatened you."

"Yes."

The warmth in his chest became hot anger. It was fortunate for Chilton that he wasn't still here. "He will be leaving today, Miss Bryant, I can assure you."

"I'm sorry, I—"

"You should not be apologising. You stepped in to help my sister, for which I am grateful. I should have made him leave yesterday, but I accepted his word that he had not intentionally bothered Lucy."

Some colour returned to her cheeks, and she relaxed further.

"Do you wish to return to the house? May I escort you?"

"Mr Chilton... I mean, I would not wish to encounter him." She tucked a stray strand of hair behind her ear, and he thought he detected a faint tremor in her hand.

She needed time.

"One moment."

. . .

Alice breathed deeply as Lord Harlford stepped outside to where Griffiths waited, trying to calm herself. Why was she feeling this way? Nothing had actually happened.

She had never been personally threatened like that before, and had been shocked at the malevolence in Chilton's expression. But the threat was gone now—Chilton would be leaving, and she would make sure she was not alone anywhere until she was sure he had gone.

The damp scent of earth and growing things was familiar and comforting. She stood, pleased to find that her legs no longer felt quite so wobbly, and wandered slowly along the glasshouse, taking her time to examine the arrays of seedlings and young plants.

Lord Harlford returned as she reached the far end. "What are these, do you know?" He was looking at the slatted shelves with their rows of pots.

Alice walked towards him. "Tomato plants." She pointed to the ones she was passing. "These are runner beans, marrows, and so on. They germinate better in warm soil, and will be planted out when there is no chance of frost."

"Why are some plants in here and some in the cold frames outside?"

"The cold frames will keep the plants free of frost but ..." Alice stopped—the gentle questions, easy to answer, had set her at ease. Had that been his intention? "My lord, are you *really* interested?"

"I am interested in many things, Miss Bryant."

That wasn't a 'yes'.

"I am happy to explain, but you may feel I have turned back into a governess."

He smiled. "I will take that risk. Why are those—?"

A rattle at the door interrupted him. Two footmen brought in a small metal table and two chairs, moving warily around Tess to set them out. A third man entered, his tray laden with tea pot, cups, and a plate of cakes.

"Would you take tea with me?"

Alice gazed at the delicate china cups, the steaming pot, and the fancy cakes, and couldn't help laughing. It wasn't only the incongruity of these things next to the thick clay pots and the traces of mud on the floor, but that Lord Harlford had thought of it.

"I would be delighted, my lord. Shall I pour?" The twinkle in his eyes as she handed him a cup showed that he, too, was amused.

He looked along the glasshouse. "I don't think I have been in here since I was a boy. I was interested in seeing things grow at one stage, before my interests turned to other areas of natural philosophy. You must miss your own garden."

He'd remembered what they had talked about at dinner on their first evening.

"I do, yes. It is lovely to have grounds like these to wander through."

"Hyde Park doesn't quite compensate, does it?"

She turned her gaze to her cup—was he recalling finding her on her knees there, looking for beetles?

"I haven't yet thanked you properly for rescuing Lucy yesterday." His face became serious as he changed the subject. "I do thank you—I had not noticed how uncomfortable she was, and she may not have had the confidence to tell me about it."

"It was nothing. Anyone would have done so."

"*Not* nothing, Miss Bryant, particularly in view of today's consequences. I'm sorry you were put in such a position. I should have—"

"My lord, it wasn't your fault. How could you know Mr Chilton would be so…"

"Vile?" He sighed. "I could not."

He would never act like that, she was sure. She sipped her tea as he talked, the hot liquid welcome and refreshing.

"As I said, I will ensure that Chilton leaves, but could I ask you not to go about the estate unless you are accompanied by Chatham or one of my men? For a few days, at least—particularly if Lucy is with you. I can see that Chilton is put on a coach from Hereford, but I cannot prevent him returning if he so chooses. If your man is not available, ask a groom or one of the footmen."

"I will, thank you." That seemed sensible.

"It does not seem fair that your movements should be restricted because of—"

"It's perfectly all right, my lord. It is only for a few days."

"Thank you. And…" He hesitated, and set his half-eaten cake back on the plate. "Do, please, let me know if you see anything, anything at all, that suggests one of the other young men might have similar designs."

"Certainly. Lady Jesson has planned to take a carriage ride to some of the nearby villages this afternoon, and was intending to ask Lucy if she wishes to come with us."

"An excellent plan. Thank you." He toyed with the cake on his plate. "When Griffiths went to order the tea, he also passed on my instructions to set someone to keep track of where Chilton is. When you feel ready to return, have Griffiths escort you to the house, to Bellingham. He will ensure you do not encounter Chilton between now and your excursion this afternoon."

"Thank you." The tea and cake had revived her, and it was a couple of hours before Maria would need her. "I was enjoying talking to Griffiths before Mr Chilton arrived. I would happily remain here for a while longer, if I have your permission to distract him from his work?"

"I… Well, yes, of course, if you wish. Now, or at any other time." He stood, smiling at the crumbs on her plate. "Enjoy your excursion. If you go to Luncot, make sure Lucy introduces you to Mrs Anderson and her cakes."

With a bow of his head, he turned and left the glasshouse. Alice poured another cup of tea, not quite ready to resume her tour.

How could Lord Harlford be a traitor when he'd arranged tea in a glasshouse just to make his most insignificant guest feel better?

CHAPTER 13

*B*ellingham approached James as he entered the Castle. "Mr Chilton—Mr Julius Chilton—is in the billiards room, my lord."

"Thank you, Bellingham." No time like the present. "Chilton will be leaving within the hour. Have someone start packing his things, order a carriage to take him to Hereford, and ensure he continues to be escorted until he is in it."

Bellingham bowed his head, and James headed for the billiards room. His mother emerged from the parlour as he passed the door.

"Where have you been, James? You should be entertaining your guests."

Damn. "I was in the garden, Mama."

"I was there with the Chiltons. I didn't see you."

"The kitchen garden. Miss Bryant… wished to see the glasshouse."

Her brows drew together. "James, why are you wasting your time with her? You escorted her to the Dower House the other day, and invited her to accompany you to the portrait gallery. You should be concentrating on your potential brides—you said you wanted to get to know them better before making your choice."

James clenched his jaw. He wanted to tell her to mind her own business, that he *was* trying—but a footman stood by the parlour door, and Bellingham was still in earshot.

"Your grandmama has invited Miss Esham to visit her this afternoon. You may escort her to the Dower House at two o'clock."

"Very well, Mama. If you will excuse me?" He didn't wait for a reply.

When he entered the billiards room, Chilton was watching a game between Lord Gearing and Miss Stockhart's father.

"A word, Chilton?" James did his best to keep his voice pleasant. "In private, if you please."

Chilton's brows rose, but he shrugged and followed James across the hall, his brows rising even further as James ushered him into the estate office. A jerk of James' head had Terring scurrying out of the way, and James closed the door behind him.

Chilton looked about him, then at James. "Interesting though your estates might be, Harlford, I don't—"

"You are leaving here this morning. Make what excuse you like to the rest of your family, but you will be in a carriage on the way to Hereford in half an hour."

"What? Why?" Chilton smiled—an ingratiating smile that put James' teeth on edge. "I have done as you asked. I have not spoken to your sister since yesterday."

"You threatened one of my guests."

"Good God, Harlford. I had a quiet word with the *companion* of one of your guests. What's the harm in that?"

Whether Chilton really thought he'd done nothing wrong was irrelevant. "I've given instructions for your belongings to be packed. The carriage will be ready in half an hour."

"You're not going to eject me on the word of an employee, surely? The woman's being hysterical if she—"

"Half an hour, Chilton. If you don't present yourself ready to leave when the carriage is brought round, I'll have you escorted from the premises. By force, if necessary." He opened the door, and waited.

"But my parents and—"

"Twenty-nine minutes."

Chilton glared at him, and James took his watch from his waist-coat pocket. Chilton stalked past, muttering curses under his breath.

James let out a breath, then headed for the stables to arrange a suitable escort to remain with Chilton until he got onto the Mail in Hereford.

~

The expedition to Luncot set out in an open carriage that afternoon. Lucy and Miss Stockhart had both brought their sketchbooks. Miss Stockhart was wary of Tess coming along at first, but once she saw that the animal was happy to doze at their feet, she relaxed. One of Lord Harlford's grooms was driving, with Chatham beside him.

Luncot was only about three miles from the Castle if you were a crow, but six or seven miles by road. Not far from the quarry, Alice estimated—close enough to walk across the fields.

She said little, listening with half an ear as Lucy and Miss Stockhart chatted. It was so good to be in the countryside at this time of year, with hedgerows in flower and apple orchards in full blossom. She'd enjoyed working for the Comte de Calvac in London, but when her time with Maria came to an end she would try to find a position somewhere outside London.

"Oh, how lovely!" Maria exclaimed as the carriage drove into the village. Houses and shops, mostly white with black timbers, clustered around a triangular green with a pond in one corner. The scene was all the more attractive for the sunshine and front gardens coming into bloom.

"Mrs Anderson sells ribbons and things." Lucy pointed at one of the shops. "She does tea and cakes, too. Jamie sometimes lets me stop here if we've been riding together, although she does talk a lot."

Alice met Maria's eyes—a garrulous shopkeeper would be an ideal person to help them find out more about Lord Harlford's assistants.

Refreshments were served at three little tables near the window, and Maria sat down while the others examined the goods, telling Mrs

Anderson when she bustled over that she would wait until her companions had decided what they would buy.

For such a small shop, there was an excellent range of fabrics, ribbons, and other dressmaking supplies. The shopkeeper was a thin little woman with greying hair, who explained in great detail the benefits of each ribbon Alice inspected. Alice chose some green ones for her bonnet, and Mrs Anderson turned her attention to helping Lucy and Miss Stockhart determine which colour silk flowers would look best to match their pelisses. Then they drank tea and ate from a selection of delicious Shrewsbury biscuits, Queen cakes, and ratafia biscuits.

When they had finished, and with no-one else in the shop, Maria looked at Alice and gave the tiniest jerk of her head towards the window.

"I need a little exercise after all that food," Alice said. "I think I'll take a walk around the village. Will you come with me, Miss Stockhart? Lucy?"

"You three go." Maria made a shooing motion with her hands. "I will sit here for a while and have another cup of tea."

Lucy hesitated, eyeing the empty plate.

"This is such a lovely little shop," Maria added. "I must ask Mrs Anderson to tell me all about it."

Alice bit her lip as Lucy stood, sure that if she met Maria's eye she'd laugh. "Is Mrs Anderson that bad?" she asked as they walked onto the street.

"Not really, I suppose," Lucy admitted. "Not the first time, anyway. But when you've heard it all before... several times..." She shrugged. "Shall we take Tess for a walk?"

Chatham held out a leash as Tess jumped out of the carriage. "She's well trained enough around deer and the like, but not ducks."

Alice hooked the leash to Tess' collar, and they set off around the green. Tess ignored most of the children playing on the grass, but her nose twitched and she gave a low growl when they passed a stocky man with a satchel going from door to door. The man looked around at the sound, then turned his back and increased his pace as he hurried on.

Tess gave another little growl before turning her attention to the ducks. Had she recognised the man's scent? At the quarry, perhaps, but this man's coat was blue, not the green of the fabric scrap Chatham had found. Alice resolved to mention it to Chatham later, to see if he thought it significant.

Half an hour later they had admired the ducklings and the stained-glass windows in the church. "I will make some sketches of the ducklings, if you don't mind," Miss Stockhart said. "I think there's a blanket in the carriage I can sit on."

Alice collected a second blanket, and they sat near Miss Stockhart —within sight of Chatham and the driver, both still lounging by the carriage.

"Have you seen the new foal?" Lucy asked.

"Not yet."

"It was out of one of Jamie's favourite mares. He said I may name him. The dam is called Athena, and the stallion is Ventus—the one he was riding yesterday. Ventus means wind—I'll see if there is a book about the ancient gods in the library to find another wind name for the colt."

"I'm sure there is, but…" Alice glanced at Lucy's eager face. "That is, many of the ancient stories are rather… improper."

"Mama might not approve," Lucy said. "But she'll never know."

"I'm glad I'm not your governess," Alice said with a laugh. Lucy could turn out to be a real handful when she was introduced to society.

"I like Miss Sullivan," Lucy said. "She teaches me things Mama wouldn't approve of."

"Oh?"

"Natural philosophy, mainly. Jamie spends most of his time doing experiments, so it must be interesting. And I like learning how he chooses which horses to breed."

"What does your brother study besides horse breeding?"

"All sorts of things—he did try to explain once, but I didn't understand. I'm more interested in plants and animals, especially small things. There's a book in the library with magnified drawings of flies and beetles. Have you seen what a fly's eye looks like?"

Lucy chattered on—describing Hooke's *Micrographia*, Alice suspected. Finding out more about what Lord Harlford did in his laboratory might have been useful, but she wasn't sorry that Lucy didn't know. Obtaining information from his young sister felt as bad as breaking into his desk.

"Did you find out anything?" Alice asked Maria. Lucy had joined Miss Stockhart on her blanket by the time Maria emerged from the shop, and they had a few minutes to themselves.

"My dear, the woman was a goldmine!" Maria said. "I must have heard the life history of every family in the village, for several generations back, as well as several from further afield."

Alice laughed. "Gossip is your business. But was there anything to the point?"

"I think so, but elimination of a possible suspect rather than anything positive. There's a blacksmith a few miles further east, by the name of Norton. One of his sons works with Lord Harlford. I questioned the 'with Lord Harlford'—"

"—as opposed to 'for'?"

"Indeed—so he could well be one of Harlford's assistants. Mrs Anderson doesn't know exactly what the lad does—to her and my regret—but says he's not got too much up here..." She tapped her head. "But he's good with his hands, can fashion all sorts of things once he's got the idea of what's wanted. She showed me a neat little rack to hold spools of thread that he made for her."

"Being... a bit slow-witted doesn't stop someone from taking bribes," Alice pointed out. "Or being threatened."

"Or having revolutionary sympathies," Maria added. "All that is true, but I suspect it might take more wit than the lad has to know what information to steal, and to do so without being found out."

"So still a possibility, really, but a very unlikely one." She felt pleased that they hadn't found anything to incriminate him, but today's efforts had done nothing to clear Lord Harlford of suspicion either, and their investigations were not at an end. She felt a weight in her chest at the idea he may yet prove to be guilty.

～

Grandmama was not alone when James and Miss Esham were shown into the parlour. The man who stood to greet them... It was like looking at an older version of himself in the mirror.

"Uncle David?" Grandmama had told him his uncle was returning, but he hadn't expected it to be so soon.

"The very same." His uncle clapped him on the shoulder, a wide grin on his face. "It's good to see you, James! Rather larger than you were when I left. Who is your pretty companion?"

James had forgotten Miss Esham, now simpering beside his uncle. "Uncle, Grandmama, may I present Miss Esham? Miss Esham, Lady Harlford and Lord David Broxwood."

Miss Esham made a curtsey, seeming unsure whether to direct it at his grandmother or uncle.

"Sit down, Miss Esham," Grandmama commanded. "David, take James away for twenty minutes, then you may return to escort Miss Esham back to the Castle. I want to talk to James as well."

"Yes, my lady." David bowed with a mock flourish, his smile undiminished. "Come, James, we have been dismissed."

They left through the doors onto the terrace, and descended into the knot garden.

"When did you arrive?" James asked. It felt rather strange, talking as an equal to a man he had last known when he was still in the schoolroom.

"A few hours ago. Mama had already arranged for Miss Esher... whatever the name was... to visit her."

"Are you staying here, rather than in the Castle?"

"I think it best, don't you? There was never any love lost between me and your mother. And I've no fancy to mix with a houseful of your guests when I've only just arrived."

"Mama's guests."

"So I gathered. Cassandra's pushing you to marry, eh?"

"She'd arranged it all before I even learned about the house party. I don't see why there's such a rush."

"She doesn't want me to inherit if anything happens to you."

Because David didn't have any heirs of his own, Mama had said. Perhaps that wasn't the real reason?

"No need to look like that, James. Whatever Cassandra says about me is like water off a duck's back. Don't let her nag you into taking someone you don't care for. No—someone you don't love."

"Love?"

"It's not so strange. I don't suppose my mother would ever discuss it with you, but she and my father were very happy together. Your parents..." David shrugged.

"I don't recall them arguing." Not the way he'd heard his mother berating David. But then he didn't recall them spending much time together at all.

"Not arguing isn't the same as being happy together." David spoke with a wistful air, then his smile reappeared. "Tell me about your research—Mama said you've been obsessed with it the last few years. You haven't blown your laboratory up again, have you?"

"Ha, no. Not yet, anyway."

"You'll have to explain what you're doing some time. I may even understand some of it."

James laughed. His memories of his uncle were fond ones—he liked this older version just as much.

"I'll show you around the stables, too. I've enjoyed breeding my own matched pairs."

"Tell me more."

"Well, James?"

James closed the terrace door behind David and Miss Esham and turned to his grandmother. She seemed to have a glow about her.

"I'm glad Uncle David is back. It's a pity he stayed away so long."

"I'm very happy he's returned, but I wasn't asking about him. What do you think of Miss Esham?"

James sat down. "Attractive, certainly. Very accomplished—or so she informs me."

"You're not smitten, then?"

"Rather the opposite."

Grandmama nodded. "And the others?"

"Miss Gearing giggles all the time—Lucy thinks she might be nervous, but she's showing no signs of getting over it. Miss Stockhart is a pleasant girl; enjoys painting. Miss Chilton...I don't know her well."

"Not a promising collection, then?"

"Miss Stockhart might do, I suppose."

"James, do *not* make an offer for someone who 'might do'. This is the rest of your life you are deciding upon. You need a wife who can be your friend as well as give you an heir."

"I'm not intending to offer for her."

"If you loved her, it would be different. But she would not thrive here, I think. Look at Arabella."

What did his late brother's wife have to do with it?

"She was of Cassandra's choosing. The poor girl—and poor Robert —were leg-shackled before either knew what was going on. It wasn't happy for either of them."

Robert had mostly ignored Arabella, as far as James could recall. It could not have been a pleasant marriage from Arabella's point of view, with a mother-in-law who still ruled the household and a husband who spent most of his time in London. When Robert was at Harlford, he took little notice of her, and his visits to his mistress in the village had been common knowledge.

"Robert might have made more effort with her," Grandmama added. "But I think Cassandra made a mistake with Miss Esham, and possibly Miss Chilton."

"Because I don't like them?"

"No. Cassandra wants you to marry another timid girl like Arabella, of course."

"Why would she—?"

"James, *think*. What normally happens when the heir marries? Who runs the household? Cassandra has browbeaten Arabella into retreating to her rooms with her baby, or spending time here with me, leaving Cassandra to run things as she pleases. David would have your mother moved out within a week of inheriting, and she knows it."

That was why Mama was so keen on him providing an heir.

"There is no need for you to marry this season, or even next, if you do not find someone who suits *you*."

Had Robert been happy with Arabella? Probably not, or he wouldn't have kept a mistress. He didn't want his marriage to be like that—he wanted someone he would be happy to remain faithful to. "Very well, Grandmama. I will be careful in my choice."

CHAPTER 14

*J*ames turned the page of the journal, marking significant passages in the text with a pencil and copying some into his notebook. Shouts and laughter drifted in through the open window, from guests playing croquet on the lawn. Inside the library, the only sounds were the occasional clearing of a throat from the far end where Lord Gearing was consulting the parliamentary proceedings again.

"Harlford, do you have a minute?"

James looked up to see Lord Chilton walking along the library towards him. He sighed, and blotted the page in his notebook before closing it. "What can I do for you, Chilton?"

Chilton fiddled with his neckcloth. "I… er, I wanted to pass on my son's thanks for your hospitality. Shame he had to leave so suddenly yesterday, eh?"

"His business must have been urgent."

"I… er, yes, it was." Chilton looked around as Gearing cleared his throat again, then nodded at James and walked away. "Gearing, why are you holing yourself up in here on such a lovely day?"

Gearing's sigh was audible even from this distance.

"Fancy a game of billiards? A hand of piquet?"

"Oh, very well." Gearing caught James' eye and shrugged as he followed Chilton from the room.

How was playing billiards supposed to make use of the good weather? James shook his head, and scanned the page of the journal, finding his place. At least now there was no-one in the library to interrupt him.

He had only read a few paragraphs when he heard the sound of footsteps again, and swore quietly. If he hadn't invited several of the guests to use the library, he'd lock himself in.

"Miss Chilton." Politeness demanded he stand to greet her, but politeness be damned. He was not going to do anything to encourage her to stay.

"Lord Harlford." She tilted her head as she looked at him. He supposed it was intended to be attractive.

"Well?"

Her smile slipped at his harsh tone. "I... I wondered if you had anything I might read."

"By all means. What are your interests? History? The classics? Natural philosophy?"

"What would you recommend, my lord?"

He tried to recall what topics were shelved in the furthest bays. "I find travellers' accounts fascinating."

She smiled.

"If you look in the last bay but one, you will find a selection. Now, if you will excuse me, Miss Chilton, I am very busy." He returned to his journals, but Miss Chilton leaned forward and rested a hand on his desk. It seemed he would not easily be rid of her.

Her smile widened as he stood. "I wish you would call me Laura, my lord."

Certainly not! "Would you care for a turn in the gardens, Miss Chilton?" He might be able to shake her off without being too impolite if they joined the croquet players.

Her smile disappeared, to his surprise. She took the arm he offered, and trailed half a step behind as he headed for the door. They were only half-way down the room when she came to a stop.

"You have such a lot of books, my lord," she said, her voice breathy. "Will you show me which ones you prefer?"

A feeling of unease began to niggle. Chilton had made sure where he was and taken Gearing away; now his daughter was trying to keep him in the room...

"Come, Miss Chilton, we are wasting the good weather." He took her by the elbow and hurried her towards the door.

Alice looked up as Lady Chilton entered the parlour. A large vase of peonies and irises partly concealed her, and she was about to resume her reading when Lady Chilton stopped close to Maria. Alice sat up straighter.

"Lady Jesson, I noticed you enjoy reading novels."

Odd—Lady Chilton had shown no sign of wishing to befriend either of them in the last few days.

"Indeed." Maria's voice carried clearly. "I find the realistic situations they describe offer relief from the fabrications of society gossip."

A look of confusion crossed Lady Chilton's face. "I... er... I believe the library here includes a stock of novels."

Maria didn't reply.

"I understand you have been in the library. Would you accompany me and show me where they are?"

Lady Chilton must want something, to be so persistent. Alice put her book down—Maria would not be able to resist finding out what was going on.

"By all means."

When Maria and Lady Chilton reached the door, Alice followed them.

"Mama!" Augustus Chilton stood near the foot of the stairs, Miss Stockhart several yards behind him. He put out a hand as if to stop them, but his mother ignored it and continued as if he were not there.

"I say, Mama..." Augustus followed them up the stairs, protesting ineffectually, and stood gaping as they headed towards the library.

"What is wrong?" Alice asked Miss Stockhart, a few steps behind Augustus.

"They... Lord Harlford is in the library with Miss... um... Augustus overheard... Miss Chilton is... wants to... to trap—"

"Come with me." Alice grabbed her hand and almost pulled her up the remaining stairs, ignoring her squeak of alarm. If Lady Chilton thought to use Maria to back up her plans, she'd grossly misjudged the matter. But there might be other witnesses. She pushed open the door that led to the servants' corridor.

"Hurry, Miss Stockhart."

~

"Laura, my dear, are you here?"

James released Miss Chilton's arm as Lady Chilton appeared at the end of the room. "Damn it!" He'd been outmanoeuvred.

Who was that with her... Lady Jesson? She'd seemed a sensible woman, but she was a gossip.

"Laura, are— Oh, what *have* you been doing, Laura?"

James turned. Miss Chilton's hair now tumbled halfway down her back, and her gown seemed to have slipped, one shoulder showing.

"Oh, Lord Harlford!"

"That is none of my do—"

"Oh, but I see how it is. Young love, so touching," Lady Chilton gushed. "I'm so pleased. Laura, you've been away for an age." She turned to Lady Jesson. "I suppose young people in love must be allowed to spend time alone together."

"Lady Chilton," James protested. "Miss Chilton came in only—"

"We found them, Lord Harlford!"

James spun around—that voice had come from behind him, near his desk.

Miss Bryant?

She emerged from the end bay with Miss Stockhart, both carrying books. Miss Bryant was smiling, but he was too relieved to see her to

121

wonder what was amusing her. Miss Stockhart looked as bewildered as he felt.

"Someone must have shelved them in the wrong place, my lord." Miss Bryant's voice sounded unusually breathy. "Oh, hello, Lady Chilton, have you come to borrow something, too? It took us an age to find the ones we wanted. We heard Miss Chilton come in and ask to borrow a book."

"I didn't know you were a bluestocking, Laura," Lady Jesson said. One brow rose as she inspected Miss Chilton's hair, then she turned to Lady Chilton. "If I were you, I'd find a new maid for your daughter. The one you have is clearly incompetent, if her hair comes unpinned so easily. Now, you asked where the novels were shelved."

"I don't want a novel," Lady Chilton forced out through stiff lips. "Come, Laura, I need to speak with you." She took hold of her daughter's arm and pulled her away. Her son stood in the doorway, gaping, but she swept past him.

"Mr Chilton, would you close the door please?" Lady Jesson turned to James as Augustus obeyed. "I've witnessed a few attempts at entrapment in my time, but I have to say that was a particularly poor effort. I assume you did not want to be pressured to offer for Miss Chilton?"

He ran a finger around his neck inside his cravat. "No, I did not." He turned to glare at Augustus. "You were party to this, Chilton?"

"Augustus tried to stop them, my lord!" Miss Stockhart put a hand over her mouth after this outburst, seeming shocked at her boldness.

"Shall we sit down?" Lady Jesson moved to the chairs near the fire.

James headed in the opposite direction, towards his desk, returning with the tray holding a decanter and glasses. Lady Jesson and Augustus Chilton accepted a drink, but the other two refused. He poured himself one and downed it in one swallow.

"Please can someone tell me what is going on?" He was dismayed at the plaintive sound of his words, and cleared his throat. "A plain tale, if you please. I was alone in here when Miss Chilton arrived."

"Miss Stockhart told... indicated that Lady Chilton and her daughter were planning something," Miss Bryant said. "I thought you might appreciate an intervention."

"Oh, I do, believe me!" And he had to admire her quick wits.

He turned to Miss Stockhart. "How did you know?"

"I... um..."

She looked terrified. James realised that his frown wasn't helping and smoothed his features. "Miss Stockhart, I am extremely grateful for your help. Please, do explain."

Miss Stockhart managed a small smile. "Augustus—Mr Chilton, I mean—told me he overheard his parents planning something, but he wasn't sure what it was."

"Chilton?" James said, trying to sound encouraging.

"We... er... well..." Chilton coughed. "Pockets to let, whole family, you know. Need to marry money. Julius... well, it wasn't right, trying to... your sister... I mean..."

Get on with it, man!

It didn't improve his mood to see Lady Jesson staring out of the window, her lips pressed together. Miss Bryant was looking at the rug with a similar expression. They wouldn't find it so amusing if they'd been the target.

"Then Mama sent Papa to find you... he told her you were in the library, then she sent Laura in and I followed her... Caroline—Miss Stockhart—was there and I told her."

"I knew the entrance from the servants' passage, my lord," Miss Bryant said. "Er... Lucy told me about it." She looked uncomfortable now, her hands clasped tightly in her lap. Why should that worry her?

"I do thank you, Miss Bryant. But they seriously misjudged. I would not let such a ploy force me into matrimony with someone like... with Miss Chilton." Being shunned by society would be no loss.

"As they misjudged when they supposed I would abet their scheme by spreading gossip," Lady Jesson said.

Chilton stood up. "I must apologise for... for the behaviour of my family, my lord. Julius, in particular. I will endeavour to persuade my parents to leave, and we will be on our way as soon as I can manage it." He gave a small bow.

"Oh!"

It was a faint sound—James wasn't sure who had made it. Miss

Stockhart's brows were drawn together and tears glistened in her eyes. Lady Jesson and Miss Bryant gazed at him expectantly.

What did they want?

He glanced from Miss Stockhart to Chilton, recalling how often he had seen them together. Until now, James had considered the man faintly ridiculous, with his colourful clothing and overabundance of fobs, but his apology had been made with dignity and the situation was not of his making.

"Chilton, you are welcome to stay if you wish."

One watery smile and two approving nods told him he had said the right thing.

"Only you, I mean," James added, not wanting there to be any misunderstanding. "Your parents and sister—"

"Oh, thank you, my lord!" Miss Stockhart leapt to her feet, and for one horrible moment James thought she was going to hug him. Lady Jesson stood and patted her on her shoulder.

"Yes. Thank you, my lord." Chilton bowed again, and left the room.

"I... I think I will go and find my family." Miss Stockhart didn't wait for a reply, but bobbed a curtsey and followed Chilton out of the room.

James looked after them. "It is not my business, but..." Miss Stockhart was one of his guests, though, and—

"I've never let that stop *me*," Lady Jesson said.

Miss Bryant made a choking sound as James suppressed a laugh. It was refreshing to come across a woman who was honest about her behaviour.

"Am I right in recalling that Stockhart is likely to give his daughter a sizeable dowry? Chilton..."

"Don't worry, my lord," Lady Jesson said. "I suspect the pair of them truly like each other. And much can be done with settlements to prevent the rest of the family taking it all for themselves. I will have a quiet word with Sir Aloysius or his wife."

"Thank you."

"My pleasure."

Lady Jesson rose to her feet. "We will leave you in peace now. May

I suggest you make use of the servants' door if such a thing happens again?"

"I feared she would follow me."

Lady Jesson smiled. "I'm sure you can run faster."

Miss Bryant gave him an uncertain smile and followed her employer.

So two more of Mama's candidates had been ruled out in one morning. Discovering Miss Stockhart's preference for Augustus Chilton hadn't caused him the slightest pang. That left only Miss Gearing, and he was not going to offer for a girl who was still uncomfortable in his presence. There was little point to this house party continuing, but he could hardly ask the guests to leave, so he'd have to make the best of it. Lucy, at least, appeared to be enjoying Miss Stockhart's company, and Miss Bryant's.

Running one hand through his hair, James looked out of the window. The sunny intervals of the morning had given way to a thin sheet of high cloud covering the sky. Good enough weather to go for a ride. His concentration had gone, and no-one would be able to trap him while he was out on horseback.

Alice finished playing a Handel suite to a scattering of applause, and turned to the stack of music on the piano to choose another piece. Lady Harlford had requested she entertain the guests after dinner, and Alice was happy to comply, even if half the guests were playing cards in the next room and the rest were talking.

She had got only a few bars into the piece when a shriek, hastily muffled, stopped the hum of conversation. Alice turned on the stool to see everyone staring at the door. A man stood there—an older version of Lord Harlford, dressed as plainly. Lady Harlford had one hand over her mouth, and Maria... Maria looked like the cat who'd had the cream. Alice hurried to sit beside her.

"Lord David Broxwood," Maria said.

"Harlford's uncle?"

"I hope you're not intending to stay here, David." Lady Harlford's strident tones carried clearly across the room as she hurried towards the door.

Far from being taken aback by this unfriendly greeting, Lord David smiled. "My dear Cassandra, I wouldn't inflict your company on myself." Maria muffled a laugh as Lord David examined his sleeve, flicking something from it. A few of the other guests looked shocked, others amused. "No, I am settled in the Dower House. So kind of you to be concerned."

"The Dower House? But—"

"Ah, James, introduce me to your guests, will you?" He walked off with his nephew, leaving Lady Harlford scowling after him.

"Very rude," Maria commented. "But really, what else could Cassandra expect after a greeting like that?"

"Has he been away a long time?"

"Fifteen years or so, I think. Enjoying life in Italy. It should make this house party more interesting."

CHAPTER 15

Three days after the incident in the library, Alice stood near the entrance to the Castle, watching as Lady Harlford ushered the female guests into open carriages. A wagon loaded with baskets of food, blankets, and several servants had already left. It was a lovely day for a picnic, with a mild breeze and warm sunshine. Maria hadn't arrived yet, and Alice was content to wait—she didn't want to share the journey with Miss Esham or her mother. Or with Lady Harlford. With the Chiltons gone, and most of the gentlemen riding or driving themselves, the three carriages would not be full.

The second carriage was ready to set off by the time Maria appeared, explaining that a maid had spilled coffee down her gown and she'd had to change. As she spoke, the carriage pulled away and Alice thought she saw a fleeting expression of satisfaction on Lady Harlford's face. Lucy waved, but her mother said something and she looked away.

"This must be for us, then." Alice admired the smart landau, shiny with new paint, its seats upholstered in soft leather. Chatham climbed up beside the driver as the carriage set off.

"I suspect Cassandra is plotting something," Maria said as they passed between the stone pillars at the entrance to the estate, and headed west through Harlford Green. "Allowing us to have the best carriage to ourselves."

"What, though? Unless she's planned a mishap?"

"I hardly think she'd arrange for damage to this." Maria ran a hand along the glossy paintwork at the top of the low door. The wheels jolted across a rut in the road, but they hardly felt it. "Nicely sprung, too."

"We'll find out soon enough," Alice said. "What are we going to do about Mr Sumner?" A pleasant excursion the day before to Woodley, the village where Lord Harlford's other assistant lived, had revealed only that he had a wife and young baby.

"If I were taken ill outside their house, his wife might let something drop, or perhaps his servants would."

Alice didn't like the sound of that. Asking for help in order to spy on someone's family felt much more dishonourable than listening to the village gossip.

"No, I don't care for the idea, either, Alice. But I don't see what else we can do."

"Report what we've found so far and go home?"

"Marstone expects us to stay for the full fortnight, unless we discover something conclusive before then. He hasn't replied to my first note yet, so his original instructions still stand. Chatham would need to stay, in any case, I think."

"To try and catch the watcher?" Chatham had been lurking in the woods nearly every day, but had not spotted anyone going to the observation place above the quarry. He'd even carefully arranged a small pattern of twigs near the quarry edge, and that had remained undisturbed. It appeared that the watcher only went there intermittently.

Alice sighed—still nearly another week to go. She enjoyed the gardens, and Lucy was entertaining, but there was always the thought of her own duplicity lurking in the back of her mind.

She turned her attention to the scenery—this was the first chance she'd had of exploring west of the Castle, where the hills were steeper than the gently rolling countryside around Harlford. May blossom in the hedgerows made splashes of white, and purple spires of foxglove brightened the verges. After less than an hour they entered a wood and the carriage halted in a clearing. The ground sloped steeply upwards to their left, and the track headed diagonally up the slope in front of them.

There was no sign of the other carriages, but a groom awaited them, removing his hat as he approached. Their driver kept his gaze rigidly to the front.

"My lady, Lady Harlford apologises, but we... we hadn't realised how narrow the track is from here. This carriage is too wide to get to the picnic... er... without... without..."

"Scratching the paintwork?" Lady Jesson suggested. She cast a quick glance at Alice, one brow raised.

The man looked at his feet. "Er, yes, my lady. My lady... that is, Lady Harlford... told me to say she would send one of the other carriages back for you."

Their carriage was no wider than the others, and the groom made a poor liar.

"How long is the drive from here to the picnic spot?" Maria asked.

The groom glanced at her then his gaze slid away. "Er, around twenty minutes, my lady. The track for carriages, it goes around the hillside, see, it's too steep to go straight up. And it's rough."

It might well be an hour or more before a carriage returned for them, and they would still have to get to the top. By then, the picnic would be nearly over.

Chatham turned around. "Do you wish to return to Harlford Castle, my lady?"

The groom pointed the way they had come. "If you please, my lady, there's a pretty spot through the woods, along there. Lady Harlford, the Dowager Lady Harlford, I mean, she used to like it there."

"Come, Alice, let us take a walk," Maria said. "It would be a shame to go back straight away." Chatham picked up a satchel from near his feet and a rug, and Alice collected their two parasols.

"Lead on, Jenkins," Chatham said, and the groom set off through the trees. They walked for ten minutes along a narrow path lit by dappled sunlight, climbing gently until they came out into an open area. To their right, the grassy hillside rose steeply, dotted with a few scrubby hawthorn trees. To the east, the view stretched for miles across fields and woods.

"View's better from the top," Jenkins explained, still apologetic. "But there's less breeze down here."

"It looks a pleasant enough place," Maria said. "We can certainly sit here for a while."

Jenkins shuffled his feet.

"Thank you for showing us, Jenkins," Alice said. "Will you wait with the carriage?"

"Thank you, miss." Jenkins almost bolted back the way they had come as Alice spread the rug out on the grass.

James sighed as Terring gathered his notes and left the room. Seeing the steward this morning had been an excuse not to accompany the carriages, but he'd promised Mama to join them later. Then Uncle David had asked if he wanted to go along in his curricle, but by that time Terring was waiting. David had been here two days now, but he'd spent most of that time in the Dower House with Grandmama. The drive would have been a good time to talk to him.

At the window, his spirits lifted. The day was fine, and he'd enjoy the ride even if he had to attempt polite conversation with Mama's guests at the end of it. Perhaps he could return with David and let one of the grooms ride Ventus back.

An hour later, he rode into the trees near the base of Hengoed Ridge, wondering whether to lead Ventus up the steep hillside or ride him up the much shallower track that the carriages would have taken. He reined in when he saw his mother's new—and very expensive— landau standing in the clearing, the horses unhitched. Two men sat a few yards away, each leaning on a tree. They scrambled to their feet when they spotted him.

"Why is the carriage here?" James asked. "Is something wrong?"

The two men looked at each other, then back at him.

"Just tell me."

He listened to their halting explanation. "So two of my... Lady Harlford's guests have been abandoned here?" What was his mother about?

"They've got their man with them, my lord," one of them said. "They went around to the meadow—"

"Very well. Do not leave here without Lady Jesson and Miss Bryant, no matter what her ladyship says. Is that clear?"

They nodded, and James turned Ventus onto the path. He'd only ridden a few yards when low branches forced him to dismount and lead the animal. It was some time since he had been here, but he knew the meadow well. In years gone by, he and Robert had raced each other up the steep hillside on foot, reaching the top long before the carriages. Those had been carefree days.

Lost in regrets, he came out into the sunshine again, the sudden increase in temperature and brightness bringing him back to the present. He stopped and blinked. Lady Jesson sat on a blanket halfway across the meadow, as he had expected. In front of her danced a vision in shimmering light.

Shaking his head, he rubbed his eyes. Not a woodland sprite, but a woman, arms out as she swirled, skirts and hair swinging around her, laughing in delight. A Persephone welcoming spring, alive and vital, a being of sunshine and air that made the day seem even more beautiful, life more worth living.

Miss Bryant?

Even as he recognised her, she stopped, one hand going to her mouth. She turned abruptly and hurried to Lady Jesson, her hands raised to gather her hair and twist it up behind her head. By the time he reached them, it was tucked into its usual neat chignon, and the only sign of her dance was the rosy blush on her cheeks.

His arrival had killed the magic.

· · ·

Alice dragged her fingers through her hair, face burning as she tried to regain some semblance of order before Lord Harlford got too close. She'd thought they were alone, apart from Chatham, who lay dozing close by.

Sheltered from the breeze, their spot on the hillside was warm, and she'd soon shed her pelisse and bonnet. Although the view was quite different from here, the steep grassy slope leading up to the ridge reminded her of her childhood freedom to wander alone over the downs. The smell of warm grass and the hum of insects recalled days spent playing with her brother, their only worries whether they'd be made to finish their lessons before dinner. Some now-regretted impulse had made her take out her hairpins and twirl, enjoying the feel of the sun on her skin and the breeze in her hair.

Crouching on the blanket, she took the handful of pins that Maria held out, managing to tuck all the loose strands in as Lord Harlford approached. His frown was visible from some distance away.

"Act as if there is nothing out of the ordinary," Maria said calmly. "After all, if we had not been abandoned here..." She broke off; Lord Harlford was close enough to hear.

"Lady Jesson, Miss Bryant." He looped the reins over his mount's head as he came to a halt in front of them, and took off his hat, running a hand across his forehead. Ventus moved off a few paces and started cropping the grass.

"How nice to see you, Lord Harlford," Maria said, as if they were in a drawing room. "Have you missed your way? I believe the picnic is at the top of the hill."

"No. I mean, yes, the picnic is..." He broke off, still frowning. "I... I must apologise for the misunderstanding about the carriage. If you wish to join the picnic, the carriage is, of course, at your disposal."

The frown was not directed at her behaviour, then? Alice relaxed. She could not pretend he had not seen her, but he was being gentlemanly enough not to mention it.

"The picnic will be well under way by now, will it not?" Maria asked. "It is half an hour or so since we arrived."

Lord Harlford looked up the hillside, then down at them. The grass was steep, but no steeper than parts of the downs Alice climbed regularly when at home. And dry—it would not be slippery.

"It will be quicker to walk up from here, I think?" she suggested.

His face cleared. "Yes, much quicker, if..." He glanced at Maria, doubt in his expression once again.

"Lady Harlford will be so pleased to see her mistake about the carriage hasn't inconvenienced us too much," Alice said to Maria.

A muffled 'hmpf' from Lord Harlford showed he had noted the irony, but he said nothing. Maria looked up the hillside, raising one eyebrow.

"If you please, my lady..."

Alice started. Chatham had woken and was standing behind them.

"If his lordship permits, you could hold onto his horse. It will help you get up the hill."

"Oh, very well."

Chatham, two parasols clutched incongruously in his free hand, led Ventus while Lady Jesson held onto one of the stirrup leathers. She was breathing heavily, and clearly becoming uncomfortably warm, but with the horse on one side and the support of James' arm on the other, she doggedly placed one foot above the other. James was impressed.

"Not far now, Maria," Miss Bryant said from his other side, hardly out of breath. A becoming glow to her cheeks seemed to be the only effect of her exertions.

"You appear to be taking it in your stride."

"This is little different from the slopes near my home, my lord." She looked up as a skylark trilled overhead, and her smile reflected some of the enjoyment he'd seen in her dance.

"It is not only gardens you enjoy, then?"

"I love all kinds of countryside, but especially hills. I expect we can see for miles from the top."

"Yes—well into Wales, when the air is clear."

"Days like this make me wish I were better at watercolours—but no painting can replicate the feel of the breeze or the smell of the air."

James could mainly smell horse at the moment, but he knew what she meant. He looked up to where the slope became less steep near the top of the hill. A figure stood outlined against the sky, then set off towards them. His uncle.

A broad smile spread across David's face as he neared them. "I wondered if you'd come up this way, James, but I didn't expect you to have company." He looked at Lady Jesson. "Cassandra gave me some rigmarole about the carriage. I'm pleased to see it didn't have the effect she intended." His smile turned into a grin. "May I escort you ladies from here? James, if you go around the hillside here, you'll stay out of sight of the rest of the party."

"Why should I—"

"A more effective riposte, dear boy, if Cassandra thinks they walked up with no help."

"Oh. Yes, I see." He supposed he did.

Lady Jesson released his arm. Miss Bryant came to her side as Chatham led the horse a few paces away. She held out a handkerchief; Lady Jesson took it and mopped her face.

"Off you go, James," David said. "I'll give the ladies a chance to cool down, then escort them on. See you up there shortly."

James rode off reluctantly—it didn't seem right to leave them there, even though they had his uncle for escort. Mama had gone too far this time. Guests or no, he would have to confront her this evening.

Further round the hillside, he rejoined the track and followed it to the top of the wide ridge. He dismounted near the waiting carriages and handed Ventus to a groom. The guests sat or stood around a spread of blankets in the shade of a stand of trees, where footmen waited by a laden table.

Uncle David strolled towards the picnickers, Miss Bryant on one arm and Lady Jesson on the other. His mother's face as they approached changed from surprise to astonishment and then annoyance. James avoided her by joining a group of male guests, glancing over his shoulder only long enough to see that Miss Bryant had found a place next to Miss Stockhart, and David was taking food and drink to Lady Jesson.

The men were discussing the merits of different breeds as hunters and carriage horses. James tried to push the image of Miss Bryant from his mind and concentrate on what they were saying.

"I say, Harlford, do you have a minute?" It was Lord Gearing. James followed him a few paces away.

"How can I help you, Gearing?" Had he come to press his daughter's case?

"Don't take this the wrong way, Harlford…" He cleared his throat. "My wife insisted I accept Lady Harlford's invitation, seemed to think you'd be choosing a bride."

"That was my mother's intention, yes."

"She had her eye on the title, of course…"

Naturally.

"… and I thought the political connection might be useful if you took a liking to my girl. But she's not comfortable in your company, I can see that."

This was not going the way James had anticipated. "I'm sorry about that." He *had* tried to make conversation with her.

"No, no, not your fault. You are a man of serious interests, and my Cecy is still young. A couple more years, and she might have done." He shrugged. "Thought I'd clear the air, you know? I want her to be happy."

"I had reached the conclusion that we would not suit, but I appreciate your honesty."

"Better to have everything above board, eh?"

James held his hand out, and Gearing shook it. "I've not paid much attention to politics so far, but I'll have to take my seat at some point. I don't know how close our views will lie, but I'll listen."

"Very good of—"

Both men turned at a loud, feminine shriek. Miss Esham was kneeling on the ground beside the rug where Miss Bryant had been sitting. People converged on her as James hurried over.

"That Bryant woman tripped me deliberately!" Grasping her mother's arm, Miss Esham got to her feet. She held trembling hands in front of her face as James approached. "My hands," she said, in a wobbly voice. She looked down at her skirts—a small tear was visible where her knee must have hit the ground. "Oh, my dress…"

CHAPTER 16

"*M*iss Bryant?" Miss Stockhart's voice was anxious, hardly audible above the babble of voices and cries.

Alice dragged in a deep breath, clutching her hand. What had happened? She'd been leaning back with her hands on the ground behind her, looking up at the clouds. Then there'd been an agonising pain in her fingers, and she'd fallen to her side.

"I'm all right," Alice said, as the immediate feeling lessened a little. Miss Stockhart's arm came around her shoulders and helped her sit up. Her fingers throbbed, and she took deep breaths to try to dispel a slight dizzy feeling.

"Head down, miss. Put your hand in this." Chatham gently took her wrist, and plunged her injured hand into something cool and wet.

"What is—?"

"Lemonade, miss. The cold will help stop your hand swelling."

That made little sense to Alice, but it did seem to ease the pain somewhat, so she left her hand there and rested her forehead on her knees. The dizziness began to fade.

· · ·

Miss Esham swayed alarmingly as James hurried closer. He was stepping forward to support her when his uncle took hold of his shoulder and turned him away.

"Don't believe her," David said, his voice quiet enough for only James to hear. "Miss Bryant is in more need."

James stared down at the women on the rug near his feet. Miss Bryant sat with her knees drawn up, one hand resting in a jug of lemonade. Her face was hidden by the rim of her bonnet. Lady Jesson's man and Miss Stockhart knelt either side of her.

"What happened?" She didn't look well, and a small knot of worry formed. There was nothing left of that vital figure glorying in the sunshine.

"The shrieking one stood on her hand," David said quietly. "Deliberately—I happened to be looking in that direction."

"What? Why?" Anger joined his worry.

"I haven't been here long enough to know," David said. "But I am positive it was no accident. If she's making that much noise, there cannot be a great deal wrong with her."

"Miss Bryant, how badly are you injured?" James knelt beside her as Lady Jesson arrived beside them.

"I'll be all right," Miss Bryant said, looking up. Her face was a pasty white, far from her usual healthy glow. "Chatham's lemonade is helping."

"Broken fingers, I reckon," Chatham said. "Or badly bruised."

"You know about such things?"

"Former boxer, my lord."

James turned his attention back to Miss Bryant. "Can you stand? We should get you back to the Castle and summon a doctor. David, can you order one of the carriages put to?"

"James, come and help Miss Esham... James!"

Mama stood next to Miss Esham, glaring at him. Miss Esham leaned on her father with one hand against her forehead. Unlike Miss Bryant, her complexion appeared its normal colour.

"She has plenty of help." He turned his back on his mother, ignoring her further protests.

"Cassandra will make a fuss if you take one of these carriages," David said. "Use my curricle to get them down the hill to the landau they came in—that's the most comfortable vehicle, less jolting. I'll send a groom on horseback to alert them to have it ready." He hurried off.

"We need to get you back," James repeated to Miss Bryant, glancing at Lady Jesson for confirmation. "I... um... my uncle's curricle is not a large vehicle."

"I'm sure the pair of us can squeeze into it for a short distance," Lady Jesson said.

Chatham tore a handkerchief into strips and bound the fingers of Miss Bryant's injured hand together. Then he and Chatham took an elbow each and helped her to her feet. She staggered as they let go and, with a muttered imprecation, James lifted her into his arms, holding her close as he carried her towards the curricle, breathing the faint lavender scent of her hair. A couple of grooms were fastening the horses to the pole.

"I can manage, my lord."

"Nonsense. We're nearly there now." He set her down, keeping one arm around her shoulders until she was steady on her feet, then grasped her waist to lift her into the vehicle. Chatham helped Lady Jesson up at the other side, and James climbed in to sandwich Miss Bryant safely between them. It *was* a tight fit, but Miss Bryant would not fall if she fainted.

He avoided what ruts he could on the way down the hillside, taking things slowly on the rough track—slowly enough for Chatham to keep pace behind them on foot. He was conscious of Miss Bryant's tense body pressed against his side, but he could not avoid all the bumps. "I am sorry for the jolting."

"It's quite all right, my lord. The jolting doesn't make it feel worse." Her voice sounded a little stronger.

He spared a glance at her—she had regained a little colour.

"Miss Bryant, I cannot tell you how sorry I am that you have been treated this way while a guest in my home. Being made to walk, and now this."

"It's not your doing."

"It is my responsibility, however."

"Nonsense," Lady Jesson put in briskly. "You could not have prevented either occurrence. It was a deliberate act on Miss Esham's part. She will deny it, of course."

"They will be leaving," he stated, and nothing more was said until they came in sight of the landau, harnessed and ready to depart. The groom who had alerted the driver and his assistant waited there, holding Ventus' reins.

"Jenkins, take Ventus and ride for the doctor in Woodley—tell him it is probably broken fingers." He turned to the other two. "One of you take the curricle back up the hill to Lord David."

Chatham had helped both women into the landau, and climbed up beside the remaining man. James took the rearward facing seat and they set off.

Miss Bryant was still paler than normal, her features drawn. Anger at Miss Esham filled him, at the change she had caused. Why would she do such a thing?

It hardly mattered, though. The whole family would be gone within a day.

He realised he was staring, and turned his gaze to one side, not seeing the passing woods and hedgerows.

Alice awoke to breath on her face. Warm, smelly breath.

"Tess, come here!" That was Maria's voice.

Alice opened her eyes as Tess gave one last sniff and reluctantly moved away. She was in Maria's room, still fully dressed, and Maria stood in the doorway with her maid and a rotund gentleman, who introduced himself as Doctor Netherton.

The doctor waddled to the bed, wheezing gently. His nose showed signs of a fondness for the bottle, and Alice reluctantly held out her left hand for his inspection. In spite of his unprepossessing appearance, his examination was thorough, and he apologised first for any extra pain he caused by prodding her fingers. "Not broken, I think, but very badly bruised. Bed rest and light food for today. Your fingers will feel more comfortable if you keep that hand elevated. Try to move them when you can—a little more each day."

"Can I get up tomorrow?" At the moment she wanted nothing more than to stay here dozing, but from past experiences of falling off her horse or out of trees, she was likely to be feeling much better in the morning.

Doctor Netherton looked over his spectacles at her. "You appear to be a sensible young lady," he said. "Rest helps healing; boredom generally does not. By all means get up, but be sure not to overtire yourself. If you feel unwell at any time, go back to bed."

"Harlford has had a suite prepared," Maria said as Simpson closed the door behind the doctor. "The one occupied by Lord and Lady Chilton before the library incident. There is a room for each of us, and a dressing room where Simpson can sleep. Do you feel up to moving?"

Alice still felt weak and tired, but well enough for that. She stood up slowly—no dizziness. They left Simpson gathering Maria's belongings, and walked down the corridor, Tess padding along behind them. Their new accommodation was much larger than the room Lady Jesson had originally been given, the curtains thicker, the bed hangings less faded. Rather than going straight to bed, Alice sat in a chair near the window and Maria rang for tea.

"Lady Harlford will be so pleased we have this chance for better rooms," Alice said, trying for an air of innocence.

"Ha!" Maria shook her head. "That's two of her candidates gone now, although I think she misjudged in selecting Marianne Esham as one of them. The girl can give a good impression of being a meek miss that Cassandra could browbeat, but she would have soon found out she was wrong."

"The Eshams have left?"

"Not quite, but they will be gone in the morning." Maria spoke with a great deal of obvious satisfaction. "I'll leave you to your tea. Simpson will bring your things down shortly, and help you into your night-rail. Ask her if you want anything else. I'll come and see how you are doing when it is time for dinner. I'll leave Tess with you. I don't think Miss Esham will bother you further, but it's best to be sure."

Alice drank her tea, and got into bed as soon as Simpson had helped her undress. When the maid had gone, Tess lay down and began to snore gently.

How considerate of Lord Harlford, Alice thought as she drifted off to sleep again. He had personally escorted them back, given them better rooms, and ejected guests, all on behalf of a paid companion. She didn't know why he'd done it, but she was very pleased that he had.

What would it be like to be courted by him? To have someone who cared for her all the time? Who would hold her close when she was hurt, and make her feel safe?

Someone she wasn't here to spy on.

James watched as his uncle took careful aim, his cue arm moving smoothly forward just as the door behind him opened.

"James!"

The cue ball bounced off three cushions—but no balls—before coming to rest. David muttered a curse. "Damn it, Cassandra, can't you enter a room quietly?" He glared at his sister-in-law.

Mama glared in return, then turned to James.

"James, what is this I hear about the Eshams?"

James laid his cue down, and went to close the door. "Mama, I'm glad you've come to find me." He'd informed the Eshams that they were leaving as soon as they returned from the picnic—and walked off as Lady Esham was still protesting her daughter's innocence. Mama had been with other guests at the time. "I wanted to know why you abandoned Lady Jesson and Miss Bryant at the bottom of the hill this afternoon."

She stared at him. "Lady Jesson? James, I've come to talk to—"

"If your new landau is too wide to get through the local lanes, there is no point having it. I will instruct Pritchard to sell it."

"Sell? Because some stupid grooms misunderstood an order?"

James felt anger rising as she failed to meet his eyes. "I'm not going to argue with you about it, Mama. You will ensure there are no further such *misunderstandings*. Am I clear?"

"But James, I'm your—"

"Am I clear?"

She pursed her lips, but finally dipped her head in reluctant agreement. "Lady Esham said you asked them to leave. How can you be so rude to your guests?"

"Your guests, Mama, not mine."

"It is your house—"

"Oh? I'm pleased you recognise that fact." He ignored a crack of laughter from his uncle, and had the satisfaction of seeing his mother struggle for words. The peace did not last long enough.

"The poor girl was deliberately tripped up by that encroaching hussy Lady Jesson brought with her. She deserves sympathy, not banishment! That companion is as bad as her employer."

"Mama—if you dislike Lady Jesson, why did you invite her?"

To James' astonishment, his mother's face turned red and she averted her gaze. "That's beside the point. That companion—"

"Cassandra," David interrupted. "Miss Esham deliberately stood on Miss Bryant's hand."

"It's nothing to do with you, David." She turned back to James, her lips pinched. "You aren't going to take the word of a nobody like that Bryant woman above Miss Esham, are you?"

"I saw her do it," David said.

Mama carried on as if David hadn't spoken. "I *demand* that you apologise, James, and tell them they are welcome to stay."

"No, Mama, I will not. As you have just pointed out, it is *my* house, and I have the final say on who is welcome here. They will be departing in the morning, as already arranged. Now, if you will excuse us...?"

"James, this is not finished. *Why* did you send the Eshams away?"

143

"David told you. I will *not* marry a woman capable of doing something like that, so there is no point in any of the family remaining."

"But Miss Esham is a sweet girl—she wouldn't do—"

David laid his cue on the table. "Cassandra, Miss Esham is a cunning baggage. She's fooled you into thinking she'd make the kind of meek wife for James who'd let you remain in control. She is far from it—it didn't take me five minutes of her company to work that out." He took her arm, but she wrenched it from his grasp.

"David, I run this household and you are not welcome—"

"*Mama!*"

She froze at James' raised voice, her mouth open in shock.

"Mama, David is always welcome here. The Eshams are not. That is the end of it, and we wish to finish our game in peace." He turned his back on her. "You should take that last shot again, Uncle."

There was silence behind him, then he heard the rustle of fabric and the door closing rather more firmly than necessary.

"She looked rather surprised," David observed. "Is this the first time you've confronted her?"

James sighed. "I'm afraid so, but I haven't really needed to until now. She mostly ignored me until Robert's child turned out to be a daughter."

"Looking forward to ruling in the heir's name, I suppose."

James would have been the official guardian, but Mama probably assumed he'd continue to spend most of his time in his laboratory. He still had to confront her about her spending, but that could wait until the remaining guests had gone.

"Not many women left to choose from, then." David walked around the table to place his cue ball ready to retake the interrupted shot.

"None," James said. "Miss Stockhart favours Augustus Chilton, and Gearing thinks his daughter is too young. But I still don't understand why Miss Esham would be so cruel."

"I do now." David bent to look along his cue. "I had an interesting conversation with Lady Jesson. But it is something *you* should be able to work out for yourself."

"I have no idea."

David straightened. "James, how have you survived unwed for so long when you take so little notice of what is around you?"

"I don't know what you mean." He was aware that his tone was defensive. "I study things around me—"

"People, James, people. Why are the Eshams here? And the other young women? To marry you—a matrimonial prize of the first order."

"Like a prize bull at a fair," James muttered.

"Or prey being hunted—in which case it would help to study the predators. In this case, the Esham chit was dispensing with a rival." David leaned across the table, aiming the cue. The red ball trundled cleanly into a pocket. "Three points."

"Rival? She's Lady Jesson's companion."

"You could do worse." David moved his marker on the scoreboard.

"What—?" James saw again the dancing sprite, her hair loose and free. Would she take similar delight in other physical—?

No—he must put that image out of his mind. "Er...my turn?"

"I've just scored three points, remember?"

"Oh, yes." James watched as David took his next shot. His uncle had not been serious.

Had he?

"She's not from a titled family. Mama wouldn't approve." Not that he would let that stop him, if he did wish to marry someone like her. Someone he could talk to easily, laugh with, who would share his life.

"Cassandra isn't likely to approve of anyone she hasn't picked for you. Two points." David moved his marker. "She won't want anyone of high rank, in any case. Haven't you noticed that the fathers of the young women she's invited are all mere barons or baronets?"

No, he hadn't. "Why?"

"She's a viscount's daughter. As the current marchioness, your future bride will outrank her. She won't want someone who is also from a higher family." David tutted as his next shot went wide.

Good grief—did Mama really think like that?

"Your turn, James."

"What? Oh, yes." He looked at the table, trying to concentrate on the positions of the balls.

Had David been serious? It wasn't done for someone of his rank to marry outside the aristocracy. There were good reasons for that, of course. Well, he supposed there must be, but he couldn't think of any at the moment.

This was not the time to think about it, not with David watching him and dinner imminent.

Concentrate.

He took aim, and watched in satisfaction as his cue ball bounced off the red and dropped into the far pocket. "Three points."

CHAPTER 17

*J*ames reined in at the top of the hill and dismounted, turning Ventus loose to find what grazing he could. This place was not as picturesque as the picnic hill, being covered only in clumps of prickly gorse and patches of heather, but it was close enough to reach on his morning ride. The air still held its early chill, and wisps of mist hung in the valleys.

He hadn't slept well, David's words refusing to leave him. *You could do worse.*

That was true—look at Misses Esham and Chilton. Then his mind had changed the statement to a question.

Could he do *better* than Miss Bryant?

Arguments for and against had spun through his mind. Half-awake thoughts were no way to make a decision of this magnitude, so he'd risen at dawn and had Ventus saddled.

Cantering across fields wet with dew had cleared his head. He picked his way through the gorse to a rocky outcrop that poked through the vegetation and found a flat stone to sit on. So many things to consider...

A list—that's what he needed. He pulled his notebook from a pocket and opened it at a blank page.

Requirements

An heir—that went without saying. But he wanted a wife he would be happy to remain faithful to, and that meant a willing bed partner. One he *wanted* in his bed.

He hadn't thought of Miss Bryant in that way until yesterday, but the sight of her dancing had been a revelation. The way her hair had swirled about her, the shapely ankles as her skirts moved, and the pleasure she'd taken in it.

She had felt right in his arms yesterday—his body had noticed that even though his mind had been on her injury.

Heir, he wrote, and placed a small tick next to it.

Intelligent. Another tick. He would enjoy telling her about his research, and he thought she would be interested in hearing it.

Easy to talk to. She wasn't boring or irritating, but it was more than that. He'd enjoyed talking to her amongst the plants in the glasshouse. She never made him wonder if he'd said the right thing, or if there was some hidden meaning in her words. And when they'd paused, the silence hadn't felt uncomfortable. Tick.

Enjoys living in the country. He thought of the dancing sprite again, and the walk up the steep hillside. She enjoyed being out of doors in the countryside, as he did. Tick.

Lucy. He wasn't going to choose a wife to suit his sister, but he did want someone who would befriend her. Miss Bryant met that requirement. Tick.

Miss Bryant. *Alice.* He tried the sound of her name a few times—he liked it.

But he had to consider both sides of the question.

Against

Their difference in station, that was the main obstacle—the one most people would see. What did that mean in practice?

Society, gossip. Not about him; he didn't care what people said. But gossip about her, and how society might treat her.

What else?

How to manage the household. Even if she had helped to run her home before she became a governess, Harlford Castle must be far larger than her family's farm.

Education.

Manners in society.

Then he crossed out the last two—they were not obstacles for Alice. And although she hadn't been trained to manage such a large household, she was intelligent and would soon learn. More crossing out.

No, the problem would be what other people did or said. He didn't let that bother him, but would she? She preferred the countryside, but not wishing to take part in events in Town wasn't the same as not being able to because members of the *ton* would not receive her.

Then his Mama's words came back to him. *You are a marquess,* she'd said, when he told her of being rejected last year.

There would be enough people who wouldn't risk his displeasure by ignoring his wife. And as for gossip...Lady Jesson was Alice's friend. As long as she approved, she would be a potent weapon.

Several reasons for, and none against—none that was insurmountable. Logic said yes, as well as his inclination.

His stomach growled, reminding him that he'd had nothing more than a few mouthfuls of coffee before setting off. Time to head back for breakfast.

As Ventus trotted along muddy lanes, he imagined having Alice beside him, galloping across winter fields or through summer meadows. How they might warm up together after being out on frosty mornings.

He would wait until the house party ended. Then he would ask her to be his marchioness.

Alice felt better the next morning, having slept hours later than usual. Tea and toast in bed improved things further, and she headed outside, finding Maria sitting on a bench in the formal garden. A few of the remaining guests walked between the beds, but all were some distance away.

Maria looked up with a smile. "I take it you're feeling better?"

"I am, thank you." She sat down, holding her left hand at her shoulder to ease the discomfort in her swollen fingers.

"Good. There has been a development." Maria handed Alice a newspaper folded to an inner page. It was creased at all angles, as if it had been screwed up and then flattened again. "Lord Harlford was reading this at breakfast. He swore, quite loudly, flung it on the floor and left. 'Stormed out' would be a better way of putting it."

"Bad news?"

"I assume so. That behaviour seems most out of character."

It was a copy of *The Morning Herald*, dated two days ago—it must have just arrived from London.

"I couldn't see anything relevant," Maria went on, "but I thought you might be able to. Of course, it may be nothing to do with our… with Marstone's business."

Alice scanned the articles, resting the paper awkwardly on her lap. The page included snippets of society news, a list of persons recently executed in Paris, and several advertisements for legal services.

"Did you see anything interesting in the society news?" Alice asked.

"No—and it's unlikely Harlford would bother reading it anyway. But as he's communicating with France, might these be of any relevance?" Maria pointed to the list of the latest victims of the guillotine.

As Alice scanned the list, a name caught her eye. Lavoisier. It sounded familiar, but she couldn't think why. Closing her eyes, she let her mind drift—trying too hard to remember never worked.

"Alice? Are you well?"

She opened her eyes. "I'm thinking." She'd come across the name recently. Was it in something she'd read in the library here? Agricultural articles… scientific journals… chemical experiments…

That was it—Lavoisier had something to do with the books and articles that Lord Harlford consulted. "I need to look in the library."

"You have seen something? What is it?"

"It's just an idea," Alice said. "I need to check some journals, and probably look at those letters again."

"I saw Harlford walk off towards the quarry. You could go now. Will it exonerate him?"

"If I'm right, it may mean the correspondence is nothing treasonous. I really hope that's so." Her feeling that he could not be a traitor had grown stronger as their acquaintance developed.

"As do I, my dear."

"It may come to nothing," Alice warned. "But if I confirm my suspicion, we can let Marstone know and he can check further."

"Very well. I will try to make sure you are not interrupted." Maria stood and straightened her skirts, then put her hand in her pocket. "I brought your picklocks."

In the library, Alice went straight to the section of shelving containing the chemistry textbooks. Running her finger along the spines, she came to a copy of *Reflections on phlogiston*, with Lavoisier's name on the spine, before a paper sticking out of a worn copy of the *Method of chymical nomenclature* caught her eye.

The paper wasn't merely a place marker, it was a letter from Lavoisier himself, addressed to Lord James Broxwood and dated from before he inherited the title. It appeared to be a commentary on some experiments, and was clearly a response to a letter from Lord Harlford.

News of Lavoisier's execution might explain Lord Harlford's reaction at breakfast, but did it have any bearing on the correspondence currently locked in the desk drawer? Might he have been attempting to bribe someone to get Lavoisier released?

There was nothing for it—she would have to look at the letters again. Seating herself at the desk, she took out the picklocks and selected the one she remembered being useful. Her aching fingers made opening the bottom drawer more awkward, but she succeeded and removed the folder. Laying the letters out in order of date, she leaned on her left elbow, holding her injured hand up, and started to read.

They were as vague as she recalled. All of them *could* have been about sending bribes to jailers and officials. On the other hand, they could equally well have been about obtaining goods of some kind. But Lord Harlford didn't seem to be the kind of person who would smuggle brandy or any of the other things normally traded clandestinely. She did not believe it of him.

Voices sounded at the far end of the library, muffled by the closed door. Then the door opened and Lady Harlford's voice became suddenly louder.

"...Eshams. James, you need—"

"Enough, Mama. I have work to do. We can discuss this some other time."

"But James, I must—" Lady Harlford's voice was cut off as the door closed with a click. She heard footsteps—Lord Harlford must have entered.

Alice looked at the letters spread out in front of her. She didn't have time to gather them up and replace them before being discovered, but she didn't feel any inclination to even try. Whatever Marstone might think, her deception ended now.

She stood up as Lord Harlford approached.

"What the devil are you doing?"

Alice swallowed hard, glancing up at his face. He looked... she wasn't sure *what* his face was showing. Puzzlement turned to anger, but there was also surprise and... hurt?

James felt a leaden lump in his stomach. Alice sat at his desk, papers spread out before her. His letters to Laurent—he was close enough to recognise them.

Letters he kept locked in a drawer.

After what he had been thinking this morning, to find her... stealing? Spying? How could he have misjudged her character so completely?

That announcement in the paper, and now this. It was too much.

"I can explain, my lord."

He didn't want to hear it. "Get out of here now," he ordered, his teeth almost clenched. "This is *not*—"

"Please, my lord, I need you to—"

"Don't bother, Miss Bryant." He made an effort to control his voice. "I cannot think of any acceptable explanation for you going through my personal correspondence. I will send someone to assist with your packing."

He turned to leave, but came to an abrupt halt a few steps down the room. Lady Jesson had entered quietly and now stood in his path, not moving as he approached.

"I think you should stay and listen, my lord. It is a matter of national security."

"Nonsense—it is a malicious intrusion." Miss Bryant was as devious as the Esham woman, or the Chiltons, although what she'd hoped to achieve with those letters was beyond him. Blackmail?

"Please, my lord, you must let me explain before we leave," Miss Bryant said.

He took a few steps back towards her—for what purpose, he wasn't sure. "*Must?* You are giving me orders in my own home?"

A rustle of skirts behind him indicated that Lady Jesson had followed him.

"Is everything all right, Maria?" David came into the room, looking from one to the other as he approached. "You hurried off very quickly."

"Would you persuade your nephew to hear what we have to say before we leave?" Lady Jesson said. "It really is in his best interests."

"Leave?"

"Yes, Uncle. Leave. Miss Bryant has been going through my personal correspondence."

David looked at Lady Jesson, who merely nodded.

"That seems somewhat... unusual. If you're not curious as to the reason, I am."

Could there be an acceptable explanation?

Miss Bryant's gaze on him was steady, and she did not avert her eyes. She didn't have that self-satisfied air the Chilton chit had worn when she thought she'd trapped him.

"Oh, very well." He gestured to a chair near the desk and Lady Jesson sat down. David brought two more chairs over.

"Thank you, my lord." Miss Bryant pushed a newspaper across the desk, and pointed to a section part way down the page.

"Is this the article that angered you this morning?"

James glanced at it again, his anger and regret resurfacing. "Yes, but what business—?"

"Do let them explain, James," his uncle said.

Alice let Maria do the talking. Although she'd managed to speak calmly, she felt strange inside, shaky. The matter had needed clearing up, but she wished it could have been done without spying on Lord Harlford.

Maria reached the point in the story at which they were invited to attend the house party.

"So you could go through my personal correspondence?" Lord Harlford's words were clipped, as if talking through anger.

"That was one activity that might have been involved, certainly."

Lord David leaned forward and picked up a couple of the letters still spread out on the desk. "You *have* been corresponding with someone in France, James. I assume there is an acceptable explanation for this?"

"I am no traitor, if that is what you are implying, Uncle."

He looked directly at Alice, as if he were addressing her instead of Lord David. There was that same trace of hurt she'd seen in his face when he found her with his private letters.

"Lord Marstone asked us to confirm that the correspondence was an innocent matter," Alice said. "He did not believe you were conducting any treasonous activity, but he had to be sure."

Lord Harlford's frown faded a little as she spoke.

She pointed to the newspaper. "Does this explain the correspondence? Were you attempting to get Monsieur Lavoisier released?"

"Yes." He slumped in his chair. "As you see, I failed. In fact, I have probably been taken for a complete fool, wasting money paying for something that had no likelihood of happening."

Lord David stood and laid a hand on his nephew's shoulder, then went to the drinks cabinet and brought back a decanter and glasses. Alice shook her head when he glanced her way, but the others accepted a small glass of brandy.

"What happens now?" Lord David asked, once he had resumed his seat.

"I will write to Lord Marstone to inform him of what we have found," Maria said. "Chatham will arrange a messenger."

"A satisfactory conclusion, then." Lord David picked up his glass.

"I'm afraid there is more," Maria said.

Lord Harlford frowned.

"What else have you been up to, James?" Lord David asked.

"Nothing!" He shot to his feet. "I have no idea what they are talking about. *You* are accusing me now?"

"No, no. My apologies; I phrased that badly."

"May we explain?" Maria said, a voice of calm.

Lord Harlford looked at Maria, then at Alice, and sat down again, one hand massaging his temple.

"Marstone also has intelligence that the French are in possession of some information that few in this country are privy to," Maria continued. "One of these people is you, my lord. He said it is connected with weapons, but did not give any further details."

"Very wise," Lord Harlford muttered.

Maria ignored him. "We have our suspicions, however. Alice?"

Lord Harlford's lips compressed in a straight line. She should not feel so dismayed—this situation was never going to end well, and she could not expect anything other than anger or disgust now he'd found out why they were here. The throbbing in her fingers reminded her how concerned he had been yesterday, but that seemed an age away now.

Alice hesitated. Their job was to find out if Lord Harlford was guilty of dealing with the French, not to tell him what Lord Marstone knew. But Maria had already let slip the second matter.

No—not *let* slip. Maria must believe, as Alice did, that Lord Harlford had no knowledge of the stolen information. She took a deep breath, realising the others were waiting for her to speak. "We assume it pertains to your experiments with explosives."

James gaped at her. "What? How...?" His voice trailed off, and he rubbed a hand over his face. These meddling women seemed to know everything.

"Your experiments are not a secret, surely?" Lady Jesson said. "That you work with explosives is common knowledge amongst the stable hands."

"Has your man been interrogating my staff?" As if Miss Bryant betraying his trust were not enough.

"Only listening, he tells me."

"Plying them with ale?" David asked.

Lady Jesson smiled. "I think he tried that, but with little success. Apparently they do not talk about Harlford matters in the village inn, only amongst themselves in the stables."

"That is something, I suppose. I... I'm afraid this is a lot for me to take in. My guests... my staff..." James ran a hand through his hair. "You are saying there is a spy amongst my staff?"

"That is one possibility," Lady Jesson said. "Chatham found a place where he believes someone is watching the quarry."

"What makes him think that?"

Miss Bryant responded. "Flattened vegetation, a tarpaulin hidden. It might be to observe any testing you do outside, or to determine when you and your staff have left so they can look around inside your laboratory."

"I take it he hasn't seen anyone there?" David asked. James was glad for his uncle's interjection; with all this talk of spies on top of his shock at finding his intended bride going through his desk, his brain seemed to have seized up.

"No," Miss Bryant replied. "But he hasn't been able to keep a continuous watch."

James got to his feet—this was too much to think of all at once.

"Thank you for informing me of the suspicions against me, Lady Jesson, Miss Bryant. You may now leave the matter in my hands. Excuse me."

He strode to the door without waiting for an answer or looking back.

CHAPTER 18

*J*ames strode out of the house and across the park. Thinking was impossible with people around, continually interrupting him. And there was much to think about.

He'd come to consider Miss Bryant and Lady Jesson as friends, even before he'd decided he would ask Miss Bryant to be his wife.

Would a friend spy on me?

He tried to think back through the events that had just unfolded. Mama had accosted him as he was heading to the library, calling Miss Bryant an encroaching hussy.

Not encroaching. Dishonest and deceitful.

He tried to regain his train of thought. Mama had been berating him, her voice strident, and he'd attempted to just walk away, pushing open the library door. Then he'd interrupted her, shutting the door on her continued complaint.

Miss Bryant *must* have realised she was about to be found. She knew about the servants' door at that end of the library, and she'd made no attempt to escape.

What did that say about her?

He didn't know.

Damn the woman. Damn *all* women, his mother included. All he wanted was to be left alone with his research.

Lavoisier—what a waste of a fine mind that execution was. He'd tried, but could he have done better? Might Marstone have helped? After the events of last year, he *knew* Marstone had links with... well, spies was the only word. Why hadn't he thought to ask if Marstone could bribe or coerce someone into releasing the man?

Would it have worked, though? *He* thought such a brilliant mind was worth risking much for, but not everyone would agree. The most likely outcome of approaching Marstone would have been the man declining to jeopardise his network of contacts for such a matter. Despite that, he should have asked.

And a traitor amongst his staff. A *possible* traitor, he reminded himself. It might be someone as yet unknown to him. It would not do to assume that Norton or Sumner were guilty.

Miss Bryant *had* said they'd been sent to clear him. So Marstone had not assumed he was guilty either.

That reduced his gloom a little, and he decided it was time to turn back—he'd walked a couple of miles while his thoughts were elsewhere. He should consult his notebooks to check exactly what information might have been passed to the French.

Mama came out of the parlour as James returned to the Castle, his head no clearer than when he'd left. She must have been waiting for him. He cursed beneath his breath—he should have come in through the servants' quarters.

"James, I'm glad you've seen sense at last about those women. Although it's a pity the Eshams have already left. You are leaving yourself rather short of young ladies—"

"What do you mean, seen sense?" Aware of an interested footman on duty by the door, he kept his voice low.

"About Maria Jesson and that companion of hers, of course."

Another argument. "Come with me, Mama." There was no sound from the billiards room, so he led the way there and closed the door. "Explain."

Her brows rose at his abrupt tone. "You mean you didn't send them away? I thought you'd finally realised how... how unsuitable they are."

"They've gone? When?" The dismay he felt clarified some of his jumbled feelings—he *didn't* want them to leave. Not yet, anyway. Not until he'd puzzled out why Miss Bryant had allowed him to discover her.

"They had their things packed half an hour ago. I didn't see them leave, but they must have gone by now."

Half an hour—they could not have gone far, yet, and it would be too late to get a place on the Mail by the time they reached Hereford. With any luck, they would be putting up in one of the local villages.

"James?" His mother must have seen some fleeting expression in his face.

"Thank you for letting me know, Mama." Did they even have a carriage? Mama hadn't mentioned lending them one to get to the nearest posting house.

"Have you not made your choice yet? You agreed you would choose a bride from the young women at this house party."

"I did not agree to the house party, Mama, as you well know." She opened her mouth, but he carried on talking. "And I certainly did not agree to choose a wife from amongst the women you invited."

"But you need—"

"No, Mama. If I broke my neck tomorrow, Uncle David would be the next marquess. He's not much above forty—plenty of time for him to get some heirs."

"But, James—"

"Enough, Mama. *You* are not the head of the family; I am."

She pursed her lips, her nostrils flaring. He'd stopped her for now, but she would bring the matter up again.

"Mama, would you be satisfied if I made a choice from any of the young women at the house party?"

"Why, yes, that's what I've always said. Although there aren't many left now. There's—"

"Mama, let me be clear. You would accept any of the young women at the house party as my bride? *Any* of them?"

"Why, yes, James. Isn't that what I have just said?"

"And if I choose one and she turns me down, that will be the end of it for this year."

"But—"

"I insist. I will have your word on this."

She glared at him, but then her posture relaxed. "Very well. But they will not turn you down. Your title, the estates…"

"Thank you for the compliment, Mama." James knew the sarcasm would go right over her head. "I have work to do." He walked to the door and opened it for her.

"You will decide soon, James?"

"Yes, Mama." Decide whether or not to ask Miss Bryant.

Now he only had to find out where they had gone.

Alice and Maria followed Lord David through the Dower House and out into the garden. The afternoon was warm, and the dowager sat at a small table under a canopy in the middle of the pattern of low hedges.

"So, you've invited yourselves to stay, have you?" The dowager raised an eyebrow as Maria and Alice seated themselves.

Alice's mouth dropped open for a moment, and the dowager smiled. "Why would a wagon follow you if not to bring your luggage?"

"I invited them, Mama," Lord David said. "I hope you have no objection?"

"And if I do, you'll persuade me to change my mind?" The dowager attempted to look stern, but her lips twitched. "Oh, get some more chairs, David, then you can tell me why the invitation was necessary."

Maria did the talking. Alice wondered if she should have kept some of the details about Marstone and what he had said to herself, but she had to trust Maria's judgement that neither the dowager nor her son would betray their country. The dowager's face gave no clue about her thoughts.

"And how have you enjoyed your spying career so far, Miss Bryant?" the dowager asked.

"Not at all, my lady."

"Oh?"

Alice glanced at the others uneasily. She'd discussed her misgivings with Maria, but the dowager and Lord David were almost strangers.

"Afraid of what would happen if you got caught?" The dowager's lips were set in a thin line.

She *had* spied on the dowager's grandson—the least she could do was to be frank now. "No. Not afraid in a physical sense, certainly." Had the dowager's expression softened a little?

"Why, then?"

"Lord Harlford has been a perfect gentleman, and I repaid him by acting in an underhand manner."

"*We,*" Maria said. "The blame is more mine—I involved Alice in this. She might have been the one who actually went through Lord Harlford's papers, but that was only because she was more adept at... at picking locks."

The dowager turned to her son. "David, you would not have issued your invitation if you did not think there was some justification."

"James does seem to have been... unwise, shall we say? In his correspondence about Lavoisier. Once that was intercepted, Marstone's investigation was to be expected." He waited until the dowager nodded before continuing. "I believe everyone's intention was to try to find the truth."

The dowager turned to Alice. "*Have* you proved his innocence?"

"Not proved, exactly, my lady, but there is now a plausible explanation for the correspondence that does not involve anything treasonous. And I do not believe he is capable of treason."

"And unless Lord Harlford is a better actor than I give him credit for," Maria added, "his reaction to the discovery has satisfied me that his explanation is the truth."

"I agree," David said.

"Very well. And you, Maria Jesson. How, *exactly*, did you get an invitation to this house party?"

"I merely suggested to Cassandra that it would be a pity if Lord Harlford found out what happened before Lord David left for Europe."

"How do *you* know what happened?"

"I don't, but..."

Alice had heard this story before, in the coach on the way here, and shifted uncomfortably in her chair. At least the dowager and Lord David seemed amused rather than disgusted.

"What *did* happen?" Maria asked. "You are not obliged to tell me anything, of course."

Lord David smiled. "Cassandra thought her... physical charms might convince me to persuade her husband to... Do you know, I've forgotten exactly what it was she wanted. Probably something as banal as spending more time in London. I left to avoid her stirring up trouble between me and Andrew, and I stayed away because I found life on the Continent suited me very well."

That was all? Alice supposed no son would care to learn that about his mother. But then, two unwanted guests at a house party was a small price to pay. One unwanted guest, really, as Lady Harlford considered her to be little better than a servant.

"Miss Bryant, would you be so good as to go and ask for refreshments to be brought out?" the dowager said. "Lemonade, I think, as it is so warm."

Alice stood. "Yes, my lady." As she left, Maria broached the subject of someone possibly spying on Lord Harlford's research activities. Glad to escape, Alice strode over the gravel and, once she had passed on the request for refreshments to the butler, sat on one of the chairs on the terrace. The three people below were conducting an animated conversation, but she could not shake off the morning's events so easily.

Lord Harlford had been kind to her, and friendly, and she'd

betrayed his trust. In spite of the patriotic reasons behind her actions, she felt ashamed. More than ashamed.

Alice shook herself. She wouldn't see him again after this house party, so she should try to forget about it.

If she could.

~

Lucy came out of the parlour as James followed his mother from the billiards room. He could tell from her face that he was in for another reprimand.

"Wait until we're in the library, Lucy." How had he got into a situation where his little sister was about to take him to task?

"Why, Jamie?" she asked, as soon as the door closed. "Why did you send them away?"

She looked truly dismayed.

"I *liked* them. I like Miss Stockhart, too, but she's not as much fun as Alice and Lady Jesson. What did they do?"

"Come and sit down, Lucy." He sat at his desk, and she took one of the nearby armchairs. He didn't speak immediately, wondering how much to tell her.

"Jamie?"

"Lucy, you will not repeat what I tell you to anyone else, is that clear?" His letters about Lavoisier need not be a secret, but the fact that he was still being investigated must go no further. Any talk might warn off the culprit before he could be trapped.

Lucy's eyes widened in surprise.

"I'm trusting you, Lucy. Don't make me regret telling you."

"I promise."

James regarded her closely—she did appear to be taking his words seriously. "Very well. In my researches, I corresponded with a well-known French experimentalist, Monsieur Lavoisier. He was arrested and—"

"For doing experiments?"

"No. Although natural philosophers are not particularly popular in

France at the moment, his crime in their eyes was being an investor in a tax collection company."

Lucy nodded. "Miss Sullivan teaches me about what is happening in France."

"She does?"

"Oh, yes. She says a well-educated young lady should know what is happening in the world, even if many men like to think they are the only ones who are capable of—" She put her hand over her mouth.

James waited, but Lucy said no more.

"The point is," he resumed, "I tried to find a way of getting Lavoisier out of prison. I sent money—bribes—to France, but nothing came of it. Some of my messages were intercepted, and..." He began to wish he hadn't started this tale; Marstone's name should not be bandied about in this context.

"Someone thought you were a spy."

"Yes. Er, not quite. They thought I *might* be." That 'might' was important to him. "They sent Lady Jesson and Miss Bryant to try to find out what I was writing about."

Lucy's eyes went round again. "They are spies? That's why they are so much fun!"

Fun? "I don't think they're really spies." When he'd encountered Miss Bryant last year in Kent, she hadn't appeared to know Marstone, and hadn't taken part in any of the discussions about the traitor in Marstone's ranks.

"So why did you send them away?"

"Wouldn't you be angry if you found someone you... er, someone going through your private correspondence?"

Lucy shrugged. "If you leave it lying ar—"

"It was locked in a drawer."

"They know how to pick locks! Oh, I wish they hadn't gone, I'd love to—"

"Lucy!"

She shrugged. "I suppose it's not something a young lady should learn. But it would be interesting. Now there are only a few left to choose from."

Only Miss Bryant—possibly—but he hadn't decided what to do yet, and he was *not* going to discuss it with Lucy. "I don't *have* to marry any of them, and would you please leave me in peace?"

She pouted, but then got up and walked down the room. She turned before she reached the door. "I *did* like them, Jamie. It's a pity you can't marry Miss Bryant."

The door clicked closed behind her and James rested his head in his hands. Now *Lucy* was telling him who he should marry.

He opened a drawer and contemplated his notebooks, then shut them away again. His mind was too busy to concentrate on scientific work. Reading—he could see if there was anything significant in the latest journals. Or, at least, mark any interesting articles for when he did have the concentration.

The door clicked again as he opened the latest copy of the *Philosophical Transactions*. Was he to get no peace?

"Jamie!" It was Lucy again. "They haven't gone. Bellingham said they went to the Dower House." She stared at his face, and her lips curved. "I can tell you're pleased!" She left before he could say anything.

Had he smiled without realising? But he *was* pleased, he realised.

It was no use trying to concentrate on anything but what he should do about Miss Bryant. He needed time to think. Alone.

The kitchen garden would do—no-one would look for him there.

An upended crate in the shade of the south wall served as a seat. The last time he'd been here was after Miss Bryant's encounter with Julius Chilton. A few days after that, one of his mother's guests had deliberately stepped on her hand. Neither of these things had been his fault, but both were his responsibility, in a way. Did that compensate for her spying on him?

He was still saddened that she had done so, but their explanation made some sense. What would he have done if he'd been asked to spy on a friend? And they hadn't been friends when she... they... had accepted the task.

She'd looked distressed in the library, worried even.

The thought that he might never see her again hurt as much as her betrayal. More. Today's events need not change his mind, although he'd sleep on it before making a decision.

His future wasn't the only problem. There was also the matter of information being sent to France. Perhaps thinking about that would take his mind off Miss Bryant for a while.

CHAPTER 19

*J*ames ordered breakfast in his room the following morning. He needed time alone to review his thoughts from the previous day; avoiding his mother and her remaining guests was a bonus.

The easier problem first—he should talk to Marstone before trying to do anything about the stolen information. The house party and the preparations for it had distracted him from his work for the past few weeks, and it had been a couple of months since he'd made any significant progress. If someone was copying his notes, they would already have details of his latest results with different propellant mixtures and casings. Locking his notebooks away more securely would serve only to alert the spy that his activities had been discovered. It would not be enough to merely stop the leak of information— if they did not find out who was responsible, the spy could try again.

A knock on the door heralded a couple of footmen with loaded trays. A trip to Town would be useful for other reasons, James thought, as they laid out dishes and poured a cup of coffee before setting the pot on the table. He had a new pair of riding boots ready for collection, and he wanted to call on the instrument maker he patronised to look at the new pressure-measuring device he'd developed. And it was always worth seeing if there were any promising colts or fillies on offer at Tattersalls.

The footmen left and he spooned buttered eggs onto his plate. He could not leave today, as such an abrupt departure would raise awkward questions and be rude to his guests. The remaining young women and their parents had done nothing wrong—Lucy liked Miss Stockhart, and he rather thought he could get to like Lord Gearing. He would tell them today he'd received an urgent message, and set off tomorrow morning.

One thing decided to his satisfaction, he turned his attention to the question that had taken most of his attention since yesterday. Sitting in the kitchen garden, he'd thought he should stick by his original inclination to make Alice Bryant his marchioness. This morning, with his mind drifting and still half-asleep, he'd felt happy, looking forward to the day. And that feeling was due to the thought that Alice would be his wife. He wouldn't wait until the house party finished, as he'd originally planned, in case they left before then. He would ask her this morning.

Alice and Lady Jesson were in the knot garden as James approached the Dower House. He ran a hand through his hair and tugged on the bottom of his coat to straighten it. Yesterday's encounter in the library seemed a long time ago now.

Alice was pointing here and there amongst the clipped hedges, explaining something to Lady Jesson. He paused to admire the enthusiasm apparent in her gestures—no passive miss, his future bride.

They turned to face him as his boots crunched on the gravel path. Lady Jesson's expression remained faintly enquiring; Alice dropped her eyes.

"Good morning, Lady Jesson, Miss Bryant."

"My lord." Alice's tone was subdued, her eyes still downcast. That was not like her at all.

"How is your hand, Miss Bryant?"

"Mending, thank you."

"I'm glad to hear it. Um, I was pleased to find that you had not completely left Harlford, in spite of my somewhat intemperate reaction in the library."

Alice looked up, her eyes widening. "Oh. You were perfectly justified—it was a poor way to repay your hospitality."

"Shall we move on?" James gestured towards one of the paths. It might be easier to talk while walking.

She fell into step beside him, Lady Jesson on his other side. The disadvantage of this arrangement, he belatedly realised, was that the rim of her bonnet hid her face from his view.

"I can see," he went on, "now that I have had time to think things through, that asking a possible spy whether or not he is guilty may not be the best approach."

A quiet chuckle from Lady Jesson made his lips twitch. He thought a little tension left Alice's shoulders.

"It still seems wrong," she said, so quietly he had to bend closer to hear her clearly.

"Well, it is done, and soon to be forgotten, I hope," James said. They walked on a few paces further. "There is also the matter of information being where it should not, to which you referred."

"Yes," Lady Jesson said. "We have completed only half of our task. Lady Harlford—your grandmother, that is—was kind enough to invite us to stay a little while longer."

"Is there any other information on the matter that you did not tell me yesterday?"

"Only that I do not think your assistant Norton is involved."

James agreed—the man was good with his hands, but he couldn't imagine Norton managing to take and pass on information without being found out.

"We have not managed to discover much about your other assistant."

"Sumner?" He frowned. "I cannot believe it of him, but I suppose the possibility should be investigated. Very well. I will see Marstone about this business, so you needn't bother yourselves with it any further. I'm sure he will have some ideas about how to proceed."

Neither woman responded. James felt uncomfortable with the silence—had he said something wrong?

"Er, I trust your accommodation here is to your liking?" he said at last, not being able to think of anything else to say.

"Yes, indeed," Lady Jesson said.

"Yes, thank you," Alice replied at the same time.

They had reached the edge of the formal gardens. From here the path continued along the edge of the lake towards the main house.

"Would you care to walk on?"

"Thank you, but no," Lady Jesson said. "Alice, you go on. The walk will do you good."

Alice glanced at Maria, not really wanting to be left alone with Lord Harlford. Not after yesterday.

"Do go, Alice," Maria repeated. "The weather's lovely and you'll only fret if you end up sitting with us older women all day."

Alice's lips quirked at the idea of Maria putting herself in the same category as the dowager, but she was right. "Very well. Thank you."

Lord Harlford smiled, but it seemed a trifle forced, not reaching his eyes. Had he really forgiven them, or had he more to say on the subject?

He held the gate open for her, and they continued around the lake in uncomfortable silence for a while, then he halted. Politeness demanded she stop and face him.

"Miss Bryant, I do assure you that I understand why you were persuaded to... ah... investigate me. And I apologise for my language yesterday."

"That is quite all right." She'd heard far worse from the farmhands at home. "I suppose our actions *did* resolve a question, but it still seems dishonourable." She turned her gaze to the lake. "Spying on the enemy seems quite different from being asked to spy on one's countrymen."

"But if I *had* been sending information to France, I would have been the enemy, would I not? Please do not refine upon it. It is done. I was perhaps unwise in the way I chose to go about attempting to extricate Lavoisier." He examined a clump of rushes at the edge of the water, appearing as ill at ease as she felt.

"I suppose methods of extracting a condemned man from a foreign prison are not generally part of a gentleman's education."

He glanced up at that, a smile lightening his face. The warmth in his eyes made her feel a little breathless. "Not of mine, certainly." He stood straighter and cleared his throat. "You... er, you are, of course, aware of my mother's purpose in convening this house party."

Alice nodded.

"I wonder if you would do me the honour of becoming my wife?"

Her eyes flew to his face—was he sincere? Surely he could not have meant it?

She'd found him attractive, and easy to talk to, and had even wondered what it might be like to be courted by him. She had not expected this—nor the growing feeling of excitement. Was he serious?

His expression was calm, and as she looked, he raised one eyebrow.

Her excitement turned to confusion. Although she had no experience of what an ardent lover should look like when asking for his lady's hand, she was sure it was not the confident half-smile now on his face.

He was making fun of her—he had to be. Waiting for her to fall into a trap, ready to laugh at her naivety in thinking a marquess would offer for a paid companion.

Hurt stabbed her as she spun around and set off around the lake again.

"Miss Bryant!" His voice was close behind.

"There is no need to mock me, my lord." Her voice verged on a wobble and she took a breath to steady herself. "I have apologised, and there is little more I can do to make amends. I can arrange to leave Harlford even if Lady Jesson desires to remain."

"Miss Bryant!" His hand grasped her arm, and she reluctantly stopped to face him.

"Miss Bryant, I assure you I made my offer in all seriousness." That confident smile had gone, his brows were drawn together.

"Why?"

"I... Well... I think we would... I mean, you can hold an intelligent conversation. You are even interested in natural philosophy, or you would not have recognised Lavoisier's name as being significant. You could help me in my research, if you wish, as poor Lavoisier's wife did."

He did seem to be in earnest.

Alice swallowed hard, her surroundings suddenly seeming dreamlike, unreal. When he'd carried her after the picnic, she'd felt safe and secure. Now she wondered what it would be like to be held by him in quite a different way.

She turned away, afraid that the sudden heat inside her might show on her face.

"Miss Bryant, I have not distressed you in some way, have I?"

"Er, no."

Did he love her? She doubted it, although he must at least *like* her. Whenever she had contemplated her future, her *married* future, she had always imagined a degree of affection warmer than mere liking. Not someone who chose her because she could make conversation.

It was too sudden—it was impossible to think things through properly with him standing there awaiting an answer. Particularly not with this strange feeling troubling her.

"I... er, I thank you for your offer, my lord. I... That is, may I have some time to consider?"

His body stiffened, but his voice, when he spoke, was polite enough. "By all means. Naturally, you should consider carefully. I... Should I leave you to consider in peace?"

"If you don't mind, I will return to the gardens." She smiled uncertainly, and set off the way they had come. Turning as she opened the gate, she saw he was still where she had left him. He stood with his hands clasped behind his back, examining the rushes once more.

Perhaps her decision *did* matter to him?

· · ·

173

James felt as if he were rooted to the spot. She hadn't said yes.

She hadn't actually turned him down, he reminded himself, only asked for time to consider her answer. But that thought didn't alleviate the sense of loss. In all his deliberations about whether or not he should offer for her, the notion that she might refuse him had not crossed his mind.

He should have known better. After last year's abortive courtship of Miss Deane, then discovering that Miss Stockhart preferred young Augustus Chilton to himself, he should have worked out that the women he contemplated marrying wanted something other than his title and wealth.

And it was Alice he wanted, not just any attractive and intelligent woman who would deal well with Lucy.

He had surprised her; that was it. She needed some time to think about it—pushing her for a quick decision might only make her refuse outright. Tomorrow's journey would have to be put off until the afternoon.

Alice made her way to one of the benches in the knot garden. Her hands felt shaky, as if she had suffered a shock.

"Alice? Why are you here? Are you feeling well?" Maria stood before her.

Alice sat up straighter. "I'm well, thank you."

"Hmm." Maria sat down. "Harlford said something to trouble you. It's unfair of him to blame only you, when we both—"

"He asked me to marry him."

"I wondered if he might." There was no hint of surprise in Maria's voice.

"What?" Alice jumped up and faced Maria. "Why would he do that?"

"Because he likes you?" Maria leaned back slightly to look her in the face. "Come, my dear, you may not have the curls and fluttering eyelashes of the other young women here, but that is quite likely part of the attraction."

"Attraction is not enough for a lifetime."

"You are not attracted to him?"

Alice's face grew hot. "I didn't say that." She sat down; that way she could hide her expression better. Maria was too good at working out what people were really thinking.

"You'd never want for money. You'd have a husband who respects your intelligence, and—"

"He thinks I'm intelligent enough that I might be able to help him with his experiments." Why had she expected anything more, though? If women's scientific interests were generally accepted, she wouldn't need to use a false name for her agricultural correspondence.

"Hmm. But be fair, my dear, he doesn't know about your interests, does he?"

Alice relaxed a little. "I suppose not."

"If you want to carry on your own research, you should tell him that. Do you think he would object?"

"I don't know—he might."

"Any of the other women he asked would have said yes for his money and title," Maria pointed out.

"Do you think I should have accepted?"

"You should think carefully before giving your answer," Maria replied. "Leaving aside attraction, or lack of it, there are other factors to consider. His mother, for one."

"She'll... She won't regard me as suitable, at all."

"No, indeed—but Lady Harlford's requirements probably bear little resemblance to what Harlford himself wants." Maria stared into the distance, a smile on her face. "I'd give a great deal to be an observer when he tells her."

"*If* I say yes." Alice didn't find the prospect amusing. "I'll have to put up with her for the next..." She waved a hand. "Decades. Another quarter century at least."

"I will leave you to it, Alice. Come and talk it over with me if you wish, but do consider carefully." Maria patted her shoulder and left her alone.

Could such an unequal match work? Would Lord Harlford come to think of her as having married him only for his money? Or for his title? What would that do to their relationship?

Would society accept her? She cared little for that, but their children...She blushed at the thought, and stood abruptly. Exercise might help her to think more clearly.

When she reached the gate near the lake, she peered through it cautiously. Seeing that Lord Harlford had gone, she let herself out and strode along the path towards the stables.

"Has something happened?" Chatham asked, when she announced that she'd come for the dog.

"No, nothing." Her voice came out more sharply than she intended.

"It's just that you looked worried. His lordship hasn't taken against..."

Oh, the spying business. "He said he can understand why we agreed to Lord Marstone's request," she said. "He didn't say anything about what will happen now."

"I'll keep my eyes open then, miss. And you, too. There's still that evidence of someone watching."

She nodded, then called to Tess and set off across the park towards a section of woodland she hadn't yet explored.

This could be hers—in a way—if she said yes. There was enough land here that a large experimental garden, or even orchards, should be possible. She shook her head—she should not let that weigh with her when coming to a decision. No amount of land for experimentation was worth tying herself—for life—to a man she didn't know well. She liked what she'd seen of him, certainly, and more than any other man she'd met. But she hadn't met many unmarried men.

Striding on, with Tess beside her or wandering off to investigate interesting new smells, she tried to list the points for and against, but an hour and several miles later she had reached no conclusion.

CHAPTER 20

The decision she had to make distracted Alice for the rest of the day. She'd planned on catching up with her correspondence, and she did try. But first she couldn't find the letter she'd started a few days ago about increasing wheat yields, and had to start again. Then she got as far as thanking the man for the samples he'd sent before her mind wandered back to Lord Harlford's offer.

She'd often dreamed of having someone to care for her, someone with a scientific mind who would accept her interests, and who she could discuss her plans with. Might Lord Harlford might be such a person? She wasn't sure. He *had* mentioned his scientific interests, but only that she might help him.

But if she accepted his offer and wasn't happy, or if *he* wasn't happy, there would be no going back. The way he had asked her made it sound little different from obtaining a new position, but one in which she could not give notice and leave if it did not suit.

She had to refuse him; it was the only sensible decision.

Although she'd come to a conclusion, the question still kept her from sleep most of the night, and she rose the next morning long before the breakfast hour. She begged a quick cup of tea and a sweet roll in the kitchen, and walked to the stables.

The sky was grey with a thin mist cloaking the view, but Tess would be happy whatever the weather. The mist brightened to white above her, promising a lovely day once the sun had burnt the moisture off.

Tess was pleased to see her, and Alice took her usual route around the back of the house and across the parkland. The mist dampened her hair, and the dew on the grass quickly soaked into the hem of her gown, but she didn't mind—the lack of visibility made her feel as if she were walking in a private bubble, alone in the world. Apart from the dog snuffling around, and hoofbeats in the distance behind her.

Bother—it must be Lord Harlford on one of his early morning rides. She'd intended to think up a proper rejection speech, but it was too late now—unless he passed by without noticing them.

Tess' bark prevented that. The hoofbeats drew nearer, then Lord Harlford appeared as a shadow looming through the mist. He veered towards her, and dismounted.

"Miss Bryant?" Fine droplets of water beaded on his coat and hat.

"My lord." She made a small curtsey.

"May I escort you back to the house? You could get lost." There was concern in his voice, rather than censure.

Following the tracks her feet had made though the dew would be a fool-proof way of returning, but she didn't say so. She turned, and he fell into step beside her, leading his horse. Wondering whether she should broach the subject of his proposal, she cleared her throat.

"My lord, I—"

"Miss Bryant, have—?"

It would have been amusing at another time, but not now. Her stomach knotted. Although she'd decided on perfectly rational grounds that she must decline his offer, part of her wanted to throw prudence to the winds and take a chance. But she must not rethink her answer now.

"My apologies, Miss Bryant. I wished to ask if you had considered my proposal."

"I have, my lord." Her hands clenched so her fingernails dug into her palms. "I am afraid I must decline. I do not... that is, we do not know each other well enough for me to take such a big step."

James walked on in silence. She'd said no.

She had turned him down.

He felt... What did he feel? Empty? In spite of his doubts yesterday, he had never really thought she would refuse him. He caught a flash of movement as her head turned towards him, then away again.

"I am sorry, Miss Bryant. I think we would have dealt well together." He stopped speaking and rubbed his forehead with his free hand. If that was the limit of his eloquence, was it any wonder she had rejected him?

He cleared his throat. "Is there something I can do to change your mind?"

"I am flattered that you wish to, my lord. But it is a decision that will affect the rest of our lives. I do not know you well enough to be sure we would be happy together."

"I see." She'd said that twice now.

Was there someone else? He'd heard no mention of a beau, and he thought she would have said so if someone else were courting her.

"Miss Bryant, I am leaving for London later today, to see the Earl of Marstone about the information being sent to France. You are, naturally, welcome to stay with my grandmother as long as you wish. In fact, I hope you *will* stay." Once he'd seen Marstone he would return and attempt to court her properly.

They had walked several more paces before she answered. "That is very kind of you, my lord." Her voice was disappointingly flat, as if she had no interest in his plans. She glanced around, pointing to the northern edge of the orchard. "I think your path lies there. I will make my way back around the other way. I wish you a good journey."

She stopped and curtseyed. He bowed in return, and she strode off with the huge dog, the pair of them becoming darker shapes against the grey mist and then vanishing.

· · ·

"Lady Harlford wishes to see you in the morning room," Bellingham told James when he returned to the house. James suppressed a curse—the last thing he wanted at the moment was another set of demands from his mother, but he might as well get it over with.

"Mama. What can I do for you?" He closed the door behind him and went to stand by the window. He wasn't going to be here long.

"James, our guests have been here for ten days, and still you have not chosen your bride."

He had fulfilled his mother's insistence that he make a choice. Perhaps now he might get some peace for the rest of the year. He turned to face her.

"Mama, you recall you said any of the young women here would be acceptable as my wife?"

"Yes, James, but—"

"And I promised I would make one an offer?"

"Yes, but—"

"And whether she accepted or rejected me, that would be an end of this business until next year?"

"Don't be silly, James, she will not turn you down. Turn down a title and—?"

"Mama." There was enough force in his voice to stop her in mid-sentence. "Yesterday I asked Miss Bryant to marry me. Unfortunately, this morning she said no."

"You asked... Bryant? The *companion*?" His mother's voice was faint.

"Yes, Mama."

"Miss Bryant?"

"Yes, Mama. Miss Bryant."

"James, you *know* I meant one of the young ladies I invited, not the hired help! Who are her people? Where does she come from?"

"They are landowners in Wiltshire, I believe." That described her family accurately, although Mama would assume a country estate with a deer park and tenant farms.

"But... what title does her father hold?"

"No title, as far as I am aware."

"Aware? Did you not ask? And what about a dowry? She cannot bring anything to the marriage if she is employed as a paid companion."

"I did not enquire, Mama. I consider neither of those things to be important."

"Not important? James, you have cancelled several of my plans to keep this place in the fashionable style, why are you—?"

He walked to the door. "*I* do not consider a dowry important. If you will excuse me, I have things to see to. I will be setting off for London this afternoon on urgent business."

Mama stood, opening her mouth to speak, but James kept talking.

"*Urgent* business that cannot be delayed. I hope to be back within the week."

"But your guests are—"

"*Your* guests. You invited them without asking me first. I explained yesterday evening that I had to leave."

"I didn't think you meant so soon, James! You promised to choose—"

"I did choose. Remember, Mama, you agreed there would be no more matchmaking once I made an offer."

"But I didn't—"

"No 'buts'. You agreed. I will not discuss this further."

She looked as though she would continue arguing, but he wasn't going to stay to listen. He left, heading for his library rather than the breakfast parlour, but she did not follow him. He would be glad to be out of her way for the next few days.

Safely alone in his sanctuary, he stood at the window as he often did when he wanted to think. How would his future wife—whoever she turned out to be—enjoy living at Harlford with Mama in the same house?

Could that be why Miss Bryant had turned him down? It was probably not the only reason, but it must have been a factor. Any other prospective bride would doubtless feel the same.

The Dower House was out of the question—Grandmama would

not readily share her home with her daughter-in-law. James could not blame her for that.

Bourton Manor!

He nodded in satisfaction. Mama had wanted the Manor near Brighton, and insisted on its refurbishment. She should make use of it.

She would object, of course, but he held the purse-strings.

That decision made, he went to sit at his desk. Now all he had to do was to help catch a spy and decide whether he should try to persuade Miss Bryant to change her mind.

And if he could.

Alice's pace slowed as she rounded the end of the orchard and headed for the Dower House. The mist was thinning, but she would be out of Lord Harlford's sight here in any case. As she walked, the sky gradually turned blue and sunshine warmed her face. Tempting as it was to stay outside, she'd have to tell Maria what she'd done at some point. Maria might convince her that she'd done the right thing.

Maria was in the breakfast parlour, a cup of tea in one hand and several slices of well-buttered toast on the plate before her. She looked up as Alice entered. "Is something wrong, my dear?"

"No, I'm well, thank you." Alice took the place beside her.

"Hmm. Did you meet Harlford on his morning ride?"

Alice nodded.

"You turned him down?"

"Yes." What else was there to say?

"What was that?" The dowager spoke from her seat further down the table.

Maria gestured to a footman to pour another cup of tea, then dismissed him. "Alice has just refused a proposal of marriage." She turned to Alice. "There's no point in trying to keep it secret. Harlford is bound to tell Cassandra, in some attempt to get her to stop nagging him, and then the whole house will hear about it."

"Hah, yes," the dowager said. "Cassandra was never the most discreet of people. A shame, though."

Alice's mouth almost fell open. She'd expected the dowager to make some comment about her unsuitability, and to say that she was pleased Alice had turned down an unequal match.

"There is no-one else, is there Miss Bryant?"

Alice sighed. Perhaps she should have stayed outside after all—until she was sure of finding Maria alone. But she was a guest in the dowager's home, and it would be rude not to answer. "No, my lady."

The dowager smiled at her. "You may as well tell us the details, my dear. Maria will get them out of you at some point."

That was true, but Maria wouldn't pass on *all* the details to the dowager. The bare facts would do.

"We have your best interests at heart," the dowager continued. "I also have my grandson's future to consider."

"But his rank, my lady? My family are farmers."

"Landowners, I think you said? That is a large disparity, to be sure, but not insurmountable. You have the manners and ease to mix with the guests here, and you will bring intelligence and integrity to the family."

"There must be any number of young ladies in the *ton* who meet that description," Alice pointed out.

The dowager shook her head. "I'm more interested in my grandson's happiness than in status or wealth." She tilted her head back and examined Alice. "Are you worried that you will not be accepted in society? Do not be. Most people will think twice before snubbing a marchioness, particularly if I make it known that *I* approve."

"But still, I'm—"

"Miss Bryant, I'm beginning to think you do not *wish* to marry my grandson."

She wasn't sure what she wanted, but the logical part of her mind told her to be cautious.

"From what I've seen of you, and Maria and David have told me, I think you would have dealt well together."

"That's what he said, my lady."

"That was *all* he said?" Maria asked.

"Well, he asked me to marry him, and said I can make intelligent conversation and I might be able to help him with his experiments."

"Good grief, the boy's a fool!" the dowager exclaimed.

In spite of her inner turmoil, Alice almost laughed at the dowager's disgusted expression.

"That was yesterday," Alice explained. "I asked for some time to think about it, but I met him on my walk this morning."

"And you turned him down?" Maria prompted.

"I said we did not know each other well enough. That is, *I* do not feel I know Lord Harlford well enough to take such a big decision."

"A pity." The dowager tapped a finger on the arm of her chair. "What did Harlford say?"

"He asked if he could convince me otherwise."

"Good, good."

"He is leaving for London today." Alice glanced at Maria. "He also said we were welcome to stay as long as we wished, but I don't think I can… It wouldn't be right to stay when—"

"Nonsense, of course you must stay!" the dowager exclaimed. "You are my guests, not my grandson's. I will enjoy your company, especially now David has gone off for a few days to deal with some business matter. Lucy would appreciate you staying, too."

Alice didn't want to encounter the marquess again—that would be awkward. Even if he would be away for some days, it still felt wrong to be accepting his hospitality.

"I think we must go," Maria said, to Alice's relief. "I was intending to write to Marstone with our findings, but we can make a better report in person. We will leave Chatham behind to make further enquiries, and Tess with him. In fact, I think we should set out this afternoon. My lady, could we prevail upon you to order a carriage for us, as far as Hereford? We should be able to get a seat on the Mail or a stagecoach."

"Nonsense. There is a perfectly good coach languishing in the stable block—take that to London."

"Won't Lord Harlford need it for his journey?" Taking his coach on top of turning him down—not to mention spying on him—would be too much.

"He'll probably drive his phaeton," the dowager said. "And if he doesn't, there is a spare coach." She looked from Maria to Alice and back. "I do insist on one additional thing, though. I want to you accept my invitation to return here when you have reported your findings."

"I will gladly do so," Maria said, before Alice could speak.

About to object, Alice subsided as Maria gave the tiniest shake of her head. There would be time enough to argue about it on the journey.

"If you will excuse me, my lady, Maria, I will pack."

CHAPTER 21

*J*ames put his pen down as his mother entered the library, and eyed the door into the servants' corridor. There was a flash of white beyond her as someone tip-toed down the room and slipped into one of the bays.

Lucy? No matter. She would find out everything eventually, so she might as well listen now.

"James, that... those women are residing at the Dower House. Does your grandmother know the kind of people who are foisting themselves on her?"

"I beg your pardon?"

She held out a paper—a letter. "This is that... This is Miss Bryant's hand—I recognise it from the slips she helped me write for charades. Your grandmother would not be pleased if she knew her unmarried guest was corresponding with men. Do you see why you should trust my judgement in these things? You are lucky she was stupid enough to turn you down."

James picked up the paper and ran his eyes over it. It was dated several days ago. "Dear Mr Cromhall," he read out loud. "Thank you for the items you sent. I have not had time to examine them in detail, but I hope to be able to ..." The writing stopped there.

"Well, James?"

"Where did you get this?"

"It was left behind in the room that encroach… that Miss Bryant was staying in."

Encroaching hussy? Mama's look of concern was an act, and not a very good one. Perhaps she suspected he was intending to ask Alice again.

But her protests made no sense. Had her fixation on his marriage unbalanced her mind in some way?

"Mama, this letter could have been written to a relative, a man of business, or even a tradesman from whom they have ordered goods. Why have you instantly put the worst possible interpretation on it?"

"What use would a paid companion have for a man of business? You must see that she is not—"

"Mama!" James waited to make sure she was not going to start talking again. "I appreciate your concern for Grandmama, but she is quite capable of judging her guests for herself."

"James, you—"

"Enough, Mama. But while we are on the subject of my marriage, there *is* something I wish to discuss with you."

"I am doing my best to find you—"

"Sit down, Mama." There was enough force in his voice to make her take the chair he indicated. "You do realise that whoever I marry will be the new marchioness, and the person who will be in charge of the Castle?"

"Yes, of course, but they will need my guidance and—"

"No, Mama. You have attempted to divert estate funds for your own purposes and—"

"For improving Harlford!"

"No matter what the reason, you had no right to pressure Terring to spend money for a project he—and you—knew I would not approve of."

"But James, I—"

James ignored her interruption. "Papa bought Bourton Manor at your insistence, and also spent a great deal of money on alterations—

also at your insistence. It is time you made use of that investment. In fact, Brighton is particularly fashionable in the summer months, I understand, so you should start to plan your removal there."

Her mouth fell open, then she frowned.

"You should be seeing to the comfort of your guests." James stood and walked around the desk, taking her arm. "I will not discuss this further."

She protested as she stood. "James, I—"

He'd had enough of these arguments. "If you persist in this, I will stop your allowance and let tradesmen know that I will not honour your bills." He escorted her along the room towards the door.

"You... You can't do that!"

"I can." He held the door open. "And Terring will not help you this time, either. Your guests, Mama?"

He stood by the door, ignoring her further protests, until she turned on her heel and flounced out. Closing it behind her, he went back to his desk. Lucy had already pulled a spare chair up to it.

He'd forgotten she was in the library, and must have heard every word. Should she move to Brighton with Mama? He hadn't considered the effect this would have on her, and he should have done.

"Lucy. I'm sorry I didn't warn you about what I was planning." He sat down.

"Am I to go with her?" Her scowl said she didn't relish the prospect.

"Don't you wish to?"

"No, not at all! Mama... Well, I hardly see her. Only when she summons me to find out whether my embroidery or music are improving. And she doesn't let me visit the other families nearby. I might be able to make some friends of my own age if she weren't here."

Guilt struck him—he should have taken more interest in her instead of trusting Mama. "I'm sorry for not realising. Of course you won't have to go if you don't wish to."

"Oh good! And Arabella will be happier without Mama in the

Castle," Lucy said, her expression thoughtful. "You're not going to send her away as well, are you?"

"No, of course not. This is her home."

Her expression lightened. "I'm glad of that. I *do* like her, Jamie, and I enjoy playing with little Mary." She leaned a little closer to him. "Did you really ask Alice to marry you?"

"I did—I thought you'd already know. Are you here to tell me what I should do, too?"

"I expect so."

He almost laughed—trust Lucy to be so honest.

"Don't be so grumpy, Jamie."

Her expression held an endearing mixture of sympathy and amusement, and he couldn't take offence. "You would be grumpy, too, if the person you wanted to marry turned you down."

Lucy nodded. "I'm not surprised."

"Thank you for your kind words." Stung, he hoped she didn't mean them.

"Oh, it's not you. Well, not entirely. Mama probably put her off a bit. It's a pity," she added. "I like her."

"Yes, you said that yesterday. I'm not about to choose a bride just because you like her."

"Did you know she's a natural philosopher too?"

"I know she takes some interest."

"It's more than reading a few books, I think." Lucy tilted her head to one side. "Does the notion of having a clever wife put you off, Jamie?"

"No, of course not." That was one of the reasons he was attracted to her—she could take an intelligent interest in his work. "But what makes you think—?"

She sprang out of her chair and went to the bookshelves in the end bay. "Miss Sullivan showed me Hooke's book of drawings," she said. "I come here sometimes to look at the fleas and flies. Alice did some reading here, too. Come here, Jamie." She pulled out some bound journals. "Do you read these?"

He looked at the spines. Agriculture? "No."

Pieces of paper stuck out in places, marking the beginnings of articles. Some had brief, cryptic notes in the same hand as the letter Mama had brandished. Crop yields, farming methods, orchard management...

"See?" Lucy said. "I've seen Alice studying these."

That didn't mean she was a fellow enthusiast, but making notes indicated more than a passing interest.

"This is all very well, Lucy, but how is this supposed to help?"

"Are you going to try to make her change her mind?"

"Yes." The word came out without thought—and it felt right. He *would* try—if he could work out how.

"Good. If you know what she's interested in, you have more things to talk to her about."

That was the problem, of course. "She said we didn't know each other."

"What did you do to make her like you?"

It could have been an innocent question, but this was Lucy. She probably already knew the answer—not much.

Not enough, certainly.

"They've gone, Grandmama? Are you sure?" Just like the morning when he'd found Alice going through his desk—except this time he would not discover them less than half a mile away.

"Of course I'm sure. I watched them leave myself."

James took a deep breath. "Why? I did say they were welcome to stay as long as they pleased."

"After Miss Bryant turned you down? You must see how awkward that would be for her."

"I... yes, I suppose so."

"Why did you offer for such a nobody, James? She hasn't the training to run a house the size of the Castle."

He hadn't expected an attack from this quarter. Although at least Grandmama had asked, rather than scolding him as Mama had. "She'll soon learn. She has easy manners, intelligent conversation..." He was *not* going to discuss wanting her in his bed.

"Many young ladies have those qualities."

"Not the ones Mama invited."

"Is that the only reason, James? That she's the best on offer here? She'll do?"

"No." He couldn't find the words to describe what he felt, and wasn't sure he wanted to open himself to Grandmama's scrutiny in any case.

She gazed at his face, her expression thoughtful. "Do you love her?"

What was love? "I don't know. Possibly."

"Then you should get to know her better before deciding whether to renew your suit."

She was waiting for an answer, so he nodded.

"In which case, their departure for London is a good thing. You may meet there without Cassandra interfering."

"Why do *you* approve of Miss Bryant, Grandmama?"

"I'm not sure I do approve of you marrying her. Not yet, at least, but that is to do with you, not her."

"Me?"

"My dear, since long before Robert died you have been so focussed on your experiments and your horses that I feared you would never take an interest in anything else. If you find you really do care for her, and the feeling is mutual, I think she will make you happy. And even if she does not accept you in the end, some good will have come from all this. It has made you take more notice of the people around you."

He wasn't so sure, but he wasn't going to argue with her.

"I offered Maria the travelling coach, James. You will have to ask for one of the other vehicles to be prepared."

The choice of carriage was the least of his worries, he thought as he walked back to the Castle. If there was the possibility of seeing Alice in London he should take his valet with him, and a reasonable selection of clothing. He would have to put off his journey until the morning.

No matter. First he had to work out what he would do in London —calling on Lady Jesson to sit drinking tea and making stilted conversation wasn't going to help. It was a shame David had left on business—he might have had some useful advice.

Back in the library, James went to the shelves holding the agricultural journals and took down all the ones with markers in them. Finding out what Alice had been reading was a good place to start.

The articles and reports concerned investigations into the best growing conditions for different crops, and attempts to breed new varieties of fruit, vegetables, and even farm animals. It was all so much messier than chemical experiments—so many factors to be controlled if a valid conclusion were to be reached. He had to admire anyone who could deal with that complexity.

What else was she interested in? She'd spent a lot of time talking to the undergardener. What had they discussed? He would go to the kitchen gardens later and ask him.

But there was more to knowing someone than shared interests. Was she still worried about his reaction to discovering her spying? He'd forgiven her, and thought she'd accepted that it was behind them. It would be easy enough to reassure her on that subject. But discussions they'd had about the spying niggled at his mind. There had been a couple of times when there had been a distinctly uncomfortable silence, such as when he'd told her and Lady Jesson they needn't bother with the investigation any longer.

He rubbed his forehead; one of Alice's attractions was her intelligence, and he'd been dismissive. To her and Lady Jesson. Well, the past could not be changed, but he would endeavour not to repeat that mistake.

He eyed his notebook lying to one side of his desk, then opened it to where he'd made his list of reasons against proposing marriage. He'd rejected them, but she could be worried about some of them.

Society, and the difference in their stations, were likely to be the main problems. Who would have thought a title would be an impediment to a courtship?

But, quite apart from the fact that it involved the death of his brother, he hadn't been best pleased to become a marquess. It came with responsibilities and obligations, although it did have some advantages…

He searched the shelves until he found a London Gazetteer and consulted it. Then he wrote a letter to Sir Joseph Banks, ready to be delivered as soon as he reached Town. He didn't know the man well, their interests being in different areas of natural philosophy, but it was only a small favour he was asking.

That would be a good start, if his plan succeeded. He should still talk to Griffiths, and hope to get more inspiration.

The undergardener was in the glasshouse, doing something to plants in pots.

"My lord?" Griffiths put down his pruning shears. "Can I help you?"

"I…" It seemed too direct to ask what Alice had been interested in, but most of his staff probably knew by now that he wished to marry her.

"What was Miss Bryant talking to you about when she was here a few days ago?"

"Well, many things. She talked about the garden at her home, and we discussed how it was different growing for a single household compared to a large estate such as this. And she was interested in my breeding trials."

"Breeding?"

"I'm trying to produce cabbages with sweeter leaves, and late potatoes less susceptible to blight. It does not detract from my duties, my lord, I assure you."

"I'm not questioning that, Griffiths. Do continue."

"Well, my lord, in addition to improving what the garden can provide for the kitchens, there may be commercial opportunities in developing new varieties."

"Miss Bryant was interested in this?"

"Yes, my lord, and very knowledgeable, too—it was a pleasure talking to her. She... I..."

"What is it, Griffiths?"

"She asked me to write down some information, but she hasn't been back for it."

"Miss Bryant and Lady Jesson had to leave suddenly. However, if you send it up to the house sometime today, I will ensure that she gets it."

"Thank you, my lord."

James looked about him. This place was of interest to Alice, so it behoved him to find out more about it. "Why does this bed have flowers growing amongst the vegetables?

"The marigolds help keep carrot fly off, my lord. It greatly increases the yield..."

James tried to concentrate on what Griffiths was saying, but all he could think of was that he wished it were Alice standing there explaining the finer details of vegetable gardening.

CHAPTER 22

*J*ames knocked on the door of Marstone House, and turned to look over the gardens in Grosvenor Square while he waited. He wanted to get this meeting out of the way so he could give his attention to courting Alice.

"I am here to see Lord Marstone." James handed the butler his card. "I have no appointment as I only arrived in Town last night, but I am sure Lord Marstone will wish to see me."

The butler bowed, a trace of a smile on his face. "Lord Marstone is expecting you, my lord. If you will follow me?"

Expecting him? James rubbed his forehead as he followed the butler through the entrance hall.

He came to a halt in the library doorway, his attention fixed on Alice, sitting on a sofa on the far side of the room. She met his eyes for a moment before her gaze fell to the tea cup in her hands. He shouldn't be surprised—he'd known they would be in London, and would naturally report to Marstone.

He bowed a greeting, not sure what to say. The last time he'd seen Alice she'd dismissed him and disappeared into the morning mist, but he'd spent a lot of time thinking about her since then—about having her in his life and in his bed, and how he might change her mind.

"I hope you had a good journey, Harlford." Marstone came towards him—James hadn't even noticed his presence. "Brandy?"

James nodded his acceptance, and Marstone handed him a glass.

"Lady Jesson has outlined the happenings at Harlford Castle," Marstone went on. "Including the explanation of your correspondence regarding Lavoisier."

"It's too late now," James said, regrets at his failure returning, "but would you have assisted if I'd asked?"

"No. I would not have risked my contacts in France for one man, no matter how good a natural philosopher he might have been."

That made James feel a little better. "There is still the matter of information being stolen."

"Lady Jesson has convinced me you are not to blame for that. However they have not been able to fully investigate your laboratory assistants. There is also the possibility that a member, or members, of your household staff may be involved. Would you explain how and where relevant information is recorded?"

"It would help if I knew what information had been passed on." As James spoke, Lady Jesson and Alice sat a little straighter in their chairs.

"I don't know many details," Marstone replied. "I have only heard reports of trials running into problems similar to yours."

"How do you know...?" James rubbed his forehead again. "I take it you've talked to the people at Woolwich?"

"Yes, once I suspected there may be a problem."

"Are you sure the information isn't being sent from there?" Lady Jesson asked.

Marstone shook his head. "No, I'm not. But given that Chatham and Miss Bryant found signs someone has been observing the quarry where Harlford conducts his trials, at present that seems the most likely source."

"My discussions at Woolwich concern mainly the results," James added. "Not the details of the changes made to the designs of the rockets or the propellant. If they are replicating my work, it does seem that the information must come from Harlford."

"Rockets?" Alice asked.

"I'm sure Harlford will explain at some other time if you are interested," Marstone said. "The exact nature of the information is not particularly important to our enquiry."

"I would be happy to," James said, and a blush rose to Alice's face, colouring her cheeks attractively.

"Harlford," Marstone went on, "could you describe how your experiments are recorded?"

"I keep a daily notebook in the laboratory, in which I record the details of the experiments undertaken and the results."

"The laboratory is kept locked, I take it?" Marstone asked.

"Yes—there are stocks of dangerous substances kept there. I and my two assistants have the only keys."

"Someone could have taken or copied one of those keys," Alice suggested. "Or picked the lock."

"I also write up my notes in a more formal way," James continued. "I keep those notebooks in the library, locked in my desk."

"A situation I assume you will remedy?" Marstone said.

James ignored him, seeing Alice's gaze fixed on the floor. "Miss Bryant, I meant it when I said we should put that behind us."

She looked up at him, and he was pleased to see a small curve to her lips. "Thank you, my lord."

"Your valet might easily have taken and copied the keys to both your workshop and your desk," Lady Jesson said briskly. "Or any of the maids routinely in your rooms."

Or learned how to pick locks, but best not to repeat that.

"None of which gets us any closer," Marstone said. "The man watching the quarry needs to be found—assuming he does return, and has not been frightened off by Chatham's activities. It seems he may only be watching occasionally, either to observe your trials or to check that the laboratory is unoccupied before he enters. With more men at Harlford, a continuous watch can be kept to apprehend the spy next time he appears."

Marstone looked at James, as if for permission. James nodded—it was time to end the leak of information.

Marstone steepled his fingers beneath his chin. "Good. I may attempt to hurry things along a little by letting it be known at Woolwich that you have made a significant breakthrough. Possibly in the War Office, too. If there are people in either of those places passing things along, that might help to flush them out."

"I will not have my family or staff put at risk."

"They would be no more at risk now than they have been for the past few months," Marstone pointed out. "These people are only after information. If anyone might be at risk it is yourself—although I think it's unlikely they'd go so far as to harm a member of the aristocracy. That would attract too much attention."

"The laboratory assistants?" Alice suggested.

"I suppose they could be abducted and made to tell what they know," Marstone said. "But doing so would alert Harlford to the fact that someone is stealing information. If you are concerned, Harlford, find a pretext to send your assistants away for a time. I'll leave that up to you. Chatham can brief the extra men. You need have nothing to do with the matter, other than continue your work."

"Or pretend to do so," Alice said. "In case they succeed in obtaining anything more of significance before they are caught."

"A good point. Are you sure you wouldn't like to continue working for me, Miss Bryant?" Marstone asked.

"Quite sure, my lord," she replied, before James could protest. But in any case it wasn't up to him to tell her what she should or should not do.

"I'm glad that's over," Alice said as they walked to Henrietta Place. She'd been happy to see Lord Harlford, but that feeling had been swamped by wondering what he thought of her now. She'd seen a brief smile when he entered, but after that he'd seemed almost as stiff and formal as when she first encountered him last year. Was he offended by her refusal of his offer, or so indifferent that he'd dismissed her from his thoughts? Either way, it seemed she had been right to say no.

So why wasn't she happy about it? Had she hoped that he liked her enough to want to become better acquainted?

"Our dealings with Marstone?" Maria said. "Yes, indeed. As you so rightly said at the beginning of this business, spying on one's host is very different from merely picking up gossip."

"That wasn't—" Alice stopped. "I mean, yes, of course."

"Weren't you the tiniest bit tempted to work for Marstone again?" Maria asked. "You needn't accept any potentially dangerous assignments. There was no danger this time."

"Apart from my fingers," she muttered, but that had nothing to do with the espionage. It was the notion of prying into other people's private lives she didn't like—many of whom could turn out to be perfectly innocent. What if Lord Harlford's desk had included letters from a lover or a mistress? She would have had to read at least a little of them to determine whether or not they were pertinent to their investigation. Reading that kind of letter from anyone would be intrusive and embarrassing—even more so if they'd been addressed to Lord Harlford.

"Well, Marstone kept his word to pay your salary for the remainder of the year, so you have plenty of time to look for a new position." Maria patted her arm as they walked. "I am enjoying your company, my dear."

"As I am enjoying yours." Going back to being a governess would be difficult.

"Now, Alice, we must take a look at your wardrobe, and see if Simpson can add trimmings to some of your walking gowns to refresh their appearance. You want to look your best when Harlford calls."

Alice stopped abruptly, causing a man behind them to curse as he swerved to avoid bumping into her. "Why would he call?"

"To repeat his grandmother's invitation for us to return to Harlford Castle," Maria suggested. "Come, the street is not the place to discuss this."

They walked on, Alice's thoughts veering from hope that she hadn't completely discouraged Lord Harlford, to fear that Maria must be mistaken. All the logical reasons she'd come up with for refusing him still held, but she hadn't felt happy about it since he'd vanished into the mist.

Should she just have asked him for more time?

"I think we will not be at home to visitors this afternoon," Maria said as they mounted the steps. "Apart from Harlford, of course."

Maria was right, of course. Lord Harlford was shown into the parlour at four o'clock, looking as unapproachable as he had that morning. Alice managed a polite greeting, in spite of her mixed feelings, then Maria took over. She described their journey, and hoped Lord Harlford hadn't been too uncomfortable in the second-best coach.

"Not at all, my lady." He finally relaxed sufficiently to produce a genuine smile. "I'm pleased to have been of service, even if unwittingly." He turned to Alice. "Miss Bryant, you told me we do not know each other well enough. I would like to remedy that, if I can."

She hadn't expected him to be so direct, and a warm feeling spread in her chest. His smile was far from the confident one with which he'd made his proposal only a few days ago—he wasn't taking her agreement for granted.

"Will you both drive with me tomorrow?" He glanced towards the window. "Weather permitting, of course."

"I...I'm not sure that..." To be seen in public with him? A paid companion being escorted by a marquess? "Wouldn't that cause speculation and gossip?"

"I care not what other—" Lord Harlford cleared his throat. "My apologies. I can see that speculation might make things difficult if you... That is, I did not have the public parks in mind."

Alice glanced at Maria, who nodded encouragingly. "I...In that case, I accept your invitation. At what time should we be ready?"

"Would eleven o'clock be suitable?"

"Yes. Thank you."

He looked relieved. "It will be my pleasure. I'm afraid I cannot stay in Town for long. As Marstone is intent on luring the spy into the open, I should return to Harlford soon." He reached into a pocket and took out some sheets of folded paper. "Griffiths sent these for you, Miss Bryant. I gather they are to do with plant breeding. I didn't fully understand what he told me about it. I wonder if you might explain it to me later? You have a knack for making plants seem more interesting than I give them credit for."

"Certainly." Their fingers met as she took them from him, and she blushed at the warm tingle. "Thank you. Do... do you have time to tell me... us... about your rockets?"

"Yes, of course." He glanced at Maria, uncertainly in his expression.

"Please, do explain, Harlford," Maria said. "I will probably understand little of it, but it is at least pertinent to Marstone's current enquiry."

"Are they similar to firework rockets?" Alice asked.

"Yes, but larger. Rockets have been used against our armies in India, to good effect." He paused. "Well, bad effect, from the point of view of the British. The only rockets I could purchase to investigate had a much shorter range than the Indian ones, and far worse than normal cannon shot. When I met you in the British Museum, Miss Bryant, I was on my way to look at some ancient Chinese rockets they have stored away."

He'd been helpful that day—not dismissive as he'd been when he talked about their future involvement in Marstone's investigation. As Maria had suggested, he might only have talked about her helping his research because he didn't know about her agricultural interests.

Maria's eyes glazed as Lord Harlford talked about cardboard and metal casings, different compositions of gunpowder used as propellant, and possibilities for their use. Alice didn't follow all of it, but she was impressed by the depth of knowledge he must have—although she should not have been surprised. The French clearly thought what he was working on was worth stealing.

"Is it not dangerous, to be experimenting with explosives?" Alice asked, when his explanation came to an end.

His fingers went to small scars beside his eye, then he seemed to realise what he was doing and took his hand away. "It can be," he admitted.

Although she was curious to know what had caused the marks—he must have been lucky not to have injured his eye—Alice didn't feel that she could ask. "Thank you for explaining. Lord Marstone said it was vital information going astray, and now I understand why he is so concerned."

He cleared his throat and stood up. "I would not like to bore Lady Jesson further, so I shall take my leave for now."

"We will see you tomorrow," Maria confirmed, and he bowed over their hands.

"He was eloquent enough on the subject of rockets," Alice said, when the door closed behind him. "I found it fascinating, but I'm impressed you stayed awake."

Maria laughed. "I should not complain. Many men of my acquaintance can talk only of horse races or prize fights. But let us hope the weather is fine tomorrow."

Alice hoped so too. She had a fluttery feeling inside her at the thought that Lord Harlford liked her enough to wish to court her still.

CHAPTER 23

The weather was indeed fine, and Lord Harlford arrived at eleven o'clock precisely. He handed them into a landau with the top down before settling himself on the rear-facing seat. Alice saw wicker baskets on the luggage shelf behind, and wondered if they were to picnic somewhere.

"Let us hope the weather remains dry," Maria said, eyeing the puffy clouds with a wary eye.

"I have brought umbrellas as a precaution."

"Where are we going?" Alice asked.

"It is a surprise." He looked directly at her as he spoke, his expression uncertain. "I hope you enjoy it."

"I'm sure I shall." Wherever their destination, the fact that he'd planned something he thought she would like was enough. She hadn't expected him to take so much trouble.

It did seem as if they were heading for Hyde Park after all, but instead of entering at the Stanhope Gate they passed through the turnpike and drove along Knightsbridge.

"I believe you often drove your own pair while you were in Town last year," Alice said, trying to think of something to discuss that would not be beyond Maria's interest.

"Yes. My main diversion is breeding horses, but my current pair is at Harlford. I would have had them brought here had I planned on staying longer. It is a satisfying process, although requiring patience. It takes several years before one can learn how successful the choice of sire and dam has been." He smiled. "With flowers, it must be much quicker."

"If breeding for flower colour or appearance, yes. Finding out if a new variety of grain is more resistant to blight, or whether a cross between apple varieties tastes better—that takes much longer."

Lord Harlford looked interested, but Maria did not, so Alice turned her attention to her surroundings. "Where are we now? I have never been beyond Hyde Park in this direction. Kensington Palace is nearby, is it not?"

"We still have some miles to go," Lord Harlford said.

"Tell me more about your horses, my lord," Maria said. "My late husband took a great interest in his horseflesh, although he did not breed them."

James was relieved to have something to discuss that might interest both ladies, and thankful for the presence of Lady Jesson. He'd invited her as Alice's chaperone, but her easy manner kept the conversation flowing well. They weren't far from their destination when he noticed Alice's gaze fix on something over his right shoulder.

"Is that the pagoda at Kew Palace?" she asked. "I've seen a print of it."

He turned to look. "It is, yes."

Her face held interest, but with a trace of wistfulness, and a pang of disappointment struck him until he realised she had not yet worked out where they were going.

"I would love to visit the gardens," she said. "But I understand they are not open to the public until June."

"I asked Sir Joseph Banks to arrange a private tour for you," he said as the carriage turned onto a bridge over the Thames.

Alice's eyes widened and then a broad smile lit up her face. "Really? Oh, thank you, my lord."

That smile had a strange effect on his insides, quite apart from his relief that he had chosen well when arranging this outing. A warm, happy feeling.

"I wish you would call me James," he said, before he could stop himself.

"I see no problem with that while we are alone," Lady Jesson said. "I, however, would prefer to continue to use your title." Her dry tone removed the slight awkwardness as the carriage drew to a halt in front of a pair of locked gates.

"I hoped you would enjoy a tour. Have you been before?"

"No." Alice's attention was diverted as a man opened the gates, then she turned her smile back on him. "I have only worked in London for a couple of years, and my time off never coincided with the days the public were admitted."

A man emerged from a building beyond the gates, clad in a plain but well-made coat of dark blue. He waited until the carriage came to a halt beside him, and made his bow. "Lord Harlford, my name is Fullerton. Mr Aiton has instructed me to direct your driver on a tour of the grounds, to see the Pagoda and the various temples."

"Aiton is the superintendent," James said to Alice as Fullerton climbed up beside the driver. "Gardener to His Majesty. He will give us a tour of the exotic plants later. Is that correct, Fullerton?"

"Yes, my lord."

Fullerton had a vast store of facts about each ornamental temple, artificial grotto or imitation ruin. His delivery was a little dry, but Alice seemed interested. Watching her face as she took it all in was more than enough to make up for Fullerton's monotone.

When the tour of the gardens was complete, they repaired to the Temple of Bellona, where the footman and driver had laid out the food provided by James' London housekeeper. Aiton joined them as they were finishing. He was younger than Fullerton, perhaps thirty or so, and had a more engaging manner as he guided them around the various beds and hothouses.

Watching as Aiton described the bottlebrush plants recently brought from New Holland, James was amused to see the man's manner change. He'd started by providing simplistic responses to Alice's questions, but his answers became more detailed and specific as it became apparent she knew a great deal about plants and their cultivation.

"This was an excellent idea, Harlford," Lady Jesson said, as Alice and Aiton drew ahead. "Although encouraging the object of your aff... your regard to walk off with another man is an unusual method of courtship."

He looked away in embarrassment—did Lady Jesson know how inept his original proposal had been? The relationship between the two women was clearly more one of friendship than companion and employer.

Lady Jesson smiled. "Tell me, Harlford, do you still think Alice would enjoy being an assistant to your scientific work?"

Alice *had* told her. "I meant it as a compliment to her intelligence."

Lady Jesson shook her head in mock sorrow, but James saw a small curve to her lips.

"I am not skilled at observing people, as you are, my lady, but must you throw all my idiocies in my face?"

She laughed, and patted his arm. "For a man, Harlford, you are doing very well. What think you to building an orangery at the Castle? Your mama was talking about remodelling the grounds."

James grimaced at the reminder. "Mama's plan would be for something designed to impress guests, rather than for growing plants. Alice didn't care for the one Fullerton showed us." Too dark, she'd said, and Fullerton had agreed. "I suspect she would prefer another ordinary glasshouse." If he were lucky enough to make her his marchioness, he would ask her what kind of glasshouse she wanted. She would most likely be capable of designing the whole thing herself.

"I don't want to bribe her," he added, then closed his mouth with a snap. There was something about Lady Jesson that invited confidences—no wonder she seemed to know everyone's business.

"This visit is a bribe, of sorts," Lady Jesson pointed out. "But an excellent one."

"There... there is something you might be able to assist me with."

"By all means."

James had a moment's doubt about taking her further into his confidence, but pressed on. "Mama... I mean, I own an estate near Brighton, and I have informed Mama that she is to move there this summer."

Lady Jesson nodded, her expression politely enquiring.

"I... I hoped you might help to persuade her in some way that... I mean..."

"That Brighton will suit her better than living at Harlford? I think that could be managed." She inclined her head to where Alice and Aiton had passed out of the hothouse and around a bend in the path. "We should catch up with the others."

Alice's head was spinning by the time Maria announced it was time to return. So many new plants to think about: fruits and vegetables as well as ornamental species.

"Thank you for your time, Mr Aiton," Lord Harlford said. "It was fascinating to listen to someone so knowledgeable."

He meant it, Alice thought. Aiton did, too, for he stood a little straighter.

"A pleasure, my lord."

Once the carriage was on the road back to London, Alice tried to thank Lord Harlford.

"No, Miss Bryant. Thank you for your company." He cleared his throat. "I wish I could stay in Town longer so I could see more of you, but I need to ensure that my assistants stay out of the way. I have some business to conduct before I leave, but hope to be on my way tomorrow afternoon."

"So soon? I feel as though I haven't had chance to talk to you much. It was inconsiderate of me to ignore you after you arranged everything so well."

"Not at all. I'm only pleased my surprise wasn't a disappointment."

"Oh, no! I've had a wonderful day." She was touched that he'd arranged something so in tune with her interests.

"I am leaving the travelling carriage you used," he went on. "Along with the coachman and groom. They will look after you should you accept Grandmama's invitation to return, and a few hours' warning to my butler will have the carriage readied. May I hope you will come?" He looked directly at Alice as he spoke.

"I..."

"You will be Grandmama's guests," he added. "And the house party guests should have gone by the time you return."

Alice hesitated. She felt as if agreeing would be committing herself to more than merely a visit. "I... I'm not sure."

"We will let your grandmother know of our intentions shortly," Maria said when Alice glanced at her for help.

Lord Harlford's mouth turned down for a moment. "Of course."

"I... We would be pleased to accept her ladyship's invitation," Alice said, the words coming out in a rush. She didn't like to see him disappointed. She *could* still refuse if he renewed his suit, but she was beginning to think she would not. His smile in response took her breath away.

"We will likely be only a day or two behind you, Harlford," Maria added.

"I look forward to seeing you both there." Having said that, he seemed uncertain what to say next, and Alice felt equally tongue-tied.

"Did you go on a Grand Tour, Harlford?" Maria asked. "I have heard much about the beauties of Venice and Florence."

"I did, yes. I met Signors Volta and Galvani. The latter allowed me to observe some of his experiments."

"On animal electricity?" Alice asked.

"That's right, although I understand Signor Volta now thinks that..." He cast a doubtful look at Maria as his words trailed off. "I beg your pardon, Lady Jesson. It cannot be of interest to you."

"Do go on, Harlford," Maria said faintly.

"I would be interested to hear more," Alice said. "Truly, my lord."

As Alice listened, she enjoyed the enthusiasm he showed for his experiences as much as the knowledge of science he was imparting, and was sorry when they reached Lady Jesson's house and had to part company.

~

James arrived at the instrument-maker's premises the following morning as the clerk was unlocking the door. Stonecroft had written to him only a couple of weeks before with news of a new device to measure gas pressure; such an instrument would be most useful if James ever had time to investigate the efficiency of steam engines.

He examined the wares in display cases while the clerk went to find his employer. In addition to measuring devices of every description, Stonecroft's cabinets held all manner of optical instruments: telescopes, sextants, microscopes...

Microscopes. He'd never needed one himself, but Alice might appreciate such a device to examine flowers and seeds. Which to choose, though?

"Welcome, my lord!" Stonecroft bustled in through the back door, his leather apron stained and his magnifying lenses pushed up to his forehead. "Have you come about the new pressure device?"

"I have, yes, but I might also be interested in one of your microscopes. You have many types—would you explain the differences between them?"

"Certainly!" Stonecroft pulled a key from his pocket and unlocked the microscope cabinet. "The choice of instrument depends on the use to which it is to be put."

"I... I have a friend who is interested in botany."

"A lady or a gentleman?"

"It's for... my sister." He had yet to persuade Alice to marry him. "Why is that relevant?"

"Ladies enjoy collecting and painting flowers, and have little need for anything more than a magnifying glass. If your sister wishes to examine her items more closely, a simple instrument such as this would be suitable." He removed a microscope from the cabinet and set it on a table. It consisted of pair of fat vertical tubes, one nested inside the other, mounted above a couple of three-legged platforms. "This is a Culpeper design, and is simple to operate." Stonecroft demonstrated how to focus by adjusting the inner tube.

Lucy might like that one, if she truly did enjoy looking at magnified objects. He wasn't sure she would have the concentration to learn how to use some of the more complex instruments in the cabinets.

But Alice's interest went well beyond simply painting flowers. "She is a serious student of botany. What about this one?" He pointed to a brass device, its tubes, mirrors and platforms mounted so their positions could all be adjusted. A little box that appeared to hold tiny lenses rested on the shelf beside it.

"Ah, that is based on a Simons design. Not really suitable for a lady, not at all."

As the instrument-maker talked of changeable lenses, moveable platforms, slides, and coverslips, James wondered what it would be like for an intelligent woman like Alice to be told she was incapable of using what, to him, looked like a relatively simple device.

"...and so, as you can see, this is far too complex for a lady to use," Stonecroft finished.

"Thank you for explaining," James said. "Now, I would like to see the new pressure device, then I will take both microscopes. I think the Simons one will suit my...sister...very well."

CHAPTER 24

*J*ames walked around to the stables while his luggage was being unloaded at the main entrance to the Castle. He'd see how the new foal was doing, then change out of his travel-worn clothing before going to see Grandmama.

"Stablemaster's with Lord David, my lord," one of the grooms informed him, pointing to a stall further down the building.

"The foal?"

"Out in the paddock with his dam. He's doing well. Lady Lucy wants to call him Zephyr."

Another wind name—a good choice. James nodded his thanks, and the groom returned to forking hay.

He found his uncle inspecting one of his own mares with the stable master. David raised a hand in greeting, but continued his low-voiced conversation with Pritchard.

"Sorry about that," David said, when he joined James a few minutes later. "I was concerned she was favouring her right front leg. How did things go in London?"

"Come for a walk." James wasn't going to say anything where the stable hands might overhear.

David collected his coat from a peg by the door and shrugged it on as they crossed the stable yard. "Are the ladies to return?"

Did *everyone* know his business?

"Come, James. I returned to the Dower House a couple of days ago —you can't expect me *not* to ask my mother what was happening." He grinned. "Or her not to tell me."

"Lady Jesson and Miss Bryant will be returning in a day or so."

"Excellent." David did look pleased. "And the other business?"

They were beyond the stable block now. "Marstone is sending half a dozen men to try to apprehend whoever is watching the quarry. Chatham will organise them, and they will pretend to be grooms here."

"Good idea—difficult to hide that many newcomers to the area otherwise."

"So if you could mention—subtly—that you're staying for a while and will be buying some hunters...?"

"By all means."

"*Are* you planning to stay? In England, I mean."

"Yes. I enjoyed Italy, but this country is home."

"That's good." David was someone he could confide in, should he feel the need. He had Grandmama, too, but some things could only be discussed between men.

"I'll be looking for an estate to buy," David said. "But for now Mama's happy to have me live with her in the Dower House. I may well find myself some new horses in reality."

"There are several Harlford estates unoccupied. Why not use one of those?"

"Good of you, but I fancy a place of my own. I've the funds for it," David added. "Investments, and so on."

"Let me know if you change your mind. I'll see you at dinner, Uncle."

James stood at the door of his laboratory, watching his assistants walk away. Norton had accepted his unexpected week's holiday without question, just grinning and thanking him. Sumner, however, had not looked entirely convinced by James' explanation that he wanted to carry out some tests that might be dangerous.

"An idea that came to me at Woolwich," James had said. Sumner didn't know he hadn't been to the explosives laboratory since March. "If you haven't enough to do, you may examine the old copies of the *Mémoires* of the *Académie des Sciences* to see if you can find any promising new lines of research."

"I... I don't think my French is up to that, my lord," Sumner admitted. Successfully distracted, he hadn't questioned James further.

Could Sumner be involved? He had a sharp mind—which was why James employed him.

The laboratory was tidy—bench cleaned, floor swept, all his chemicals and instruments stowed in their cupboards. Exactly as it should be left. And exactly as the spy would expect to find it, if he were in the habit of breaking in overnight.

But if Marstone's tale of a new breakthrough had been passed on from someone in London, the spy would expect to find some new information at the very least, even if not experiments in progress. On the other hand, if it really was such a breakthrough, would a spy expect him to leave his day to day notes here in the workshop with only a padlock on the door?

James rubbed one temple. Attempting to work out what someone else might think was giving him a headache.

A spy would look for new information here first. If he succeeded in evading Chatham's men and found nothing here, he would assume the information was at the house.

Would a spy attempt to break in there? It was possible, but he would post footmen as guards overnight. No-one would find guards strange if he mentioned hearing reports of thieves being abroad.

That settled, James picked up his current notebook and left, inspecting the padlock before he turned the key. There were no unexpected scratches or other marks on it, but that didn't mean anything. A skilled thief must be able to pick a lock without leaving a trace.

~

"It should be good weather for our village tours," Maria said.

They were less than an hour's drive from Harlford Castle; Alice had been gazing at the passing scenery and the streaks of white clouds against a blue sky. She brought her attention back to her companion. "Village tours?"

"Marstone sent a note asking us to continue our investigations into Harlford's assistants."

"Oh." Alice's pleasant anticipation of the coming visit faded. She'd thought this spying business was done with.

"Chatham's extra men will take care of some of that." Maria was clearly not concerned about Simpson overhearing. "They'll do any following and watching required, naturally. But discovering more about the backgrounds of the assistants is another line of enquiry. Sumner, in particular."

Reluctant though she was to resume their spying activities, the situation did need to be resolved—and at least this time she would not be spying on Lord Harlford. "Won't people become suspicious if we keep visiting those two villages and talking to people?"

"We will visit others as well. But Mrs Anderson's cakes should be sufficient reason to go to Luncot again."

"Lord Harlford said we could leave it all to him." The high-handedness of that statement had irritated her at the time, but she didn't want to ignore what he'd said. Not now she was beginning to change her mind about marrying him.

"How well do you think Harlford would succeed in discovering possible motivations for treachery in his assistant?"

Alice had to chuckle. "He'd probably just ask him outright."

Maria smiled. "Each to their own. I wouldn't know one end of a rocket from the other."

"He... do you think he will mind if we continue? He did say..." What exactly had he said? Only that they needn't bother with it. "He didn't forbid us to continue."

"I should hope not. He has no right to give either of us orders."

He would have the right to give her orders if she accepted his offer. Would he, though?

"Maria, we should tell him that Marstone asked us to continue."

"It would be impolite to do otherwise," Maria agreed, but the gleam in her eyes suggested that Lord Harlford would not have an easy time of it if he tried to stop her.

Alice returned her attention to the passing countryside, recognising the village of Harlford Green as they passed through it, before they swept past the stone lions guarding the entrance to the estate.

The butler showed them into the parlour, where the dowager sat in her usual chair, overlooking her garden and the lake. "Welcome back," she said as Alice and Maria were announced, and ordered tea and cakes.

Alice eyed the gardens with regret—she'd been in the coach for hours, and had no wish to sit and drink tea.

"Why don't you go and say hello to Tess?" Maria suggested. "Take her for a walk. I can pass on all the news."

"Yes, do go, my dear, if you want some exercise," the dowager added. "Now, Maria, tell me…"

∾

James slowed Ventus to a walk as he turned through the gates to the estate. As he rode along the drive, a woman left the stable block on foot.

He drew Ventus to a halt, a giddy sense of relief surprising him. Alice—he would have recognised her even without the huge dog beside her. Although she had accepted his invitation, he'd still had a lingering doubt about whether she really would come back.

Alice passed out of sight behind the Dower House, so he turned Ventus onto the grass to circle around the other side of the building to meet her.

She saw him and stopped, one hand going to her bonnet and then smoothing down her skirts. His uncertainty rose as he dismounted, his pleasure in seeing her here countered by the fear that he would say something wrong.

"Welcome back," he said, as she dipped a curtsey. "I hope you had a good journey." The dog snuffled around his boots, then wandered off.

"Thank you, yes. It was very kind of you to leave your coach for us, my lord." Her smile seemed hesitant.

"James. Please."

"I... very well. You... you must call me Alice, then."

"Thank you." He felt awkward, standing facing her like this, each seeming as tongue-tied as the other. "Shall we walk on?" He led Ventus with one hand, and she took his other arm. "Have you been here long?"

"No, we've only just arrived. I always want to take a walk at the end of a long journey."

He grinned. "As do I."

She smiled briefly.

"Is there something wrong?" he asked, when she said nothing more.

"Er..." She stopped and faced him again. "Lord Marstone wrote to Maria and asked us to continue to investigate your two assistants, my... James."

Is that why she's here? He dismissed the sudden doubt—if Marstone wrote to them, his request must have been made after she'd agreed to return.

"What is it that worries you?" He wasn't going to allow them to endanger themselves, but some caution made him keep that to himself.

"I hoped not to have to deceive..." She waved a hand. "And you said we should not investigate any further."

"I undoubtedly said many things I shouldn't have, for which I apologise. I was rather dismissive, I admit, but I will try to do better in future." Her tentative smile cheered him. "How do you and Lady Jesson intend to investigate?"

"We will visit the nearby villages and Maria will talk to people. She can extract an astounding amount of information from people without them minding, or even noticing sometimes." There was amusement in her eyes as she glanced up at him. "I think you have been spared the experience, so far."

"For which I am suitably grateful, believe me."

Alice chuckled. "She means well."

"And needs to be kept safe, as do you." He hoped she would not take his next statement amiss. "I do not like the idea of either of you putting yourselves at risk..." He felt the hand on his arm tense. "...but I will not try to stop you." The hand relaxed. "I wish you would consider having your man with you if you are doing anything that might put you in danger."

"That would be sensible, yes. And Tess." Alice looked around as she spoke. "Tess!" The animal darted out of a nearby coppice and ran up to them. "She doesn't really belong to Lady Jesson. Lord Marstone sent her to give me or Chatham an excuse to explore the grounds."

She was looking straight ahead, as if not wanting to meet his eyes.

"It did seem an unlikely legacy." He stopped and stood in front of her, so he could see her face. "Are you really her companion?"

"I am, although Lord Marstone paid my wage for a year. Monsieur le Comte decided Georges needed a tutor to prepare him for school. I could have returned to my home while I looked for a new position, but Lord Marstone presented this task as my patriotic duty, and also to clear you from suspicion." She looked away.

"Alice, I meant it when I said that should be put behind us. Although if you have any further secrets...?"

"No."

"No stock of invisible ink?"

Her lips twitched.

"No bodies buried in the garden?"

She shook her head. "Tess eats them."

He laughed out loud. "No cellars full of stolen treasure?"

"Now you are being ridiculous!" But she was laughing.

"Tell me more about your home, Alice. Is that where you acquired your interest in botany?"

CHAPTER 25

*A*lice reined her horse in at the end of the field, laughing with the exhilaration of the gallop. Lucy's mount pulled up beside her, skittering a little. Further along the hedge, James and Lord David jumped into the next field and galloped on.

"Oh, well done, Alice." Lucy's face showed the same enjoyment that Alice felt. "On a strange horse, too! The gate's this way." Alice fell in beside her as they rode along the hedge at a walk, flexing the fingers of her left hand.

"She's a lovely animal." Alice leaned forward and patted the mare's neck. "And it's a beautiful day." The warmth of the sun didn't quite take the bite from a fresh breeze, but that wasn't a problem while they were riding.

She'd been wary of accepting James' invitation, issued at dinner last night, as she hadn't ridden often since she started working for the Comte de Calvac a couple of years ago. When she mentioned that, James promised to select a docile mount for her, but one with energy to spare when called for. Even so, she wasn't going to risk jumping without practising somewhere more private first, not to mention her stiff fingers not allowing her to grip the reins properly.

The gate into the next field stood open. "Are you staying long?"

Lucy asked, as they went through to see James and Lord David cantering towards them.

"I'm not sure." She was becoming more certain that she would accept if James renewed his addresses. *If* he did—she tried to ignore the hollow feeling caused by the idea that he might not.

They had walked and talked for nearly an hour yesterday; they had started discussing their scientific interests, but had soon moved onto their favourite walks and rides, and then to music. He'd dined with them, too, although the conversation at table had been mostly about Lord David's time in Italy. At whist, after dinner, she had been paired with James and they had lost badly, the warmth in his expression when their eyes met destroying her concentration. He hadn't seemed to mind.

James had a good seat on a horse, she reflected, watching as the men approached. The grin on his face was as wide as hers must have been—it was lovely that they shared an enjoyment of riding.

He halted beside them. "Time for some refreshment? The Golden Lion in Woodley serves a fine table."

"Are we so close?" Alice remembered the inn from her trip with Maria to try to find information on Sumner. The seed cake had been particularly good.

"We've looped around." James brought his horse up to ride next to her, and pointed with his whip. "The Castle is only a couple of miles that way, beyond those woods."

"I will have to look at a map." Her mind hadn't been on their route this morning, but on the pleasures of the countryside. And the company.

"Come to the library this afternoon," he said. "There are plenty of maps there of the local area, and of other parts of the country. I also bought something for you—and for Lucy—before I left Town."

"I can't..." She cleared her throat. "I mean, I'm not sure about..."

"You do not commit yourself to anything by accepting a gift."

She looked away. "I'm sorry, I didn't mean to presume—"

"You didn't presume. If you wish, think of it as a gift from a friend."

Alice nodded. He'd mentioned Lucy as well, so it didn't seem as if he might wish her to make her decision today. Her feelings were telling her to say yes, but her head still recommended caution.

"Come on, you two!" Lucy called from ahead. They were in Woodley now, and dismounted outside the Golden Lion. Lord David stayed with the horses until a groom came to take them. Inside, out of the breeze, the landlord was taking payment from another customer, but bustled over when he recognised Lord Harlford and showed them to a private parlour.

Alice wandered to the window, watching as the horses were led away and the previous customer left. The man turned, and their eyes met briefly as he pulled his collar up and walked off. There was something familiar about him, or his clothing, perhaps, and the fleeting scowl on his face made her wonder if he recognised her. But she couldn't recall where they might have encountered each other.

"Alice, come and choose. There's apple pudding, or seed cake."

Distracted momentarily by Lucy's call, Alice turned back to the window but the man had gone. She would ask the landlord about him before they left.

The afternoon sun slanted through the library windows. James stood looking at the gardens below, as he often did when he had something to think about. This time he was waiting to see if Alice would come, although he'd done his best to ensure she would.

He heard Lucy's voice in the hall, and moved to the table where he'd set up the basic microscope.

"Here we are, Jamie! I've brought Alice, like you said." She almost bounced along the library. "Is that my…. Oh!"

She gaped at the microscope, and James wondered if he'd made a mistake.

"You said you enjoyed looking at the drawings in *Micrographia*," he said. "I thought you might like—"

"A microscope, for me? Oh, this will be fun. Thank you!" She pulled up a chair and examined her gift more closely.

Alice turned a smiling face to him. "It was too bad of you to tell Lucy she could not have her gift if I did not come!"

"I wanted to be sure you would be here. I thought it might interest—"

"How does it work?" Lucy asked.

James sighed at the interruption, but Alice didn't seem to mind. "You need to make a thin slice of what you wish to examine." Lucy and Alice listened carefully as he explained about glass slides, mirrors, and how to focus the image, managing to recall most of what he'd been told.

"The man in the shop assured me it was simple enough for even a young lady to use," he added, keeping a straight face.

"Jamie!" Lucy was suitably indignant, and scowled at him.

Alice frowned, and he hurriedly retrieved the box containing the more elaborate instrument from a cupboard behind him . "That's why I bought this one for Alice." Taking it out of its case, he set it on the table.

Lucy peered at it. "Ooh, that looks complicated."

"You said you were interested in fleas and flies, Lucy, and I think yours is better for that. Alice's is for looking more closely at tiny parts of things."

Alice put a hand out as if to touch it, then drew back. "I... This must be expensive. I cannot—"

"Do you like it, though?" He tried to keep anxiety out of his voice, surprised at how much her answer mattered to him.

"I would love to have an instrument such as this, but I cannot accept it. I thought you were going to give me something small, such as a book."

She wanted it. Her reluctance to accept—well, he'd anticipated that.

"There is a book," he said, pushing the instruction pamphlet towards her.

"You know what I meant." Alice reached out to touch it again.

"I do, and I'm sorry for teasing you. If you must, please consider it as something for you to use while you are here. A loan, if you will."

He delved into the cupboard and took out the final box. "I didn't know what you might wish to examine, so I had Griffiths send some things from the garden." He spread a cloth on the table, then set out a jar containing a selection of different seeds and several small pots with plants. "He assured me these are things you showed an interest in, but just ask if you wish for samples of anything else."

Alice swallowed a lump in her throat at the care he'd taken over the gift. "Thank you. It's… it's a perfect… gift." With Lucy listening, she could not say more.

"Jamie, help me to look at this leaf," Lucy commanded, and James sat in the chair beside her. Alice opened the instruction pamphlet and began working her way through the explanations. Although Lucy's excited chatter faded into the background, she was aware of James sitting across the table from her, and giving only half his attention to his sister. He smiled when he caught her looking, and she felt her cheeks blush as she returned her gaze to the microscope.

He had bought everything needed. The case for the instrument included a small box containing glass slides, and a cunning device with a sharp blade for taking thin slices of plants.

"This is wonderful." She had managed to focus on a sample of pollen from some delphinium blooms. One of her correspondents had been discussing ways of breeding wheat to improve the amount of grain per plant—she could examine slices of different seeds to see if anything could be discovered that way.

Who had it been? Someone she'd written to recently. "Cromhall. I'll write to Mr Cromhall and—" She realised she had been thinking aloud, and looked up to find the other two staring at her.

"Who is Mr Cromhall?" James asked. "After you and Lady Jesson moved to the Dower House, one of the maids found a half-written letter from you to a Mr Cromhall."

"Someone I correspond with about agriculture," Alice admitted, relieved to see that James looked puzzled rather than censorious.

"A neighbouring farmer?"

If he was going to object to her writing, best to find out now before she... before she came to like him even more.

"No, I have never met him. He sent a letter in response to something I'd written."

"Oh!" The exclamation came from Lucy. She dashed down the library, and reappeared a few moments later with one of the bound copies of the *Journal of The Society for the Improvement of Agriculture* that Alice had referred to a couple of weeks ago. "You marked these pages, didn't you?"

"Yes. I... I've had several articles published in the journal."

"Really?" James pulled the volume towards him, opening the pages.

"I'm 'Mr Eden'," Alice admitted, before he could ask the question.

James turned the pages, stopping at an article she'd written the year before. "I read some of these before I set off for London," he said, his expression thoughtful. "The ideas were very clearly expressed. But why the false name?"

"Don't be silly, Jamie," Lucy said. "Do you think the men in charge would publish something from a *woman*?"

"It seemed wiser not to risk rejection," Alice admitted. "I could not then submit similar articles under a false name without arousing suspicion."

"Sadly, I suspect you are correct."

Alice felt suddenly light, as if a burden had been removed. Although they had talked about her interests, she'd still wondered what he would think about her engaging in public correspondence.

"So you *were* still keeping a secret yesterday?"

Oh, yesterday's walk. "We'd been talking about Lord... about other things." In truth, she'd forgotten about it at the time. "There really are no more secrets now."

"You told me you wouldn't mind a clever wife, Jamie," Lucy said, before James could reply. "I hope you meant it."

Alice blushed.

"Not only do I not mind, young lady, but I relish the prospect. You, however, need to learn tact and discretion."

Although his words sounded stern, the tone was not. Lucy laughed. "I'll do that when you learn to stop scowling, Jamie! Can you find me a dead fly to look at?"

"Find your own dead creatures—you'll have to touch a fly to examine it, so there's no use being squeamish about finding one."

Alice tried to keep her attention on her microscope, but the banter between brother and sister was endearing, and she felt a rush of pleasure at the idea of being able to call Lucy a sister.

"You seem distracted," Maria said that evening as they sat by the glass doors in the parlour, looking out as the fading light changed the colours in the garden to shades of grey. The dowager had retired for the night, and James and Lord David had gone to the main house for a game of billiards.

"Just admiring the view," Alice said. Which she was, although the view was not foremost in her mind.

"All that could be yours." Maria tilted her head towards the Castle and its reflection in the still waters of the lake.

"That's not why I would..." Alice stopped—Maria knew her better than that. "There is no need to tease me. Besides, he hasn't repeated his offer."

"He will. Why else would he go to the trouble of arranging the visit to Kew, and buy you a microscope?" Maria regarded her more closely. "That's not all that is bothering you, is it?"

"Lady Harlford," Alice said. James' mother would not approve. If she accepted, James would be caught between his wife and mother. She was not going to let Lady Harlford ride roughshod over her in the interests of domestic peace.

"Cassandra. I can see why you might not wish to live in the same house as her, but don't worry about it. I understand she is to remove to another estate. However it would be rather... delicate, for him to discuss domestic arrangements for his future wife until you are actually in that position, don't you think?"

"Yes, I suppose so."

Maria stood, and patted her shoulder. "Sleep on it, my dear. There is no hurry to make a decision."

And there was still the business of the spy to deal with.

CHAPTER 26

"I'm afraid you'll have to listen to Mrs Anderson's gossip this time," Maria said to Alice as the carriage came to a stop by the village green in Luncot. "You won't want to wander around the churchyard in this breeze."

What started as a sunny morning had clouded over, and the wind was cold for late May. Alice thought she might prefer the outside chill to an hour or so of gossip, but she accompanied Maria into the haberdasher's shop, leaving Tess with Chatham. The groom—another of Marstone's men—walked the horses.

They went straight to the table near the fire, Maria announcing that she had come to sample Mrs Anderson's wonderful ratafia biscuits again. The other occupants of the tea room—a mother and daughter, Alice guessed—fell silent, inspecting Maria's clothing and bonnet, then moving on to Alice.

"Please, do not let me interrupt," Maria said. "This is such a lovely village, I just had to come back. Do you take tea here often?"

"I... er... once a week, when we come to do the marketing." The younger woman spoke hesitantly.

Maria adjusted her chair a little to face them. "Do you have to come far?"

That was all it took. Alice marvelled at the way Maria managed to set them at ease and listen with apparent interest while they described their house in a neighbouring hamlet.

Not *apparent* interest, she corrected herself. Maria really was interested in all the details. The chat was doing nothing towards their goal of finding out more about James' two assistants, but Maria would get around to that eventually. And in the meantime, the ratafia biscuits were very good indeed.

They were deep into a discussion of Mrs Yaxley's married daughter's latest baby when Alice noticed Chatham walking past the window. He met her gaze, then gave a small jerk of his head before walking on.

Alice was quite happy to join him. "Excuse me, Maria. I need to fetch something from the carriage."

She didn't wait for a reply, but stood and slipped out of the shop. Chatham was waiting a few yards down the street, out of sight of Mrs Anderson's windows.

"Is something wrong, Chatham?"

"Don't look round right now, miss, but there's a cove going door to door across the other side of the green."

Alice almost did look, but managed to keep her face towards Chatham.

"Thing is, miss, I reckon I've seen him before, on that track through the woods from Harlford Green. He's got his back to us now. Tess took an interest when he walked by."

She turned her head. The stocky figure in the green coat looked like... no, it *was* the same man she'd seen in the Golden Lion the previous day. He had a satchel slung over one shoulder. And now she recalled where she'd seen him before—here in the village when they'd come with Lucy and Miss Stockhart a couple of weeks ago.

"He was in Woodley yesterday," she said. "I asked the landlord about him, but all he knew was that the man drank there from time to time. He could have business in all three places."

"That's possible, miss. But that coat looks the right colour to match the scrap I found by the path the watcher uses. Can you find out what his business is without drawing attention?"

Alice smiled. "If anyone knows, Mrs Anderson will," she said. "I'll see what we can do."

"That's Mr Thompson," Mrs Anderson said half an hour later, when the two Yaxley women had finally left. "He comes around every month to collect life assurance money."

That would also take him to the surrounding villages, and explain Chatham seeing him on the track. There must be many men with green coats, although she didn't recall seeing any of that particular shade.

"I've seen notices about that in the papers," Maria said. "But I thought people subscribed annually, or half-yearly."

"There's some men would drink the subscription money if they had to save it for that long," Mrs Anderson said. "He comes around collecting once a month, so people can pay a little at a time."

"Does he live here?" Alice asked.

"No. He tried to sell me assurance when he first came, but I've no use for it. About a year ago, it was, or a little longer. He was very nice —has a snug little house in Hereford, he said, and a wife. Said he enjoyed the job in the summer, but it wasn't as pleasant having to ride around the county in the winter. Can't say as I like being out of doors myself, whatever the weather, but there's no accounting for taste."

"I thought I saw him here last time we came," Alice said. "That was only about three weeks ago, or a little less."

Mrs Anderson fell uncharacteristically silent, her brow creased in thought. "You're right," she said at last. "That's strange—he usually comes regular as clockwork."

"That's very dedicated of him." Maria pushed her cup and plate away. "I've enjoyed our little talk, Mrs Anderson, but I'm afraid we must be going. Would you be so kind as to wrap up four of those little cakes for me? I cannot get enough of them."

. . .

"I saw him yesterday in Woodley," Alice said as they walked towards the carriage, and reminded Maria about the scrap of green material. "Do you think we should try to find out if he calls on Sumner?"

"That would be sensible," Maria said.

Chatham agreed, after they told him everything they had learned. "It's him breaking the pattern that's suspicious. If someone in London got word of Lord Marstone's story about a new discovery, they'd be looking into it about now. Maybe I'll have a pint or two in the inn."

"It's a hard life, Chatham," Maria said, with a sad shake of her head.

"Indeed it is, my lady." Chatham kept a remarkably straight face as he touched his forehead and climbed onto the box next to the driver.

"I assume we will be calling on Mrs Sumner?" Alice asked, as the carriage set off along the road to Woodley. "What excuse can we give for calling?"

"Hmm. Taking a note from Harlford to Sumner would get us inside, but we'd have to avoid leaving it there."

"And if Sumner is at home, you'd have to give it to him right away," Alice pointed out.

"Not one of my better ideas," Maria admitted. "One of us will have to feel faint right outside their door. Enough to need a sit-down and a glass of water." She looked at Alice's face. "I think it will have to be me —you look far too healthy to be feeling faint."

Alice still didn't like the idea of using deception to talk to Mrs Sumner, but now they did have something specific to enquire about. "Very well, we can try that."

The Sumners' house was one of the pretty half-timbered buildings in Woodley, with a bow window either side of the door and a narrow strip of garden along the front, bright with sweet Williams and delphiniums, and fragrant with the scent of roses. Alice and Maria walked past it on the other side of the street before returning for Maria's little piece of play-acting. The spits of drizzle in the air would help their subterfuge.

Although no-one was about, Alice still hesitated before knocking. But they'd decided this had to be done.

A plump maid answered the door, and Alice asked if her friend could have a glass of water. The maid looked at Maria, leaning against the low gate-post, and stood back.

"Best bring her in, miss. I'll tell Mrs Sumner."

Maria leaned convincingly on Alice's arm as they entered. The maid showed them into a parlour, then disappeared down a passage towards the back of the house. A table at one end of the room held a bowl of fresh roses, and a clock ticked gently on the mantelpiece above the crackling fire.

Mrs Sumner was a pretty young woman with soft blonde hair and a shy smile. She carried a glass of water in one hand, and offered it to Maria.

"Jenny says you aren't feeling well. I'm Mrs Sumner; is there anything else I can get you?"

"It's very kind of you to allow strangers in," Alice said, as Maria sipped the water. "I'm Alice Bryant."

"Maria Jesson," Maria introduced herself. "Thank you, my dear. If I may sit for a little while?"

"Would you like some tea?"

"Thank you, that would be lovely."

Mrs Sumner was gone for only a few minutes, and returned with a baby in her arms. "I hope you don't mind." She sat in a facing chair, bouncing the child gently on her knees. "Dora's teeth are beginning to come through, and she's not happy about it."

"Of course not," Maria said. "What a darling baby. How old is she?"

Alice had little to do as Maria talked, but rose to pour the tea when Jenny brought the tray in. By the time they had drunk it, Maria had worked around to hearing how lucky it was that John had such a good position working for Lord Harlford, and how reassuring to know that they would not be destitute if anything should happen to him, thanks to the policy he paid into. Dora lay quiet in her mother's arms, seemingly soothed by the gentle voices.

They were interrupted by a knock on the front door. The baby stirred, and Mrs Sumner walked to the window. "Why, here is Mr Thompson again. I didn't expect him to come back today."

Thompson?

Alice stood—the man hadn't seen Maria before, as far as she knew, but he had seen *her*. It would be better if she were not here.

"Excuse me." She slipped out of the room as Jenny trod along the passage to open the front door. If all was well, she would return when Thompson left. If not, she could fetch Chatham.

The passage led to a kitchen, filled with the smell of hot linen. A couple of flat irons stood on the stove, and a pile of folded sheets rested on the table above a basket of crumpled ones.

Hide or leave?

Leave—she could explain that by saying she'd needed some fresh air. A door to one side of the kitchen stood ajar, and a draft of cool air told of a rear entrance.

But the back door, when she reached it, was blocked by a large man with ginger hair in homespun coat and breeches. Someone she'd never seen before. He stepped forward as she paused, and one hand shot out to grip her upper arm.

"You're staying 'ere."

~

James ascended the stairs in cheerful anticipation. He'd had a good meeting with one of his tenant farmers, and now he hoped to find Alice in the library with her new microscope.

He'd ridden out with Terring to check on the steward's claim that barn repairs were needed—something he should have started doing long ago. The farmer and his wife had been pleased to see him, and happy to show him their fields. Terring's diligence should improve if he knew James might check on his activities at any time.

Or if Alice might.

James smiled—if they married, it was likely she would prefer to spend her time supervising the tenant farms rather than running the household.

A fire kept the outside chill from the library, but the place was unoccupied. The microscope was missing too—had Alice taken it down to the glasshouse, to be closer to the things she wanted to examine?

Halfway to the kitchen garden, he paused to wonder why it felt so urgent to locate her.

He wanted to see her, that was all. He could tell her of his morning, or ask about hers.

"She was here, my lord," Griffiths said, when James ran him to earth in the potato patch. "Left a couple of hours ago. Said something about Lady Jesson, but to leave her microscope set up if it wasn't in the way."

Were they out on Marstone's business? He was tempted to go to the stables to check, but Alice had promised they would not go alone. Instead he went into the glasshouse to take a look at what she'd been doing.

He regarded the tidy pile of glass slides with approval—each labelled with a square of paper pasted to one end. Putting one onto the stage, he was soon absorbed in hitherto unknown structures of plant stems and roots. There might be more to botany than he'd thought.

Alice's heart raced as the man pulled her towards the parlour, where the baby was wailing. Thompson stood behind Mrs Sumner's chair, one hand gripping her shoulder. Alice took in the woman's white face before she noticed the pistol in Thompson's other hand. She swallowed hard.

"Caught 'er trying to escape." The man thrust Alice towards the sofa where Maria had her arm around the maid. Jenny's head was bowed, hands clenched so the knuckles showed white.

"Can't you stop that damned brat wailing?" Alice's captor added.

"Why don't you let the maid take the baby away?" Maria suggested, only a tiny waver in her voice.

As Alice sat down, Thompson looked from the baby to the maid. "Stand up, girl."

With a sob, Jenny did as she was told.

"Take the brat upstairs and keep it quiet." He waved the pistol. "See this?"

Jenny's head bobbed but she didn't speak.

"You do anything stupid, like try to leave, or tell anyone, and your mistress will be dead."

"Do as he says, Jenny," Mrs Sumner said.

The maid sniffed and wiped her nose on one corner of her apron, before taking the crying baby from Mrs Sumner's arms. She looked back uncertainly as she reached the door.

"Get on with it!" Thompson spat.

With a final sob, Jenny left. They followed her progress by the creaking of the stairs and the fading sound of the baby's cries. Then there was only the crackling of the fire and the ticking clock, and faint whimpers from Mrs Sumner. That meant two people less likely to be hurt, at least.

Thompson let go of Mrs Sumner and pulled up a chair to sit beside her. Mrs Sumner buried her face in her hands.

Alice's heart slowed and she tried to think. How much did these men know?

"Why are you doing this?" Alice felt a movement beside her leg and put her hand down. Maria gripped it tight, but with a perceptible tremor. Her friend was nowhere near as composed as she appeared—which didn't help calm Alice's fear at all.

"That man of yours is asking questions in the pub. You've been following me around—I've seen you near the quarry and in the villages. You should have minded your own business."

"I don't know what you mean."

Thompson shrugged. "Doesn't matter. Keep your mouth shut or you'll die. Bill here can do that without making a noise."

Alice glanced at the pistol—a shot would attract attention, perhaps bring Chatham to help. But that was too dangerous an option.

Bill cracked his knuckles and Alice gritted her teeth. Where *was* Chatham? The spies hadn't captured him as well, had they?

Thompson turned his attention back to Mrs Sumner and prodded her shoulder with the muzzle of the pistol. "Let's try again. Where's your husband?"

The woman's shoulders rose as she took a deep breath, then she put her hands down. Her face showed resignation now.

"He went to talk to a neighbour." Her voice was so quiet Alice had to strain to hear it.

"So he'll be back soon?"

Mrs Sumner nodded, her lips trembling again.

Thompson got up and drew the curtains almost closed, then threw another log onto the fire. "We can wait."

CHAPTER 27

*J*ames straightened and rubbed the back of his neck. If he were to spend any more time peering through a microscope, he'd have to set it on a higher bench, or get a better chair.

He'd gone from looking at plants to examining sand and grit, wondering if anyone had used a microscope to investigate the grain sizes and shapes of different mixes of gunpowder. Something to ask about, definitely—that might affect the burning speed.

One hand went up to finger the skin beside his left eye. He'd been lucky last summer—if he'd been any closer to the exploding glass vessel, or looking directly at it, he could have lost the sight in that eye. If he managed to persuade Alice to accept him, it might be time to think of investigating something less dangerous.

"My lord!" Griffiths burst into the glasshouse. "Come quick, my lord, there's one of the new grooms needs to speak to you."

He hurried outside to see one of Marstone's men doubled over, one arm braced against the wall. As James broke into a run, the man stood upright, chest heaving.

"Chatham sent me, my lord. The... Lady Jesson and...They've been..."

"Breathe, man." James's stomach knotted—Alice was in danger.

He tried to put from his mind the prospect of her being harmed, of living his life without her if she were killed.

Think!

"Griffiths, run to the stables and tell them to saddle a couple of horses."

The gardener took off at a run.

"I already asked for horses, my lord," the groom gasped out between breaths.

"Lady Jesson and Miss Bryant?" James prompted impatiently.

"They're in Sumner's house, in Woodley, with Sumner's wife. Thompson and another man are holding them there."

Damn—he should have taken more precautions to keep them safe. Sumner had a baby, too.

"Who is Thompson?"

"Chatham thinks he's the one we're after."

"How did you and Chatham let—?" He broke off. How it happened didn't matter, not now. The groom's breathing had returned to normal, so James set off for the stables, the groom striding along beside him. "Where is Chatham? And why are you on foot?"

"He's keeping watch. I rode one of the carriage horses back—left it in the stables. Had to ask where to find you."

"Sumner?"

"Don't know, my lord. Chatham sent me off as soon as we found there were two armed men in the house. He looked through the window while that dog was making a noise at the back."

"How many are at the quarry?" They could collect them on the way to Woodley.

"Four. Bates should be in the stables here."

"And you are...?"

"Doyle."

That was all six of the men Marstone had sent.

"Are you armed?"

Doyle nodded. "We all are."

"I'm going to fetch my pistols. Wait for me in the stable yard. Get enough horses saddled for all of you, in case we need them. Oh, and send one of my grooms to find Lord David." He wasn't sure what his uncle could do, but then he wasn't sure what he could do either. Not without risking someone getting killed.

~

The air in the parlour felt heavy, stifling. They had only been waiting twenty minutes, but it felt much longer.

Alice moved a little way along the sofa, wondering if she could change position sufficiently to allow her to see through the gap in the curtains. They must have been missed by now—would Chatham try to rescue them?

She had thought he might earlier, when a dog barked behind the house. It had sounded like Tess. But apart from Thompson sending Bill to check that the back door was bolted, nothing had happened.

There was nothing she could do now, except stay alert in case an opportunity presented itself. Beneath the cover of their skirts, Maria's hand gripped hers again.

Thompson sat with his pistol in his lap—watchful, but not tense. Bill fidgeted in his chair.

The sound of the latch on the front door was loud in the silence.

Chatham?

"Sally, I'm back!"

Alice's brief, irrational flash of hope vanished. Sumner had come home.

Mrs Sumner lifted her head, then returned her eyes to the floor as Thompson raised his pistol. He looked at Alice and Maria, laid one finger across his lips, and silently moved to stand behind the open door, gesturing for Bill to join him.

Footsteps sounded along the hall, then Sumner stopped in the doorway. He was a fresh-faced young man, with fair hair tied loosely back. His cheery smile faded and his brows rose as his gaze fell on Alice and Maria. Alice turned her head sideways in an attempt to warn him, but it was too late.

Thompson stepped out from behind the door and held his pistol to Sumner's temple. A little whimper came from his wife.

"Sit down and say nothing." Thompson pushed him into a chair.

"Thompson? What—?"

Thompson cocked the pistol with a loud click, and Sumner fell silent.

"You will do exactly as you are told," Thompson said, bending so his face was within inches of Sumner's. "In a minute, you're going to accompany me to the laboratory. You are going to walk through the village as if nothing is wrong, and you will not attempt to warn anyone."

Sumner's throat worked as he swallowed hard, turning his face towards his wife.

"Your brat is upstairs with the maid. Bill will stay here. If I am not back in two hours, it will be the worse for them. If you want them, and your wife, to stay alive, you do exactly what I say." He thrust his face even closer. "Clear?"

Sumner nodded. He reached a hand towards his wife, but Thompson grabbed his arm and jerked him out of the chair before he could make contact. The two men left, the slam of the front door behind them sounding very final.

Alice twisted around in her seat to see if they passed the window, but turned back at the sound of a pistol being cocked.

Bill wasn't pointing it at her, but at Mrs Sumner.

"You do anything you shouldn't, Missy, and I kill 'er, then the babe."

"We're not going to do anything," Maria said. "But someone will be searching for us by now. You won't get away with this."

"She'll die." Bill jerked his head towards Mrs Sumner without looking away from Maria.

"Do you think Lord Harlford will care about someone like her getting hurt?" Maria asked, and Bill's brows drew together. "And are you *sure* Thompson will come back for you?"

"'Course 'e'll come back." But Bill looked less certain than he had before.

"Once he's got what he wants, he can escape much more easily alone," Alice put in. "If you leave now, you might get away before anyone finds out what you've done."

"Shut your mouth! Both of you!"

Maria pressed Alice's hand. They'd sown doubt, Alice thought, seeing the way Bill's glance moved nervously from one of them to the other. It might not make any difference in the end, but it had been worth a try.

Someone would come to help.

They must.

James and the two grooms rode for the quarry, leading horses for the other men. He'd have to find Chatham in Woodley before he could plan a rescue.

He turned at a shout from behind, to see David galloping towards them. James waved the grooms on, and slowed his horse to a walk until his uncle caught up.

"What's happening, James? I got some garbled story—"

"Alice and Lady Jesson are being held hostage in Woodley. Two men, that's all I know."

David patted his pocket. "Brought my pistols. Ride on."

They'd only got a few yards into the woods when they came to Bates and Doyle talking to a third man.

"Harris has been watching, my lord," Doyle said.

"Your man Sumner is here," Harris reported. "Had someone else with him. Didn't see no gun, but Sumner, he didn't look happy. They went inside."

The women were at Sumner's house, Doyle had said. If that were the case, the second man could be one of the ones who had been holding them.

"They left the door open, my lord, and Adams got close. He's trying to listen."

"Mount up, Harris," James ordered. "We'll leave the horses outside the quarry so they don't hear us coming."

James spotted Adams listening outside the door as soon as he walked around the bend in the path leading to the quarry. Adams had seen him, too, for he raised a hand in acknowledgement. He stayed by the door for a few minutes longer before picking his way towards James across the loose rock on the quarry floor. He said nothing until they had retreated along the path to the clearing where they'd left the horses.

"He's trying to get Sumner to tell him about new findings, my lord." Adams kept his voice low, even though they were some distance from the building. "Sumner claims he doesn't know anything."

"Green coat?" Doyle asked, and Adams nodded. "That's Thompson, my lord."

"He said it would be the worse for Sumner's wife if he didn't find the notebooks," Adams went on. "Said there was only an hour left now before Bill started hurting Mrs Sumner."

James rubbed a hand across his face. Alice was in danger, as well as Lady Jesson and Sumner and his family. But now the two men—if there were only two—were separated.

Numbers—he must think about the number of men he had at his disposal, and *not* about Alice being frightened and in danger. He needed to keep a clear head.

There were plenty of men here to capture Thompson. But Thompson was expected back, so killing or capturing him would risk the lives of three women and a baby in Woodley. More than three, if the Sumners had servants.

Attempting to use Thompson as a hostage would not help. What motivation would he have for convincing his associate to let the women go? As a traitor, he would hang, and only a fool would believe a promise to let him go free.

If he could get into the house somehow, could he and the women prevail against Thompson and the other man? He would have men outside ready to take a hand.

It was all he could think of.

He turned to David. "Chatham is probably still in Woodley. Will you take some men and see what the situation is there? Rescue the women if you can see a way of doing so without endangering them."

"What are you going to do?"

"Go in there and find out more about what's happening. Possibly get myself taken *into* the house with Thompson."

David's brows rose. "Is that wise?"

"They want to know what they think I know—now they've learned that Sumner can't help them, they're not going to kill me." He hoped that was true.

"We could capture this spy," David suggested.

"No." James explained his reasoning. "And if we break into the house, even if there is just the one man there, he could shoot one of the women before he was overpowered."

"Very well." David nodded.

"Doyle, you heard? Take two men and go with him." David could find more men to help him in Woodley, if that became necessary.

As the small party left, James turned to the remaining three.

"Adams, when I go in, listen if you can. But stay hidden unless I give you a signal."

"Yes, my lord." Adams had an air of competent determination about him, as did all of Marstone's men.

"I can't tell you what to do after that. It depends what happens."

Adams nodded, and James mounted his horse. The watcher—if indeed Thompson was the watcher—would know he usually arrived on horseback. He made no attempt to keep quiet as he rode up to the laboratory. If he was unsuspecting, he wouldn't be expecting to see the door ajar, so he called out as he dismounted.

"Sumner, is that you?"

He got no reply. Surprised at how he was managing to think clearly despite the lump of dread that had settled inside him, he pushed the door open.

Sumner stood at the far end of the room, white faced. A man in a drab green coat stood a few paces from him, his pistol pointed at Sumner's head.

"What the devil is going on, Sumner? Who is this?"

"He's got my wife, my lord. And two of your guests." Sumner's voice wavered. "He'll kill—"

"That's enough, you." Thompson stepped away from Sumner, and turned the pistol towards James. "Turn out your pockets. I want to see you're not armed."

James' hand went towards the pistol in his coat pocket.

"Stop! Take off your coat. Put it on the floor."

Perhaps that was just as well—he couldn't have taken a shot before Thompson fired, and would probably have only got himself killed. That would not help Alice.

Thompson stepped forward and patted the coat, taking out the pistol and transferring it to his own pocket.

"Information about your research, *your lordship*—that's what I want. This man claims he doesn't know anything."

"He doesn't," James said. "Why would I tell him anything? He just washes the glassware."

Sumner's eyes widened a little at this lie, then his shoulders straightened. Good man—he might be of some use.

"Information," Thompson repeated. "I want your notebooks."

"By all means," James said. "My notebooks are at the Castle; you'll have to come with me to fetch them."

"I'm not that stupid," Thompson spat. "You always keep them here —where are they? They're not in their usual place."

"Do feel free to look." James waved a hand at the cupboards lining the walls.

"You show me. Open the doors."

"May I?" James asked, indicating his coat. Thompson gave a brief nod and James put it on. He walked along the row of wall cupboards first, leaving each door standing open. He'd never had a gun pointed at him before, but he wasn't too worried as long as Thompson thought he needed him to get the information he was after.

Ten minutes later, Thompson had peered into most of the cupboards, ordering James to empty a few of them and flick open some of the books. He was competent, James had to admit—he didn't allow either of them to get close enough to attempt to wrest the gun from him.

A distraction…

Not for now, because the women were in danger if Thompson did not return. But a distraction might be useful later, even though he didn't yet have a plan. He backed down the row of cupboards, stopping by the one that held stoppered jars of various chemical compounds and mixtures. Sumner was watching—he knew as well as James what was stored in there. He tilted his head to one side, a slight movement, and James gave a small nod.

"You said two hours, Thompson."

Thompson turned towards Sumner at the unexpected statement, and Sumner stepped backwards, knocking over a stool and falling to the floor.

It was enough. James reached swiftly for a bottle, and had it safe in his coat pocket before Thompson looked back.

"I told you my notebooks are at the Castle," James said. "I can fetch them."

"You can write down what you know. I'm not letting you come back here with extra men."

"Two hours," Sumner repeated. "You said we would be back in two hours."

It was a couple of miles from here to Woodley—half an hour if they'd walked fast. Half an hour back, plus the time they'd already spent in here…

"It'll take me an hour or more to write it all down." James wondered if he was sounding too compliant. But Thompson must have been confident in the effectiveness of his threats.

"We'll do it at his house, then." Thompson gestured at Sumner. "If either of you try anything on the way, the women will suffer."

CHAPTER 28

he clock on the mantel ticked the seconds and minutes away. Alice had moved from her place beside Maria once in the hour and a half since Thompson had left, and only after gaining Bill's permission to add a couple of logs to the fire.

Tess had barked again, half an hour ago. At least, it had sounded like Tess, outside the front window this time, and she'd felt hope that a rescue was imminent. Bill had looked out of the gap between the curtains, but turned his gun on her as soon as she attempted to stand. She'd half expected Chatham to break in, but the sounds of the house had settled back to the slow tick of the clock, and the hope changed back to the feeling of dread that seemed to fill her chest.

By now, Alice thought she would be able to draw the pattern on the rug by heart in spite of the dim light. She'd surveyed the room for possible weapons, and come to the same conclusion each time. The poker and a heavy brass lamp atop a bookcase could be useful—but both were well out of reach. Should she manage to get hold of one, she doubted she'd have the strength to overcome Bill even if she took him by surprise.

Help *would* come.

How precise had Thompson intended his two-hour threat to be?

And what would happen when Thompson did return? She'd been trying to ignore the thought that he'd have no reason to let them go, and every incentive to leave no witnesses to his actions.

With fifteen minutes to go, Bill went to the window.

Alice couldn't take the waiting any more. It was foolhardy to push the man's patience, but help didn't seem to be coming. This might be their only chance of escaping from the house before Thompson returned. "What will you do if they don't come back?"

"Keep quiet, woman." He scowled at her and returned to his seat.

"I'm only curious," Alice said. "It's been a long time. He might have gone off and left you. If you do as he said and he doesn't come back—"

Bill pointed the gun at her. "I said keep quiet!"

Maria squeezed her hand in warning, but Alice pressed on. Once Thompson returned they would have no chance of talking their way out of the situation. "Do you really trust him to split the money with you when he could just take it all while you hang for murder?"

There was a sound from the gate and Bill turned to the window. "Ha—told you! They're back."

"It's me, Bill," Thompson called as the front door opened.

"Sally?" Sumner rushed in and knelt by his wife's chair. "Sally, are you harmed?"

Mrs Sumner said something in between sobs, but Alice didn't hear it. James stood in the doorway, his head turning as he scanned the room. He'd come for her!

Her relief at seeing him lasted only an instant. What was he doing here? He'd put himself in danger, walking in like this.

"Are you well, ladies?" James came into the room, and removed his hat and gloves as if he were on a social call. But the intent look he turned on Alice belied his apparent lack of concern.

"Quite well, thank you," Maria said, a quaver in her voice.

"No one's been hurt." Alice managed to keep her voice steady.

James nodded, but the intensity of his gaze did not change. "I've come to write some notes for Thompson, then we'll all be free to go."

"Less talking," Thompson growled from his position by the parlour door. "There's a table. Get on with it."

"May I open the curtains?" James asked. "It's far too dark in here." He waited until Thompson gave a reluctant nod, then walked to the window and pulled both curtains back. Alice blinked in the sudden brightness.

"Paper? Ink?"

"See to it, Sumner," Thompson ordered.

Sumner looked at Thompson, then at James. "They're in the other room."

James nodded. Hope rose in Alice—it seemed James had a plan.

"Go with him, Bill," Thompson ordered, and the two men left.

James looked at Mrs Sumner, still sniffling into a handkerchief. "My dear chap, I really cannot concentrate with that noise. Why don't you send the women upstairs?"

"You think I'm stupid? They're what'll keep you in order."

"She's only a workman's wife," Maria pointed out. "I told—" She put her hand to her mouth, as if she'd said something she didn't mean to.

Thompson's gaze fell on Alice. "She stays. You..." He pointed at Maria. "Take her upstairs and keep her quiet."

"Very sensible," James said, as Maria rose and helped Mrs Sumner to her feet.

"Remember, you can't escape, and your husband'll suffer if you try."

Maria put her arm around Mrs Sumner. "Come, my dear." Thompson stood back to give them room to pass, then resumed his position by the door.

The stairs creaked as they ascended. Alice was relieved that her friend was now out of danger, as well as Mrs Sumner, and tried to suppress a wish that she'd been the one sent upstairs.

"I'll need a lamp," James said, looking at the one on the bookcase. The lamp that she'd identified as a possible weapon. Her pulse began to race. Was he about to try to overpower Thompson? But Thompson was too far away—James would be shot before he could get close enough to attack him.

"Bill will move it when he comes back."

Alice could still hear creaks from the stairs, but now it sounded like someone coming down. Thompson didn't seem to have noticed—his attention was all on James, now rubbing his hands.

"Can I put another log on the fire? Can't write with cold fingers."

Thompson merely nodded, waving his gun.

James bent over the fire, placing a log carefully. He met her eyes as he stood, and made a small shooing motion with his fingers.

He'd put something on the fire! She shuffled to the far end of the sofa, her heart beating faster still. He worked with explosives…

"About bloody time," Thompson muttered, backing towards the fireplace as Sumner returned. There was a curse and scuffle from the hall just as a strange fizzing noise came from the fire.

"What—?"

Alice threw herself to the floor as a sheet of flame shot from the fireplace, then there was a bang and all she could hear was a ringing in her ears.

The fizzing gave James a second's warning. Thompson spun around, pointing his pistol towards the fire, and James vaulted over the back of the sofa and flung himself towards him, the two of them falling to the floor.

The gun—where was the gun?

Thompson's mouth was moving but James couldn't hear anything beyond the ringing in his ears. He pressed on Thompson's shoulders to push himself up, one knee on the spy's chest while he grabbed the flailing arm that held the pistol. Thompson heaved, tipping James sideways. James held on and pulled Thompson with him—better keep hold of the gun hand, even if he ended up on the bottom. The fire…

He kept rolling, kept hold of his opponent. The clatter of fire irons as Thompson fell into them penetrated the buzzing in his head. There was a howl of pain and the hand holding the gun went limp. Crashing sounds must be someone else fighting—Alice? Was Alice safe?

Pushing himself away, James saw that Thompson lay unmoving on the burning embers that had been scattered across the hearth and rug by the exploding gunpowder, and a trickle of blood ran from one temple. James picked up the gun and scanned the room, looking for Alice.

Bill lay on the floor, with two of Chatham's men tying his hands behind his back. Alice was picking herself up—James strode over to her, uncocking the gun and putting it into his pocket. He took her hands in his. He saw no trace of blood, but—

"Are you hurt?"

"No." Her voice was quiet. Although she'd appeared calm, she was trembling, and he pulled her close. She rested her head against his shoulder as he put his arms around her. Thank God his improvised distraction had not harmed her.

She felt right in his arms, where she belonged. Safe. The tension in her began to relax, and he turned his attention to what was happening around him.

David came down the stairs, Lady Jesson behind him.

Down the stairs?

"Glad to see you managed this one on your own." David poked Thompson with the toe of one boot. Chatham had found some cord and was trussing up the spy, ignoring his moans of pain. One of the other men threw a bucket of water over the burning embers on the rug, adding the smell of wet wool to the stench of sulphur and burning. James looked up—the mantel and the wall above it were blackened, and there were scorch marks on the ceiling.

His distraction had worked, but it might easily have made things worse.

Alice stood safe in the circle of James' arms, her hands resting on his chest. His solid closeness calmed her—warming her from inside as the ringing in her ears gradually subsided.

She'd looked up after the explosion to see James wrestling with Thompson, but there was nothing she could do to help. Sumner had vanished from the doorway, and Bill staggered into the room, one arm twisted behind his back by Chatham.

How had that happened?

It didn't matter now. She was safe.

More than safe. Content. Happy, even, in spite of the stink of gunpowder and burning wool, and the sounds of distress from upstairs.

"Alice?" Maria appeared at her side, gripping her arm.

"She is well." James' voice rumbled in her ear.

"I am... I am uninjured." Alice reluctantly removed herself from James' embrace. She wasn't quite sure yet that she was well. "How are you? The others?"

"Mr Sumner is comforting his wife," Maria said. "The baby and the maid have been with a neighbour for the last hour, apparently. Chatham and David used Tess as a distraction and put a ladder up against a back window to get them out. When I got upstairs with Mrs Sumner, they were waiting."

That explained some of the creaking she'd heard—Chatham creeping down the stairs to tackle Bill.

"Alice, I'm so sorry I involved you." Maria put a hand on her arm. "I never thought—"

"It's over now," Alice said. "Neither of us thought it would come to this."

"What happened here?" Maria asked, looking at the blackened wall.

"A minor diversion," James said.

Alice stifled a giggle at James' understatement. Then she put a hand to her mouth—that giggle had held more than a hint of the vapours.

"Explanations later," James said. "Alice... You and Lady Jesson need to get back to the Dower House. David?"

"I'll have the landau brought round," Lord David said, and left.

"Four of the grooms will accompany you," James added. "They are all armed. I don't think there will be any more spies, but please stay in the Dower House once you arrive."

"I will have no desire to leave the house," Alice said firmly.

"Nor I." Maria shuddered.

"I would come with you, but I need to make sure all is settled here."

"We will be all right," Alice said. Although she wished for nothing more than to be held in his arms again, he had things to deal with here.

~

It was late afternoon by the time James was shown into the parlour in the Dower House. To his relief, he found only Alice and Lady Jesson there, looking out at the rain now obscuring the view. They turned towards him, then Alice blushed and smiled.

"I will inform her ladyship you are here, my lord," the butler said.

"No!" James cleared his throat. "I mean, I have called to see A... Lady Jesson."

"Is all settled?" Lady Jesson asked, when the butler had gone.

This wasn't the main reason he'd come, but the two of them deserved to know what was happening.

"As far as it can be," he said. "Thompson and his associate are both injured, but not too badly to travel. Chatham has already set off for London with them so Marstone can question them in person."

"Are they the only two involved?" Alice asked.

"Chatham thinks so, but it is not certain. I suspect Marstone will find out more."

"Is Mrs Sumner well?" Lady Jesson asked. "Poor woman."

"Sumner has taken her to stay with her mother for a few days, while their parlour is repaired. Sumner..." Sumner had been hurt to learn he'd been kept in the dark about the spy plot. "He... Well, it wasn't..."

"He wasn't happy to find he'd been a suspect," Lady Jesson suggested.

"No. Understandably."

"Thompson..." Lady Jesson said. "Did he not make himself rather conspicuous by posing as a life assurance man? I assume it was a pose."

"I imagine so," James replied. "I will enquire, but I wouldn't be surprised to find he's unknown in the villages a few miles further from here. As to being conspicuous... he would probably have drawn more suspicion if he was seen in the area regularly with no obvious reason for being here. Calling at Woodley and Luncot may have allowed him to gather information about my two assistants. He most likely pocketed the subscriptions he gathered."

"So all those people have not been providing for their future after all," Alice said.

"I've sent a note with Chatham for Marstone to extract as much detail of that fraud as he can, and get his man of business to look into it. I'll make sure no-one loses by it."

"Good of you, Harlford," Lady Jesson said.

"The estate can afford it," he said, but his mind was no longer on the spy.

The way Alice had stepped into his embrace this afternoon... Did that mean she would accept him if he asked again?

He'd come here to see her, to reassure her that she was in no further danger, but also to renew his addresses. The limp way she sat in her chair, and the signs of strain on her face gave him pause. If she were to accept him, he didn't want it to be the result of a decision made when she was tired and still recovering from what must have been a terrifying experience.

As he was gazing at Alice, Lady Jesson stood. "If you will excuse me, Harlford, I think I'll take Tess for a walk."

She left the room before he could point out that it was still raining. But this was Lady Jesson, who noticed *everything*—and whom he'd never seen walking the dog alone.

"Not very subtle," James said. "I do wish to talk to you alone, Alice, but I don't think now is the best time. Would you accompany me on a drive tomorrow?"

She looked up, that lovely blush reddening her cheeks.

"I would like that."

CHAPTER 29

$\mathcal{A}$ lice was idly examining the box hedges in the knot garden when James walked around the lake from the Castle. She'd managed to eat some rolls with her morning coffee, but suddenly the food sat leaden in her stomach. The weather was fine, so there was no reason for him not to have brought his phaeton around to the front entrance for their drive. Had he changed his mind?

He came through the gate and approached her. "Good morning. I trust you slept well?" His face was serious—worried, even.

"Yes, thank you."

"I'm sorry for the change of plan, but it struck me as rather unwise to drive around the countryside without an escort until Marstone has satisfied himself there is no further threat."

She was touched by his concern. But why did he appear uneasy?

"Will you take a turn in the gardens with me?" He held his arm out, and she laid her fingers on it. Then his other hand rested on hers, and her doubts began to dissipate as they walked.

"Miss Bryant... Alice. I... I should inform you that my mother will be removing to an estate near Brighton within a few weeks."

Alice nodded. "Maria said something about that, yes."

"I wondered if her presence might have been..." He cleared his throat. "That is… I mean, I think we have got to know each other a little better during the last couple of weeks."

Warmth grew inside her, but he rushed on before she could speak. "My feelings towards you have changed. Deepened, I mean, not…" He drew a breath. "I… I did not realise how much until yesterday, when you were in danger. Am I too precipitate in renewing my addresses? I said many things that day that I regret—"

"No."

His arm stiffened, and he came to a sudden halt.

Heavens, had he misunderstood? "I mean, no, you are not too precipitate." She pulled her hand free and stood facing him.

"I… Oh. Good. I mean…" He swallowed hard. "I… You… I am not expecting you to help me with my work, as I said before. Unless you wish to, of course. I would not discourage you at all. But you may have…I wish for you to feel free to—"

"James." Her words had not been loud, but he stopped speaking. "Yes."

"Yes?"

It might be forward of her, but she couldn't let him continue to tie himself into verbal knots. "If you are asking me to marry you, my answer is yes."

He appeared dazed, then her heart turned over at his smile.

"I think I had decided before yesterday," she admitted. "But I knew for certain, in that cottage, that I love you and could not bear to lose you."

She held her hands out and he took them. Then he did as she had hoped, and drew her into his arms. This time there was no comfort involved, but a fizz of excitement at the feel of his body against hers.

"I love you, too, and I will do my best to make you happy," he promised. "And not to tell you what you may or may not do."

"There is one thing you may forbid me to do, with my hearty agreement," she said, smiling at the surprise on his face. "You may forbid any further involvement with Lord Marstone's business."

"Forget Marstone," he said softly. He bent his head towards hers, and their lips met. The kiss was gentle at first, but when she responded to the brush of his tongue along the seam of her lips, he drew her closer. Or she pulled him, she wasn't sure. This was a new sensation, warmth gathering in her belly as the kiss deepened and his hand on her back held her closer still.

They broke apart at the sound of steps on the gravel path. Breathless, Alice turned to see Maria approaching, a broad smile on her face. "I take it I am to wish you happy?"

"You are." James drew Alice's arm into his again.

"Your grandmother will be pleased." Maria glanced back at the house. "If you wish to walk on, might I suggest the woodland?" She waved at the patch of trees that bordered the path around the lake.

James looked around—celebrating Alice's acceptance in full view of the Dower House might not have been his best idea, but he couldn't regret it. Not even seeing her blush of embarrassment.

"I will come in and see Grandmama soon." He waited until Lady Jesson was out of earshot before turning to Alice. "Much as I would like to resume our... activities, there are a number of practicalities to discuss. Shall we walk?"

She sighed, but smiled up at him as she took his arm and they strolled along the path, their bodies closer than before. "Do you... I mean, where will we be married?"

"Do you wish to be married in London?" He didn't want a wedding in full view of the *ton* in Hanover Square, but he would arrange it if that was what she wanted.

"I would prefer to be married here, at the church in the village."

"Not from your brother's house?"

Alice stopped, gazing across the parkland. "No. This will be my home—for most of the time, I think?" She turned her face up to his, a question in her eyes.

"I hope so, yes. I will need to spend at least part of the season in Town each year if I take up my seat in the Lords, but I prefer living here."

"Good."

She did have a lovely smile.

"The local people—your tenants, the villagers—many of their lives depend on the Castle. I think it would be nice to... to not hide away on the estate. Having the wedding here will be easier for your grandmother to attend, too."

He tore his attention away from her mouth. "It would, yes. She would be disappointed not to come, and although she will not admit it, she would find a journey to London or Wiltshire too tiring."

"You could have a feast for the staff and villagers as well."

"*We* could..." He stopped and turned to face her. "Alice, I mean for our life to be a partnership."

"I... thank you." She still appeared uncertain, her gaze now on the Castle. "There is one Lady Harlford who will definitely not be happy."

"Mama. No, she will not be pleased, but she will not be here."

Alice still had a small crease between her brows. "There's your sister-in-law, too, and all the staff in the house. I've never—"

"Arabella will be happy to have another young woman in the house. She has the training to run the place, too, even though Mama never relinquished control when my brother married. I'm sure she'll help, if you need it, and Grandmama can provide advice. Besides, a competent housekeeper should be able to manage things without much supervision." There would be time enough later to ask if she wished to oversee the farms. "You will have plenty of opportunity for your own pursuits. Or Mr Eden's pursuits."

The worry disappeared, and she smiled, properly this time, with a twinkle in her eyes. "May I have a new hothouse?"

He wasn't sure if she was being serious, but he was when he answered. "As large a hothouse as you wish. Consider it your wedding present."

"I... really? Oh, thank you." Her smile widened, and she took his arm, turning him to continue along the path. "There are many things to be decided, or planned. But we can take as much time as we need to."

"That is true."

"I expect there are many interesting trees in the wood."

He laughed: at her demure expression—which he didn't believe for a moment; at the knowledge that he was to marry a woman who wanted him as he wanted her. He suspected—hoped—they would study a great deal of nature, in one way or another, in the years to come.

One year later

At first glance, the new building against the outside of the kitchen garden wall looked like a random assortment of scaffolding poles and building materials, but James could discern order in the chaos. The structure itself was finished, and workmen were fitting the final pieces of glass in the long south wall. The piles of left-over building stone would become the edges to raised vegetable beds—or so Alice informed him—and it wouldn't take the workmen long to clear away the rest of their tools and scaffolding.

Things were considerably more organised inside. Alice sat in a chair directing footmen where to place the heavy benches that would be used to hold seed trays and arrays of pots. Tess lay on the floor beside her. The animal had been a wedding present from Chatham, who had decided that she would be happier living in the countryside, and he would get himself a smaller dog.

James turned to survey the inside of the building. The stone-flagged floor had been swept, and several of the maids from the Castle were busy cleaning the windows.

"It's looking good." He stopped beside Alice and gave her shoulder a squeeze. "Are the pipes hot yet?"

The building was long but narrow, with a series of pipes running along the back wall. James put a tentative hand on one—warm, but not hot.

"Warm enough to show the boiler's working," Alice said. "I shouldn't need the heating until the autumn."

"It certainly feels like a hothouse already." James ran a finger inside his cravat. "How's the little one? This heat cannot be good for you or him."

"Her." Alice patted her swollen belly. "But you're right about the heat. I can send Griffiths to supervise the rest."

"You are pleased with your wedding present, then?"

She smiled as he reached to help her up from the chair—she was becoming ungainly now, although as beautiful as ever to his eyes.

"How could I not be pleased?"

He was glad of it. She'd spent weeks working on the plans, writing letters as Mr Eden to ask advice from other horticulturalists, drawing and redrawing, and consulting Griffiths, before finalising the details. This was her domain for experimental plants, leaving the existing glasshouse to Griffiths for the fruit and vegetables required for the castle. He hoped she wouldn't spend *too* much time in here without him, but perhaps there might be some chemical investigations connected with agriculture that they could work on together.

Alice took his arm, surprised when he set off for the east end of the building instead of the door to the orchard. That end of the hothouse was walled off to make a little office, already furnished with a desk, shelves to hold record books, and a bench under the window where she would use her microscope.

She paused as they entered. A tea pot, cups, and plates of cakes were laid out on the desk, and an extra chair set ready.

His face reddened slightly. "It is a year to the day since we had tea and cakes in Griffiths' glasshouse."

She was touched—not only that he had remembered something from a time when they hardly knew each other, but that he'd thought to repeat it. "Thank you, James. That's lovely."

He held the chair for her, and poured the tea. Leaning over tables was becoming more difficult, and she would be glad when the baby made an appearance and she could sit and stand properly again.

The time since their wedding had been idyllic. They'd gone to his Northumberland estate for a wedding trip. James had promised her castles, beaches, and heather-clad hills, but it was the time they'd spent alone together that she valued the most. Time without the distractions of home.

"This time next year, you'll be fighting off suitors for Lucy's hand," Alice said, and chuckled at his grimace.

Lucy had matured in the last year, helped enormously by the absence of her mother. Without Cassandra looking down her superior nose at them, the local gentry were happier to visit and bring along their sons and daughters, and invite Lucy to visit them in return.

"Not to mention trying to stop Mama marrying her off to someone chosen for his rank alone," James said. "I'm relying on Maria and David to help out there."

It would be Alice's debut in society, too, as a marchioness. By that time, she hoped, any gossip their marriage had caused would be long forgotten.

But those problems, if they were to be problems, were a long way off. Before then, there would be a child. A boy, James insisted; a girl, she proclaimed. But neither of them minded—God willing, there would be more to come.

HISTORICAL NOTES

ROCKETS

I've changed history here, for the sake of giving James something interesting to research.

Rockets for use on the battlefield or on naval vessels were designed by Sir William Congreve in 1804, so around a decade after this story. They *were* based upon rockets used against the British in India, as James said. Research and development took place at the laboratory at the Woolwich Arsenal.

LAVOISIER

Antoine Lavoisier was a real scientist (although that term was not in use at the time), and what James says about him in the story is correct. Some of you may remember learning about his work on theories of combustion and other matters in science lessons. His wife did help him with his work, as a laboratory assistant. She was involved in making notes and accurate diagrams of his apparatus, and translating scientific works from other language to help him keep abreast of new developments—a task that involves a fair degree of scientific knowledge. She was also responsible for publishing much of his work after his death.

FRENCH REPUBLICAN CALENDAR

The cryptic note James receives at the beginning of the story mentions Germinal—the name of one of the months in the French Republican Calendar. This was in use from 1793 to 1805, and started at 'Year 1'. If you look at French fashion plates from the time, you may see 'An.1' or similar—these are years in the Republican Calendar.

In some ways, it is a pity it is no longer in use, for I like the names of the months. For example the spring months are Germinal (from the French for germination, starting in March), Floréal (flower, starting in April), and Prairial (meadow, starting in May). Other months translate loosely as harvest, summer heat, fruit, vintage, mist, frost, snowy, rainy and windy! They are much more descriptive than the names we use.

THE POT AND PINE APPLE

You may be more familiar with this establishment as Gunter's, but it was called the Pot and Pine Apple until a change of ownership in 1799.

LINNAEAN CLASSIFICATION

For the real bluestockings (like me!):

The Latin names given by Alice in the museum were the classifications at the time. As knowledge of biology and genetics has advanced, scientists have found links between different species not apparent from their physical features, and the biological groupings have been changed.

Swallows are still *Hirundo rustica*, but common swifts are now *Apus apus* rather than *Hirundo apus*, and house martins are *Delichon urbica* rather than *Hirundo urbica*.

AFTERWORD

Thank you for reading *The Fourth Marchioness*; I hope you enjoyed it. If you can spare a few minutes, I'd be very grateful if you could review this book on Amazon or Goodreads.

The Fourth Marchioness is Book 4 in the Marstone Series. Each novel is a complete story with no cliffhangers.

Find out more about the Marstone Series, as well as my other books, on the following pages or on my website.

www.jaynedavisromance.co.uk

If you want news of special offers or new releases, join my mailing list via the contact page on my website. I won't bombard you with emails, I promise! Alternatively, follow me on Facebook - links are on my website.

ABOUT THE AUTHOR

I wanted to be a writer when I was in my teens, hooked on Jane Austen and Georgette Heyer (and lots of other authors). Real life intervened, and I had several careers, including as a non-fiction author under another name. That wasn't *quite* the writing career I had in mind!

Now I am lucky enough to be able to spend most of my time writing, when I'm not out walking, cycling, or enjoying my garden.

THE MARSTONE SERIES

A duelling viscount, a courageous poor relation and an overbearing lord—just a few of the characters you will meet in The Marstone Series. From windswept Devonshire, to Georgian London and revolutionary France, true love is always on the horizon and shady dealings often afoot.

The series is named after Will, who becomes the 9th Earl of Marstone. He appears in all the stories, although often in a minor role.

Each book can be read as a standalone story, but readers of the series will enjoy meeting characters from previous books.

SAUCE FOR THE GANDER

Book 1 in the Marstone Series

A duel. An ultimatum. An arranged marriage.

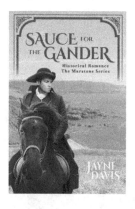

England, 1777

Will, Viscount Wingrave, whiles away his time gambling and bedding married women, thwarted in his wish to serve his country by his controlling father.

News that his errant son has fought a duel with a jealous husband is the last straw for the Earl of Marstone. He decrees that Will must marry. The earl's eye lights upon Connie Charters, whose position as unpaid housekeeper for a poor but socially ambitious father hides her true intelligence.

Connie wants a husband who will love and respect her, not a womaniser and a gambler. When her conniving father forces the match, she has no choice but to agree.

Will and Connie meet for the first time at the altar. As they settle into their new home on the wild coast of Devonshire, the young couple find they have more in common than they thought. But there are dangerous secrets that threaten both them and the nation.

Can Will and Connie overcome the dark forces that conspire against them and find happiness together?

Available from Amazon on Kindle and in paperback. Read free in Kindle Unlimited. Listen via Audible, audiobooks.com, or other retailers.

A WINNING TRICK

A Winning Trick is a short novella, an extended epilogue for *Sauce for the Gander*.

What happens three years later when Will has to confront his father again?

It is available FREE (on Kindle only), exclusively for members of my mailing list. Sign up via the contact page on my website:

www.jaynedavisromance.co.uk

If you don't want to sign up, a paperback is available on Amazon.

A SUITABLE MATCH

Book 2 in the Marstone Series

Both are seeking a suitable match. Just not with each other.

England 1782

Lady Isabella is bound for London, in search of a husband. While excited at being free of her father's ruthless control, her joy is overshadowed by knowing her aunt will arrange a match that will benefit her father. His requirements are for a title and influence—not the things a young girl dreams of.

All is not lost. Bella is no stranger to subterfuge, and she knows her brother will help her avoid an unwelcome union. But when he is called away on urgent business he asks Nick Carterton to stand in for him.

Nick, a reserved scholar who relishes the quiet life, has avoided marriage for years but is finally giving in to his father's request he seek out a bride. Keeping a headstrong miss in check is not the way he'd choose to spend his time. Instead of looking for a wife, he finds himself accompanying Bella on a series of escapades around the city. Meanwhile, Bella's eye lights on a totally unsuitable young man. It seems neither is set for matrimony any time soon.

A more than suitable match is right in front of them... if only they could see it.

Available from Amazon on Kindle and in paperback. Read free in Kindle Unlimited.

PLAYING WITH FIRE

Book 3 in the Marstone Series.

Phoebe yearns for a love match like her parents'. Revolutionary France is not where she expected to find it.

France 1793

Phoebe's future holds little more than the prospect of a tedious season of balls and routs, forever in the shadow of her glamorous cousin and under the critical eye of her shrewish aunt. She yearns for a useful life, and a love match like her parents'.

But first she has to endure the hazards of a return home through revolutionary France. Her aunt's imperious manner soon puts them into mortal danger.

Alex uses many names, and is used to working alone. A small act of kindness leads him to assist Phoebe's party, even though it might come at the expense of his own, vital mission in France.

Unexpectedly, as he and Phoebe face many dangers together, his affections grow for the resourceful and quick-witted red-head, despite their hopeless social differences. Alex dismisses the possibility of a match between them, not realizing that she feels the same way about him.

Before they can admit to their affection for each other, they must face the many difficulties that lie ahead.

Available from Amazon on Kindle and in paperback. Read free in Kindle Unlimited.

THE FOURTH MARCHIONESS

Book 4 in the Marstone Series

He's looking for a suitable wife. She's looking for a traitor. It could be a most unusual courtship.

England, 1794

James, Marquess of Harlford, wants nothing more than to be left alone with his scientific research. Unfortunately his mother is determined to see him married and with an heir to secure the succession. Faced with a house party of her selected candidates, he finds himself drawn towards the least likely—and most thoroughly unsuitable—of the guests.

While the other ladies are fluttering their eyelashes, Alice Bryant is sensible, kind and intelligent. Although he knows little else about her, James decides that Alice would do nicely as his wife.

For Alice, an out-of-work governess, taking up a position as a lady's companion would be ideal—if that was all the post entailed. Espionage, no matter how righteous the cause, sits ill on her conscience.

Alice does not wish to believe that the seemingly honourable and increasingly attentive Lord Harlford is capable of treason, but it's her duty to find out if he really is selling secrets to the enemy.

They could make an ideal match… if not for the espionage. Can love prosper, or will deceit and subterfuge carry the day?

Available from Amazon on Kindle and in paperback. Read free in Kindle Unlimited.

THE MRS MACKINNONS

England, 1799

Major Matthew Southam returns from India, hoping to put the trauma of war behind him and forget his past. Instead, he finds a derelict estate and a family who wish he'd died abroad.

Charlotte MacKinnon married without love to avoid her father's unpleasant choice of husband. Now a widow with a young son, she lives in a small Cotswold village with only the money she earns by her writing.

Matthew is haunted by his past, and Charlotte is fearful of her father's renewed meddling in her future. After a disastrous first meeting, can they help each other find happiness?

Available on Kindle and in paperback. Read free in Kindle Unlimited. Listen via Audible or AudioBooks.com.

AN EMBROIDERED SPOON

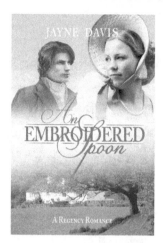

Can love bridge a class divide?

Wales 1817

After refusing every offer of marriage that comes her way, Isolde Farrington is packed off to a spinster aunt in Wales until she comes to her senses.

Rhys Williams, there on business, is turning over his uncle's choice of bride for him, and the last thing he needs is to fall for an impertinent miss like Izzy – who takes Rhys for a yokel. But while a man may choose his wife, he cannot choose who he falls in love with.

Izzy's new surroundings make her look at life, and Rhys, afresh. As she realises her early impressions were mistaken, her feelings about him begin to change.

But when her father, Lord Bedley, discovers the situation in Wales is not what he thought, and that Rhys is in trade, Izzy is hurriedly returned to London. Will a difference in class keep them apart?

Available on Kindle and in paperback. Read free in Kindle Unlimited. Listen via most retailers of audio books.

CAPTAIN KEMPTON'S CHRISTMAS

A sweet, second-chance novella.

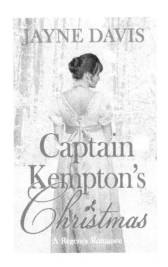

Can broken promises ever be forgiven?

England 1814

Lieutenant Philip Kempton and Anna Tremayne fall in love during one idyllic summer fortnight.

When he's summoned to rejoin his ship, Anna promises to wait for him. While he's at sea, she marries someone else.

Four years later, he is a captain and she is a widow. When the two are forced together at a Christmas party, they have a chance to reconcile.

Can they forgive each other the past and rekindle their love?

Available on Kindle and in paperback. Read free in Kindle Unlimited.

CPSIA information can be obtained
at www.ICGtesting.com
Printed in the USA
BVHW040849310521
608469BV00026B/1776